Going Postal

A Texas Trailer Park Mystery

Amy Eastlake

BooksForABuck.com

2008

Going Postal

A Texas Trailer Park Mystery

Amy Eastlake

Published by BooksForABuck.com

January 2008

ISBN: 978-1-60215-092-8

Chapter 1

"Miss. Hey, post office lady. Know where this dog came from?"

The speaker was a teenaged boy, maybe fifteen and angry with the world. His greasy hair hung down over his face under a ratty hat advertising Japanese animation. "This dog" was Andrew, a Dalmatian that lived about four blocks away. "Post office lady" was me, Kimberly Walsh, postal carrier.

I didn't recognize the kid but I knew the dog. Andrew had never bitten me but not through want of trying. And rumor had it he'd bitten several of my predecessors--including one the previous week while I'd been out on vacation.

"That's Andrew." I stepped away from the animal. Andrew had been prancing around, happily but when he heard me speak, he growled and lunged. "He lives over on Clinton."

"Good." The kid shoved the end of a gnawed rope leash my direction. "I've got stuff to do."

Andrew almost got me that time, but I stuck my leather postal bag in his mouth and he worried at it, possibly thinking he'd finally reached his dream.

"I'm a postal carrier, not lost-and-found." It was too late. The kid took off down the street leaving me with a hungry looking Dalmatian.

"Well, Andrew. I guess you'll have to come along with me while I finish my route."

I wasn't especially worried. Escaped dogs are just part of a letter carrier's day. Andrew, though, had never strayed so far from home. I tugged on my bag, then showed him my pepper spray.

Andrew growled at me but he didn't seem to have his heart in it. After a couple more chomps on my bag, he pulled on the leash to water a fire hydrant and trotted up exactly as if he was out for an afternoon walk, practically dragging me behind him.

In the suburbs, postal carriers drive from house to house, leaning out the doors of their vans to slide mail into oversized mailboxes. In the city, where I worked, we walk. Lots of carriers prefer the driving, but not me. I'd spent enough years locked in darkened cubicles during my corporate America days to appreciate a job that lets me be outside, getting paid to get my exercise. Of course, by the end of August, I was ready for a break in the heat. Texas summers last about six months with both heat and humidity averaging in the nineties all that time.

All of which meant He got to bark at every other dog in the neighborhood as we walked, and he was prancing with his tail held high before we'd finished on Edgefield and I was ready to drop him home on Clinton. As I headed for my van, we left behind a cacophony of barking so loud the sound set off a couple of car alarms.

* * * *

Sean Herbert, Andrew's owner, lived in a two-story half-timber house built in the 1930s when labor was cheap and architectural frills were considered clever. It looked like Hollywood's version of the house where grandparents would live.

In this case, looks were deceiving. Like many grandparents, Sean kept his windows covered. Unlike my grandparents, he didn't do it to protect the antique velvet of Victorian furniture. He used the darkness to hide his secrets.

I knew Sean well because he was a major eBay dealer, always shipping and receiving merchandise. But eBay was his hobby--his real job was drugs. He supplied much of the south Dallas market for Ecstasy, illegal steroids, amphetamines, and other manufactured drugs I'd never heard of. Everyone in the neighborhood knew about Sean's business. But the cops had never found anything and after a few raids, they'd given up and waited for him to mess up. Which he hadn't. Yet.

I pulled my van in front of Sean's place.

Andrew lunged for my hand off when I reached for his leash but I was ready for that trick. I showed him my pepper spray and he backed off quickly. Postal carriers can't take guff from dogs.

Andrew looked nervous when I tugged him up the pathway to Sean's place, his eyes rolling back a little and his breath coming even faster than normal for an August heat wave. I would have thought he'd be happy to be home but maybe he and Sean were on the outs. I'd call animal control if Sean looked like he was going to give Andrew a rough time. Not that I liked the dog--still there are limits.

"Almost home, buddy," I told him. He hadn't bit me yet so we were good friends.

Nobody answered when I leaned on Sean's doorbell.

That wasn't strange--if I were in the drug business, I wouldn't hurry to answer, either. I opened his screen door and banged on the solid steel door behind it.

When that door swung open, I realized what I should have an hour earlier when I'd first found Andrew loose--something was wrong. Sean would no more have left his door ajar than I would go outside without my sunscreen.

The day's mail was piled inside, under his mail slot. That wasn't like Sean either.

I pushed past the mail, stepping a few feet into his hallway. "Hello? Mr. Herbert? Sean? It's Kimberly Walsh, your mail carrier. I found your dog."

From somewhere, I heard the sound of water dripping, the buzz of an air conditioner pumping out chilled air. No reply.

"Mr. Herbert?"

Still nothing.

Andrew tugged on his leash but I didn't let him go. For the first time ever,

Andrew felt more like an ally than an enemy.

"Is anyone here?"

This wasn't my job. I delivered the mail. Snow, rain, or heat of day--that kind of stuff. I didn't want to see what Sean had in his house. If I spotted any drug paraphernalia, I was supposed to report him, but a postal worker who turned in people on her route got unpopular real fast.

I decided to compromise. I would walk to the stairwell and shout up the stairs. If Sean didn't respond by then, I'd call animal control and let them take responsibility for Andrew. I wouldn't win any popularity points for that, but I was too scared to care. Something was wrong and Sean might have set booby traps set for unwelcome intruders.

I kept my eyes forward as I stepped down the hallway. I opened my mouth to shout but Andrew beat me to it. He gave a wail of absolute anguish, and jerked on his leash.

I had been trying not to look but I couldn't help it this time. We'd found Sean.

Sean had been a good-looking guy. Early thirties, like me. Not too tall, maybe five nine, but in good shape, with jet-black hair and piercing blue eyes. Now, that good-looking body draped over the foot of the stairs, his face distorted by pain.

Blood, black in the dim light of his house, covered his white t-shirt and the beige carpets of his landing.

I bent and felt for a pulse.

Instead, I discovered that Sean's body had cooled to the air-conditioned chill of his home.

Andrew sniffed at his master's body and whined--an almost human sound of grief and loss. I yanked the dog away quickly away. Seeing Sean dead couldn't be good for the pup. Besides, Sean wasn't a drug dealer or dog owner any more, he was evidence. I needed to make sure that neither I, nor the dog, disturbed it.

"Oh, shit. We're in trouble," I told the dog.

He gave me a quizzical look, as if asking, "What's this *we* stuff?"

I may be blonde, but I managed to remember the numbers to 9-1-1. The police told me to stay put, not to touch anything, but to see if C.P.R. would help.

I knew Sean was way past C.P.R., but checked anyway. Mistake--one look at the deep gash on Sean's throat and I fainted.

* * * *

When I woke up, I was still in Sean's place but I wasn't alone. A couple of paramedics stood over me with disapproving looks and a dozen of Dallas's finest guarded the entryways and were poking around in Sean's place.

"What happened?" The female paramedic glared at me like this was my fault.

"I was returning his dog."

She shook her head. "I don't care about that. What happened to you?"

"Oh." That was a good question. I'd never fainted before. Then again, I'd never discovered a dead body before, either.

"I guess I fainted."

"Do that often?"

I shook my head.

"You should see a doctor. Make sure you're okay."

Well, that was helpful.

A couple of detectives shoved the paramedics aside, dragged me outside to an unmarked Ford, and sat me in the back seat.

"Name?" The detective was a middle-aged African American. He was good looking if you like the short-haired military type.

"Sean Herbert," I told them. "Is someone looking after Andrew?"

The second detective, a white guy who looked to be eighteen but was probably older wrinkled his nose. "You have the same name as the dead guy? Is this some sort of joke?"

It definitely wasn't a joke--in fact, it had become a nightmare. "No, that's the victim's name. I'm Kimberly Walsh."

The two detectives exchanged glances, like they'd really got a dumb one this time. "Well, Kimberly," the first detective drawled, "I'm not Sean Herbert either. I'm Marcus Poll and my partner here is Erik Sarno. But what we really need to know is what the Hell were you doing in Herbert's house?"

I told them about Andrew and got another doubtful look.

"There was no dog," the young-looking detective, Sarno, said.

"Well then he's wandering around the neighborhood. He's got to be distraught after losing his human."

"Interesting that you're more worried about a dog than you are about a dead person. Want to tell me about that?"

I started to answer, then stopped abruptly. "Surely you don't think *I* would hurt Sean. I just got here and I called the cops as soon as I found him."

"We're trying to establish the facts," Poll said. "Scene of the crime is working the evidence now. Once we get that, we'll have more to go on. For right now, though, you're the first person who saw Sean dead."

"Except whoever killed him."

"Yeah. Except for him." Poll paused. "Or her."

"Maybe I'd better get a lawyer."

"That's your right, of course."

Sarno snickered. "Sort of makes me wonder, though. Why would you need a lawyer if all you did was discover the body? Guilty conscience?"

One reason I'd decided to become a postal carrier after working ten years as a telecom engineer is that I was tired of dealing with overbearing people. Like the time one of my bosses jerked me off a million dollar project so I could write a *voluntary* nomination for him to win a corporate award for 'focus on the customer.' I didn't like it any better when it was cops doing the leaning, but I didn't want to be labeled as uncooperative. Besides, if I could help, I wanted to. Sean may have been a drug dealer and a lowlife scum, but that didn't give anybody the right to kill him.

I took a deep breath.

"Maybe we can start this over," I suggested. "I didn't kill Sean. I discovered his door was open when I tried to return his dog. When I came inside, I discovered Sean's body. Having seen the body, I immediately called the police. That's my entire involvement."

"So how did you end up with blood all over yourself?" Sarno took a swab, wiped it on my elbow, then put the result in a small brown-paper bag which he scribbled something on.

"Oh, hell." I had to swallow hard to keep my stomach down in its place. Sean's blood had soaked through my uniform all the way to my skin.

I didn't know for sure that Sean used drugs, but he was a dealer. What if I'd gotten AIDS from lying in his blood. Was that possible?

"Well."

"I must have fallen onto a pool of Sean's blood," I said.

I couldn't believe I was talking to the police while looking like a slasher victim. I wanted to stand in the shower and attack myself with sandpaper.

"The paramedic found me on the floor. She'll tell you how I got bloody. Or ask your crime scene unit. They'll probably find my elbow print in the middle of a blood puddle."

Poll frowned. "We'll do that. Now, let's go over the sequence of events again. Exactly what time would you say that you discovered the alleged dog wandering the streets?"

I think it would have gone on like that for hours if a rap on the car window hadn't stopped their questioning cold.

Sarno rolled down his window. "Yeah."

"I'm Preston Rolin with the Post Office Police. I understand you have one of our employees in custody."

I didn't know Rolin very well. Postal cops don't hang out with carriers. But I'd seen him around the post office and the credit union. He was a weightlifter type, overbulked, and losing his hair. He always talked about how the postal service was a stepping-stone into the F.B.I. and I'd never really given him much thought before. Now, I was happy to see him. I needed some support and he seemed willing to give it.

"Ms. Walsh discovered a murder victim." Poll seemed defensive all of a sudden. "We're trying to ascertain the facts and chronology."

Rolin didn't look impressed. "Is that right? The postal service is always anxious to cooperate with local law enforcement. According to her supervisor, you've had Ms. Walsh for a couple of hours. It looks to me like you've moved past simply ascertaining the facts. Now you're interfering with delivery of the mail."

Poll shook his head. "Not a chance. Walsh says she finished delivering her mail before coming by Herbert's place."

"Mail carriers don't just deliver mail, they pick it up, as well." Preston gave the older detective a grin. "Suppose I just call the local postmaster and get the official word from him." He pulled out a cell and punched a couple of buttons.

"If we have to, we can go through official channels and get this cleared up."

Poll's knuckles whitened as he gripped down on his steering wheel. "Hell. More bureaucracy is just what we need. You can go, Walsh. Just be ready to come down to the station to sign your statement when we get it typed up."

"Fair enough."

"And Mr. Rolin?"

The postal cop nodded.

"We're not the only ones who can interfere. We've got a murder investigation here and we're going to find the killer. If your little Kimberly Walsh killed him, she's going to jail no matter what you and the post office think."

Rolin looked serious. "I appreciate that, sir. I'll speak to my supervisor but I'm sure the P.O. Police will do everything we can to cooperate. After all, we're involved."

"Yeah, sure. Help from the Feds. That'll be the day."

Poll didn't say anything when Rolin opened the back door to the unmarked police car and let me out.

Rolin walked with me silently, back toward my van until we were out of earshot from the detectives. When we got to my truck, he stopped. "You all right?"

"It's been a rough day."

"Need me to drive you to central?"

"I need to bring back my van," I said.

He considered that. "I can call for another driver."

Oh, no. This girl brings in her own mail. "I'll be all right."

He considered me, finally coming to a conclusion. "If you say so. I'll follow you back. Good thing I was listening on my scanner on my way home. Those guys didn't even bother making a courtesy call to P.O. management."

That was lucky. Otherwise, I might have ended up spending the night there and getting in trouble for failing to return postal equipment. "Thanks, Preston." I barely knew the guy, but right then, he was my best friend.

"You'd better talk to your supervisor soon as you get back, though. He seemed worried and he'll be even more worried if he learns the cops think you might be a suspect from the newspaper. Wouldn't do much for our reputation."

So much for him being my best friend. Even if he was right. Postal workers had developed something of a reputation for violence. I had a nasty feeling that reputation was going to cause me trouble.

Preston followed me back to central, his hot yellow Corvette staying close to my bumper. I got my supervisor, Buddy Jorden, on the cell.

Jorden met me at the loading dock. He was a decent guy for a supervisor. He'd been a carrier for years before recurring skin cancer persuaded him to take the promotion that would get him away from the sun. His blotched pink face was all the reminder I needed to be religious about my sunblock.

Jorden slung one of my mailbags over his back when I'd unlocked the back. "You should have called animal control at once," he reminded me as soon as I told him what happened. "Let them discover the dead bodies. It isn't your responsibility to return lost pets. No stamp, no delivery, remember?"

"Very funny, Buddy."

His blotched face took on a serious tone. "Kimberly, this is serious. Homeland Security wants to convert postal carriers into spies. The only way the Postmaster General headed them off was by reminding everybody that we do just one thing--deliver the mail. Start running around discovering bodies and you kick that theory in the nuts. So, this is a lot bigger than just the question of a lost dog." He opened the mail pouch and flipped through the pickup, tossing letters, packages, and metered mail into the appropriate bins. I squatted down next to him, opening the second pouch and keeping him company in the sorting.

After a few months, sorting the mail becomes something your body does without fully engaging your brain. Which meant Buddy could talk to me without any problem.

"So, what happened to the dog?"

I told him I'd called animal control on my way in and that they said they'd have somebody drive around the neighborhood looking.

"I'll check out a few streets myself," he told me. "You go home and stay away from there."

He must have realized I planned on finding Andrew. I didn't like the dog, but that didn't mean he deserved to be homeless.

"I don't mind."

He held up a hand. "Mrs. Jorden has always wanted a dog. Maybe finding Andrew will help keep *me* out of the doghouse."

It would have been nice to have a dog to come home to at night, but a trailer is really not a great place to keep a pet. Buddy could give him a better home than I could. "Thanks, boss."

He blushed, turning from bright pink to a sort of dusty rose. "Hey, it's my job. Now, are you okay to get home or should I have somebody give you a ride."

* * * *

I rode my bicycle home, getting caught in one of the evening storms that roll in during the second half of summer as tropical moisture from the Gulf of Mexico bashes into the cooler air coming down from Canada.

The heavy drops of rain felt good as they soaked through my uniform. Each drip falling on my body felt as if it washed away a bit more of the touch of death and the stench of blood that had stuck to me since I discovered Sean's body.

When I got back to my trailer, I stripped off my wet clothes, draped them outside the trailer to let the rain clean off the rest of the blood, and stood in the shower scrubbing until my skin turned pink and raw. Only when the water turned cold did I come out and whip up a two egg-white omelet.

I tried to eat. Intellectually I knew that I was skinny, that the workouts I do and the fifteen miles I walk every day require me to take in more calories than

I'd allowed myself when I'd been an engineer lump in telecom. After what I'd been through, food lacked appeal.

I glared at those egg whites, with cheese and mushrooms oozing out the side and all I could think of was Sean Herbert's body.

It wasn't even close. I tossed the omelet down the sink, ground it up in the garbage disposal, flopped myself onto my couch, and mashed the power button on my TV remote.

No escape there. Sean's death was the talk of the news.

The local reporter, a gorgeous blonde with eyes so green they had to come from contact lenses, spoke breathlessly about the death of a drug lord. They cut away to the Chief of Police who gave some blather about the war on drugs and about how evildoers often fall out amongst themselves.

I was at the point of turning off the tube when an aide rushed in and handed the police chief a note.

He glanced at it, then faced directly into the camera. "This case has been complicated by the presence of a quasi-governmental agency, the U.S. Postal Service. Because of this, I asked for the formal assistance of the Federal Bureau of Investigation. My office just received a call from the FBI Director in Washington D. C. who assures us that he'll lend all assistance possible. If there is a connection between the postal service and the drug lords, rest assured, the Dallas Police, working hand-in-hand with the FBI will discover it, delineate it, then destroy it."

I stood there with my mouth open as the blonde came back on and redirected the program to the status of the Texas Rangers baseball team. They were, as usual, fading under late-summer intensity of too much heat in Texas.

The U.S. Postal Service is supposedly non-political. Still, I guessed it would take about three minutes for my phone to ring.

I was optimistic. It took less than two.

"Hello."

"Ms. Kimberly Walsh?"

"This is Kimberly."

"This is Vito Lindner. Postmaster for the Dallas region."

The big boss. I'd expected a flunky.

"Yes, sir."

"I understand that you've been less than fully cooperative with the police investigation."

"No, Sir. I told them everything I know."

I might as well have kept my mouth shut. "Postal employees are not above the law, Ms. Walsh. I expect, and the Postmaster General demands, absolute cooperation between our employees and those of local jurisdictions, let alone the FBI. Do you understand?"

He hadn't strained my intellect yet, but I simply agreed that I did understand.

"I'm happy to hear that, Ms. Walsh. Employment with the postal service is a privilege, not a right."

"I'm with you sir."

His voice dropped an octave. "You'd better be with me. The Dallas Post Office isn't going to get the kind of reputation some other post offices have."

I'd gotten support from Buddy and from Preston Rolin. I should have realized this positive string couldn't continue. Still, it was frustrating that the big boss would be so willing to believe the worst of his own employees.

"I'll be fully cooperative with the police," I told him.

"If necessary, I will suspend you without pay so you can make more time."

I gritted my teeth together to stop myself from saying anything stupid. I loved my job.

I'd never dealt with Lindner before and, with luck, I never would again. But he was a man who could make my life miserable. He was a man who could toss me out on the street--again, just as the high-tech company I'd worked for had done during the recession.

"I can and will make time for the police while I continue to handle my work responsibilities," I promised.

I could almost feel his doubt leaking through the phone. He paused so long I wondered if we'd gotten disconnected before he finally responded. "We'll see, Ms. Walsh."

* * * *

I arrived at the main post office at my usual time the morning after I'd found Sean's body and picked up the mail for my first delivery.

It's located just off I-30, barely a quarter of a mile from the trailer park where I live, and it's always a hive of activity, even though budget cutting means it's no longer open twenty-four hours a day. The mail delivery trucks were an ocean of blue and white and dozens of carriers elbowed their way to their mail, shouted out complaints, or flirted.

Nobody paid any attention to me, and I hoped I'd completed my fifteen minutes of fame.

Larry Mueller, who works my route when I'm on vacation leaned on my van when I jogged up with my mailbags.

My heart dropped. He wouldn't be there if I weren't in trouble.

Larry was a decent enough guy, despite hair down to his waist and an occasional crazed look in his eyes. I did try to stay upwind of him, though, because he had a rather distant relationship with his shower.

"Hi, Kimberly."

I nodded. "How's it hanging, Larry?"

"I heard you had some problems."

I'd been able to force down half a carton of yogurt for breakfast but it threatened to come up now. "You and the rest of Dallas, I guess."

He sidled closer--too close for my comfort. "Finding a dead body has gotta be the pits, know what I mean?"

"You're the master of understatement."

He looked puzzled for a second, then blinked. "I wanted to let you know that we're behind you. We have rules about these things."

I tossed my mailbags into the van. He hadn't said anything about taking over my route. "I know you're trying to be supportive, Larry, and I don't want to be unappreciative. But I have no idea what you're talking about."

He scratched something out of his hair, looked at it, then flicked it to the ground. "The union, Kimberly. We're backing you on this. If management tries to fire you, they'll have the entire union to deal with. I already sent an e-mail with the national union. It won't just be us in Dallas."

I'd forgotten that Larry was our local union rep. Most of the time, I forget that I'm in a union, except when the paycheck comes in with a hunk carved out of it for dues. Now I was glad I belonged. Lindner could only be so arbitrary before he ran into the contract. Unlike in telecom, where plenty of workers I'd known got sacked for no better reason that they wouldn't go to bed with an exec, the union means we have protection.

"Got it, Larry. I appreciate the union backing me but I think I'm in good shape. I didn't do anything so once I get the police off my case and looking for the real killer, I'll be in the clear. I'm planning to drop by the police department's office on Bishop during my lunch break, sign the statement, and that should be the end of it."

He looked doubtful. "Just remember we're here, Dude. *In Union, there is power.*"

He shook my hand, then headed toward his own van. I noticed he was limping a little and had a large bandage around his right thigh and instantly felt bad. He'd come over to offer me support and I'd been so caught up in myself that I hadn't even noticed he was hurt.

"What happened to you, Larry?"

"Huh?"

"Your leg."

He looked down as if surprised to see he even had a leg. "Oh, yeah. This. Had a little accident the other day."

"Really? What happened?"

"I got bit by a goddammed dog is what happened."

Going Postal

Chapter 2

My regular morning route took me through the apartments, auto repair shops, hair salons, and by-the-hour motels of south Dallas. Although it's not as pleasant as my afternoon circuit through the Winnetka Heights historical district, it has its own interests. I got to see a part of America I hadn't even been aware of back when I'd been a sheltered telecom worker spending my life in a darkened cubicle.

Postal carriers are supposed to be blind to the mail we carry but I didn't think any of us are. I'd flipped through some of the hair style magazines the salons subscribe to and theorized with some of the other female postal workers that if the guys who subscribed to dirty magazines spent as much money on taking women out on dates as they did on their magazines, they wouldn't have had to take their sex lives into their own hands.

One of the worst offenders in the dirty magazine service was Fred Turley who ran one of the by-the-hour motels along the route of what had once been U.S. Highway 80.

A couple of generations ago, U.S. Highway 80 had been one of the main east-west passages between the east coast and California. Like Route 66 to the north, U.S. 80 had carried Hollywood hopefuls, farmers dispossessed from their land by the collapse of the 1930s, and post-war families seeking their fortunes in the golden west.

Like Route 66 further north, U.S. 80 had once been home to hundreds of roadside attractions, neon-lit motels, enterprising diners, and quick repair places. When the interstate system had bypassed the old highways, the businesses that supported the old highway didn't all collapse. Instead, they hung on, hungry and mutating like something at the bottom of a lagoon.

Fred's Rock Cliff No-Tel Motel was at the bottom of that food chain and Fred himself was pure scum.

It wasn't so much that he subscribed to dirty magazines. Learning how many guys subscribed to that kind of thing had been one of the first surprises I got when I'd started delivering the mail.

They generally came wrapped well enough that you could ignore them if you worked at it. But letting me ignore them wasn't Fred's idea.

Just about every other day, he'd call me in for what he called "compare and contrast." He'd show me photos of naked women and point out unlikely similarities between them and me. He always ended with a leer and the question of whether I was sure I wasn't making the big bucks by moonlighting as a *nekkid* model. Half those pictures were cut off at the head, showing only

13

dehumanized torsos, private parts stretched open for public viewing.

He'd gotten a bit subtler after I'd reported him for harassment. Of course, the whole incident had made me a joke at the post office. Tough mail carriers aren't supposed to care about perverts giving them a hard time.

Bells jingled as I pushed his door open. "Fred, I've got your mail." His bundle included the usual mix of bondage magazines, young stuff, and hotel/motel management material.

I stepped into the hotel lobby where he worked and which, as far as I could tell, he never left.

"Fred?"

Then I saw him.

Talk about *déjà vu*. The dead body, the deep gouges across his throat, even the way he was draped over the chair behind his counter reminded me of Sean.

Nobody ever got killed in Telecom. Maybe I hadn't realized how good I'd had it.

A fly landed on the pool of congealed blood under Fred's neck and my knees started shaking so hard I could hardly stand. What were the odds of finding two bodies in two days? I'd gone my entire life before without even finding one.

I was tempted to dump Fred's mail and run, pretending I hadn't seen anything. I knew what would happen if I called in the police. But a girl's got to do the right thing even though she knows it's going to hurt. I dialed 9-1-1 on my cell.

The operator wanted me to stay on the phone until the cops arrived but I wasn't having any of that. I hung up on her and called Buddy. The mail must go through.

"Jorden here."

"Buddy, it's Kimberly. I'm going to need a backup."

"Police giving you trouble?"

"Uh, not yet. But they're going to be--I found another body."

The pause was painful. "Oh, shit."

"No kidding. I'm at the Rock Crest No-Tel on Sylvan. My van is a block away."

"You don't mean Fred the pervert, your prospective agent to the world of porn?"

"Right the first time." I swallowed again. "H-he's dead, Buddy. And the really scary thing is, the way he's laid out, it looks almost identical to Sean."

"Well, crap, Kimberly. You have a motive for Fred. We'll have to tell the F.B.I. about the harassment charges. You're in deep shit. Double murder is lethal injection for sure in Texas. Even for a woman."

He wasn't telling me anything I didn't know. "I didn't kill anyone, Buddy, you've got to believe me. But here's the thing. I've got to stay here until the cops arrive. And when they do, I doubt they'll let me get on with my route. I need a fill-in."

"I'll send someone out. And I'm going to put you in for a personal day so

14

you can deal with this. No sense in getting Vito's shorts in more of a knot than we have to."

"Thanks, Buddy. Oh, and if you see Larry Mueller, you might mention this to him. He said the union was ready to help me. I think I'm going to need all the help I can get."

"Larry couldn't help a racehorse piss."

I wasn't sure I could help with that much either, but I got his idea. "I'm open to other suggestions."

The silence was finally broken the insistent two-toned whine of police sirens.

"Sounds like I've got company, Buddy," I said. "Make sure whoever comes to finish my route has keys for my van. I'm not likely to be in a position to hand them over."

"Right. Oh, good luck, Kimberly. For what it's worth, I don't think you killed either of them. Even if you did, the world is better off without those two assholes. Even if Sean did have a nice dog."

"Buddy? Nice?"

"Thanks to bringing him home, I'm off the sofa and back in my own bed. Course the dog sleeps between us."

"That's way too much info, Buddy."

"Well, anyway, motive or not, I'll put in a character endorsement when it comes to a trial."

That third-rate vote of confidence didn't help much but it was a lot better than the police response.

"We have the building surrounded. Come out with your hands up." The bullhorn was loud enough to rattle the glass in Fred's windows. I followed the instructions, opening the door slowly because I didn't want any trigger-happy cop to think I was a threat.

The glimpse I got of the Rock Cliff No-Tel parking lot would have been a laugh if I hadn't been the one in big trouble. 'Guests' in various states of undress were emerging from a dozen or so of the motel rooms. From the mix of balding gray and peroxide blonde heads in the lot, I suspected that relatively few of the couples were married--at least not to each other. News reporters who had probably been listening to their police scanners quickly snapped photos, possibly hoping for a story even juicier than murder.

But I didn't have much time to look. As soon as I'd cleared the door, a beefy cop shoved me down onto the gravel parking lot, twisted my arms behind my back, and sealed my wrists together with some sort of plastic device. He shoved a heavy black shoe on my face, keeping me flat on my stomach, then fished a card out from a pocket in his tunic.

"You have the right to remain silent." He ran through the rest of my rights so quickly I couldn't make out the words, especially with the continued blare of sirens and the shouting of the No-Tel customers as the affluent males in the group called out threats to the reporters snapping their pictures and the prostitutes posed, hoping that and that Hollywood might happen to glance through the pages of the *Dallas Observer* and that this might be their big break.

While the big beefy cop kept my face mashed into the gravel, another uniformed officer walked into the No-Tel lobby, shotgun locked and loaded at his side.

I heard the retching noise almost at once.

He bolted out from there and lost his breakfast over an already dying bush. "Oh, shit. It's a dead body all right." A pause for more puking. "Not just dead, either--chopped up. Somebody hated the guy--this looks personal. Anybody know who this guy is, uh, was?"

I took a breath to tell him about Fred, but my cop put a bit more weight into his foot and I thought better of it.

"The detectives and scene of the crime are on their way," my cop said. "If it's too late to help the vic, we've just got to secure the scene."

He let up with his foot fractionally. I still couldn't get my face out of the dirt but at least it wasn't being ground into it.

"Make sure nobody gets away," my cop continued. "Somebody see if they can find a master key and check to see that nobody's hiding in any of the units."

I hadn't looked at Fred's body that closely but it was obvious he'd been dead for hours. I doubted that anybody would kill him and then decide to spend those hours hanging in a really funky motel waiting for the police to show up. Then again, how many Johns spend hours with prostitutes? Fortunately, nobody was asking me for detecting advice. The last thing I wanted in the world was to be a detective.

* * * *

"Let's see you talk or politic your way out of this one, shall we?" Detective Marcus Poll's baggy brown suit looked like it had been slept in. From the bloodshot glaze in his eyes, if he'd slept at all, it hadn't been for long. His partner, Detective Erik Sarno, looked pretty good, though.

They'd arrived about ten minutes after the patrol cops and let me get up off the ground. I had abrasions on my knees and my face from being shoved into the gravel parking lot and the police detectives took a bunch of photos of the damage they'd done. It didn't take long for them to disabuse me of any notion that they were planning an apology. Instead, they were looking for evidence of a struggle. Thanks to my over-active cop, I looked like I had been in a fight. Everyone wanted to believe I'd been fighting with Fred.

Poll and Sarno turned an ancient picnic table under an even more ancient live oak into a makeshift office and plunked me down on one end. After bringing in a female officer to give me an all-too-thorough body-search, they finally cut off the handcuffs and let me rub some circulation into my arms.

"Just how did you happen to discover another body?" Sarno demanded.

"This is my normal route," I explained. "I come by every morning. Today, I discovered Mr. Turley's body and immediately notified the police, following Post Office procedure."

Sarno laughed. "You find two bodies in less than twenty-four hours and you expect us to believe you're just doing your job. Or maybe you think it's an

16

unlucky coincidence?"

If that was a question, I didn't know the answer to it.

I tried to explain that I wasn't dumb enough to kill two people, let them sit around for hours, then go *back* to the scene of the crime and call the police.

They gave me indifferent stares. "Or maybe," Poll suggested, "you just want us to think you're not that stupid."

My brain reeled with trying to make sense of that but eventually I gave it up as a lost cause. As Sarno pointed out, criminals aren't known as intellectual shining lights.

Poll glanced down at his notebook. "Right. From when you got out of the car last night, I want every detail of your evening, night, and morning. Where you went, who saw you there, and when you left."

For once, I was glad I didn't have an active social life. It didn't take me five minutes to detail twelve hours of my life.

So they had me go through it again. And again.

Buddy showed up on the seventh run-through.

I'd never seen Buddy outside in the sun before. He covered up in a big floppy safari-style hat with a towel on the back like something the French Foreign Legion would wear, along with long sleeves and long pants. He looked odd for a Dallas August, but he was a welcome face at a time when I needed one.

Beat cops were still swarming over the place, checking out the prostitutes, getting addresses from their johns, and generally getting a charge out of watching the scene of the crime scene folks do their work. Buddy bulled through them like, well, like a postal supervisor on a mission.

"Walsh, you need me to call you a lawyer?"

I thought a moment. If I lawyered up, they'd probably let me go for now. But it would also make them more likely to view me as a suspect.

"Does Mr. Lindner have anything to say on the subject?"

Buddy frowned. "He wants you to continue full cooperation with the local police. But he can't take away your right to have a lawyer."

He could make my job miserable, though.

"Oh," Buddy continued. "I'm sure you detectives will be happy to hear that Mr. Lindner, chief of the Dallas Postal Service, has assigned the P.O. Police to look into these cases also, so you'll have extra help."

Sarno shook his head. "We don't need--"

"He had one of the D.C. lawyers give him some sort of jurisdictional authorization based on the felonies occurring on a regular mail route."

"Joy," Poll said. "More federal cops."

"Since your own police chief has already invited in the F.B.I., you're hardly in a position to refuse additional assistance," Buddy informed him.

I hoped that Lindner would realize that clearing my name would be better for the post office than framing me, but I wasn't so sure. He had sounded almost anxious to throw me to the wolves. Still, I read Buddy's warning loud and clear. If I was to ask for a lawyer now, Lindner would not only throw me to the wolves, he'd add some of his own wolves into the mix.

Sarno stood. "I'm gonna get some coffee. Want me to send over a couple of uniforms to watch these two, or can you handle it on your own, Poll?"

My coffee mug was still in my van and I was tempted to fish out a couple of bucks and put in my order. For once, though, I had a common sense moment and I kept my mouth shut.

"The day I can't handle a couple like Twiggy and the mummy is the day I'll turn in my badge," Poll growled.

Twiggy and the mummy? I should have been offended but I decided to take it as a good sign. Nobody would think of Twiggy as a killer. Would they?

Sarno returned ten minutes later with two coffees, a box of donuts, and a seriously angry face.

"Give me that statement." He ripped the notes from Poll's hands.

"Just what I thought. You said you came here in your mail delivery van. Just doing your job delivering the mail, right? So, where the hell is it? I've looked everywhere within three blocks of this place and there's not a van in sight. What other lies have you told us?"

My explanation that I'd called Buddy to send out someone to finish my route didn't go over well--even when Buddy backed me up.

Sarno got the police dispatcher on the phone and sent out an all points bulletin for my truck--as evidence unlawfully removed from a crime scene. It didn't seem to matter to Sarno that my van had never been within a hundred yards of the body and was well outside the area now taped off by the uniformed officers.

I put on my most apologetic face. "Right. Sorry. Can I go now?"

Sarno slammed his fist down on the table, knocking a hole through the picnic table's aging wood. "We know you did it, Walsh. We don't know your motive yet, or why you made it so easy for us to track you down, but we're going to get those answers. And when we do, you're going down."

Chapter 3

The cops were winding down, as bored by the repetition as I was scared by it, but Vito Lindner showed up that evening, making a fuss about protecting the Post Office's reputation.

As I could have predicted, he pissed Poll and Sarno off. Since they couldn't take out their frustration on him, they went after me a couple more times.

I didn't make it home until midnight.

Both detectives seemed happy with the theory that I was the killer although only Sarno came out and said it. Lindner didn't seem prepared to fight that conclusion very hard--as long as the Post Office could be shown to be actively cooperating in the investigation.

The only good news that came out of it was that they did let me go home.

Sarno was itching to throw me in jail for a while, but Poll held him back. It wasn't like I was going anywhere and the mail had to get delivered. Not that they cared. I suspected the only mail those two got were bills.

When I got home, I stared at my refrigerator for a while but went to bed without eating. Dead bodies wrecked havoc on my appetite.

There was a silver lining in the very dark cloud. Normally I got up at five each morning to ride my bike, in the dark, to the post office. Since I'd been put on personal days, I'd be able to sleep in the next morning. Lindner had made it painfully clear that I was to stay well away from the Post Office, stay out of my uniform, and generally pretend that I had nothing to do with the USPS. I wasn't fired, exactly, but only because of union rules. And Lindner was having his office stooges read through those rules to find a loophole that would let him get rid of me for good.

The silver lining suffered a rainout pretty quickly. My phone started ringing around four and twenty minutes later, there was a knock at my door.

Television lighting dazzled my eyes when I peeked out my door. At least thirty reporter types and five separate camera crews tried to get my attention. They went wild when I cracked open the door and didn't quiet down much when I slammed it.

I pulled on a top and a pair of jeans and went out to face the music.

"Ms. Walsh, do you have any comment on being named as a leading suspect by the police?" That was an older news reporter, spiral notebook in hand and one of those funky hats I'd only seen in vintage movies.

"Do you think that killing a couple of lowlifes is justified?" This was a television reporter for the local 'fair and unbiased' affiliate.

"Isn't it the case postal workers are exposed to an alien substance that increases their tendency toward violence?" The last question had been asked by a really gorgeous woman with enough of a figure to make all the male reporters stop looking at me and start paying attention to her. I wasn't sure who she wrote for but it sounded interesting.

The moment of silence was enough for me to break in.

"I didn't kill anyone," I announced. I wasn't going to touch the question about whether it was okay to murder people just because they were scumbags. "As far as alien exposure is concerned, I suggest you talk to the local Postmaster, Mr. Vito Lindner." I read them his number off my cell. "I'm not aware of any such alien-related substance, but I'm not authorized to make any official comment."

I wasn't surprised when my answers only generated more questions. The reporters hadn't left their comfortable beds in their rich suburbs to put up with a boring denial.

I didn't have anything else to give them, although, from the way Lindner had acted, maybe the alien theory wasn't too off-base after all. I parried a few more questions, realized it was a hopeless battle, then finally retreated inside and shut my door.

Trailers don't have a lot of soundproofing. So I figured it would be okay to call the park manager to complain. The reporters and the big camera trucks would have awakened her without my help.

Nobody has much respect for a postal delivery person. But my trailer-park manager, Tina Anderson doesn't let anyone push her around. Generally she minds her own business and lets us residents get on with her life, but when she has to, she can be pretty persuasive.

It took her about three minutes to clear out the parking lot and let darkness and quiet descend on our little patch of heaven.

It didn't last, though.

Tina knocked on my door and barged in, two cups of coffee in one hand and a sack of donuts in the other. "Want to tell me what the hell is going on?"

I shook my head. "I take it you haven't been watching the news."

She shrugged. Like me, she was a high-tech dropout. Unlike me, though, she'd left years before after being involved with successful startup. She probably got her news from the web.

"A couple of guys on my route got murdered--stabbed and sliced. I was the one who found each of their bodies."

She nodded, opened the bag, fished out a chocolate and peanut donut, and shoved the rest over to me. "The person who finds the body is always a suspect. Still, what motive--"

"I reported Fred Turley for sexual harassment."

"He showed you his dirty pictures and asked if you were the model?"

"How'd you--"

"I'm not psychic. He does it to any woman he can get to stand still. It's pretty weak as a motive."

20

"The police don't seem to need much."

Tina shook her head. "They won't. From what I've seen, most perps are dumb. In general, the most obvious person did it. Not like in novels."

If Tina thought she was encouraging me, I had to doubt her insights into humanity. Unfortunately, I thought she was right about the police.

"Still," I said, "I didn't do it. So--"

"So, nothing. They have a lot of cases to work. They can't afford to spend weeks looking for the real killer when they have a perfectly good suspect."

"Even if that's true, what can I do?"

Tina's gaze just might have been tinged with pity. "What you *can* do, I'm not sure. What you *need* to do is find out who really killed those two guys."

"I'm not a detective, I'm a postal carrier."

She swallowed the last of her donut and spoke with her mouth full. "Maybe they'll let you deliver all of the mail on death row."

I'd hated the cell-like cubicles of the telecom engineer, I was positive I'd hate the actual cells of a Texas prison at least as much.

Like it or not, Tina was right.

I would have to track down the real killer. Worse, I didn't have that much time. I figured I had a week or so before the police decided they had all of the evidence they were going to get and had me arrested for good. Once that happened, I'd be in jail and my investigating days would be over.

"I guess you're right," I admitted. I sipped on my coffee and shredded a donut so I wouldn't look ungrateful. "Any suggestions."

"You have any enemies? Because what are the chances two guys on your route get killed and you're the person who finds both of their bodies?"

I shook my head. I wasn't person-oriented, but surely I'd know if anyone hated me enough to set me up for a murder charge. Nobody came to mind.

"Well, think about it. And if you need help, give me a call."

I thanked her, promised to bring back her coffee cup, and locked the door behind her when she headed back to her own trailer.

Then I looked out my window to make sure nobody was sticking a camera in before flushing the donuts she'd left down the toilet, then undressing and showering.

The trailer's tiny shower stall wasn't much but at least I was alone. Unless I took Tina's advice, by some time next week, I'd be showering in a prison shower and worrying about whether the girl under the next outlet had a knife and an attitude.

When I couldn't scrub myself any more without losing skin, I toweled off and pulled on a clean t-shirt and a fresh pair of jeans. My jeans fit looser than they were supposed to and my stomach gave a little growl.

Dumping the donuts hadn't cured me of my craving, though. Just when I thought I had myself under control, all of a sudden I'd get this overwhelming urge to poison myself with junk food--the more fat, the more salt, the more preservatives the better.

My refrigerator contained the usual--bottled water, carrot sticks, and plain non-fat yoghurt.

I considered the yoghurt--I generally saved it for my splurge moments, but even it wasn't going to do the job this time.

My craving put me on my bike, and I rode to the local *Funny Guy in a Hat*. There I ordered the most decadent thing I could find on the menu--a sausage biscuit sandwich breakfast on a biscuit made from pure lard and white flour, along with a greasy slab of hash browns and a cup of coffee.

I even considered using half and half in my coffee--something I hadn't done even when I'd been a chunky telecom engineer. I didn't do it, of course. Still, even thinking about it said something about how frazzled I'd become.

Once the food arrived, I pulled a notebook from my pack, and sat down at one of the tables. I was an engineer, for goodness sake. If I knew one thing, it was getting things organized.

Logic said I could track down the killer. It had to be someone I had some kind of connection to.

After all, Tina was right. It couldn't be a coincidence that I had discovered two bodies in two days. Somebody was setting me up. That somebody knew my route, knew the people in my route and which ones caused the most problems, and definitely didn't care if I took a fall.

There were plenty of people in the post office and in the neighborhood who knew both my route and my troublemakers, but the list wasn't in the millions. It was probably no more than hundreds.

I licked my pencil, stared at the blank notepad, then took a look at my breakfast sandwich.

The cheese looked like plastic, pressure-molded over a hunk of browned sausage. The hash browns oozed grease. The coffee might have been fresh three days earlier.

"I thought I recognized your bike." Larry Mueller slopped himself down in the chair across from me.

If I hadn't already lost my appetite, getting a whiff of my colleague would have done the job.

I spilled about half the coffee on the table in my surprise at seeing an unexpected familiar face. "What are you doing here, Larry?"

He gave me a grin that showed expensive orthodontic work marred by cigarette stains. "I'm working your route today. I just happened to be passing the *Funny Guy in a Hat* when I saw your bike and I figured, hey, take a break and catch up on the news. Besides, I want to help you out. I told you, the union…"

Larry had only gotten appointed union steward a few weeks before but apparently he had gotten into the political swing of things in a hurry. "Have a seat, then, Larry."

He looked, noticed that he was already sitting, and grinned.

"A guy has to eat, you know. And there's got to be something I can do to help you out. Do you need the union to find you a lawyer?"

"Thanks, Larry. But Lindner would fire me if I lawyered up."

"He can't do that. The union--"

"The union would protest. In the meantime, I wouldn't have a paycheck."

Larry thought about that one. "I guess you're right. So, we've got to find the real killer, right?"

He stopped and got thoughtful again. Either that or he was having a constipation problem. With Larry, thoughtful looked purely painful. Finally he stuck a finger in the air. "Got it. I mean, if you think about it, it's got to be someone from the neighborhood, right? I mean, what are the chances that two people *you* know just happen to get wacked?"

"I don't…"

"Then there's the issue of them being guys you had problems with, right? That makes it suspicious. Still…" he snapped his fingers. "Got it. Troublemakers for one person are troublemakers for other people, too. Gets back to someone in the neighborhood."

I looked down at my blank piece of paper. Here I'd been certain my engineering mind could come up with answers and Larry's stoner-brain had done better than I had.

"You might be--"

"So, you and me, we know the neighborhood, right?"

"I gue--"

"Here's what we need to do. We'll put our heads together and come up with a list of potential killers." He snapped his fingers again--and look, you've even got a pad there to write the names on. Talk about being prepared. So, we do the list, then we check them out. Interrogate them, talk to their neighbors, find out if any of them has been burning their clothes or something."

Putting my head together with Larry sounded scary--and smelly. But everything else he'd said made sense. Except for I wanted to include people from out of the neighborhood--people whose connection was to me rather than the route.

"That sounds logical," I said. "So, here's my list so far." I handed him my empty page and stepped back. I could only hold my breath for so long.

He stared at it, glanced at me, then chuckled. "You got me, dude. I thought you really had some people in mind."

"Not yet. But someone did it and, like you said, that someone should be from around here."

Larry scratched his scalp, dislodging a number of split ends. "That isn't a very good start, dude."

"I know." I wiped the lip of my coffee off before taking another sip. "You know the people on my route. They're just regular folks. It's hard to figure that any of them are killers."

Larry shook his head slowly. "That isn't a positive attitude, Kimberly. With the right motivation, just about anyone could be a murderer. It's really an equal opportunity crime. Not like drug pushing or petty theft."

This wasn't helping and my notebook was still blank when I grabbed it back from him. I took another sip of the coffee and glanced at the hash browns. The grease had soaked through another napkin. What had I ever seen in those things?

Larry must have been following my gaze. "You going to eat those?"

I shoved both the sandwich and the hash browns his direction. "You eat, I'll write down the ideas you have."

If I hadn't seen it, I wouldn't have guessed that anything other than a snake could open its mouth as wide as Larry did.

He shoved in half the hash browns in one bite.

I think he would have taken in the whole bar if I hadn't dropped my own mouth open.

His face froze in mid-chew. "What about the Reverend?"

I wiped the spray of hash browns off my face. Steven Nagle wouldn't have been on my list. "He's a minister. Why would you suspect him?"

"He's always sending letters to the editor about the drug problem in Oak Cliff. Twice, when I was working your route, he, along with some of the other kooks from his congregation, were picketing outside of Sean's place. And I heard his daughter died of some overdose thing back in the late eighties."

Losing a daughter to drugs would be plenty of motivation for murder if you had a drug dealer living just a few doors down the street. "Could be," I admitted. I wrote down his name. "And," Larry continued, "while he was on the other side of turning the cheek, he could have killed Fred Turley for running a hooker motel."

I jotted down the possible motives next to Nagle's name. "Or maybe Fred harassed one of his parishioners. So, Nagle is on the list. Who else?"

He finished the hash browns and picked up the biscuit sandwich. "Maybe Fred Turley got wacked because he was taking pictures at the No-Tel motel."

That wouldn't connect to Sean's murder but running a hooker motel couldn't have been lucrative. Maybe Fred had turned to blackmail to supplement his income. I tried to remember if he'd ever gotten anything that looked like thick stacks of cash.

I wondered, though, if Larry was making this up, or if he had something more concrete to go on. "I'd think there would be evidence of that. You know, cameras in the rooms or video monitors in Fred's office."

Larry inhaled the entire sandwich. "Uh huv fres en ee polic?" Biscuit crumbs sprayed the air as he spoke.

I moved a bit farther away, trying not to be obvious. "Huh?"

He swallowed, grabbed my coffee and took a deep gulp. "Sorry, my mouth was full."

He shoved the cup back my way.

"Keep the coffee. I had all I'm going to drink." Especially after Larry had put his lips on my cup. Gross.

"I just wondered if you had any friends in the police. Somebody who would let us know if they found any evidence that Fred was voyeuring in on his clients."

I didn't think *voyeuring* was a word. But Larry was on a roll and correcting his grammar might distract him. "All the cops I know think I did it. They aren't going to tell me anything."

"Bummer." He licked the crumbs off the wrapper the biscuit had come in, looked around to make sure there wasn't any more food, then grinned at me and shrugged. "Well, that's all I can think of. You want the list?"

A glimmer of an idea from the cop shows I watch finally penetrated my skull. "Didn't Sean used to have a wife?"

He scratched his head with a hand still dripping with grease from the sausage and cheese in the sandwich. "Don't know. Why?"

"What if Sean wasn't killed over drugs? I read somewhere that it's generally money, sex, or love that cause murder. When there are ex-spouses involved, you get all three."

"I don't remember an ex-wife."

"I never met her, but I'm pretty sure there was one."

I'd delivered mail addressed to a Lauren Herbert. Same last name generally meant a wife or family member. Either way she was worth looking into. I added her name to the list and then scribbled something about cameras in the Rock Cliff No-Tell. I didn't know how I was going to look into that, but I didn't know how I was going to investigate the Reverend or Lauren either. At least I was consistent.

"I've got to get back to your route," Larry told me. "Hope I don't find any dead bodies. I'd hate to have the cops after me the way they are after you."

"Right. I'll see you around, Larry. I appreciate your help on this."

"No problem." He got up and headed for the door, then returned and grabbed my coffee cup. "Guess I'll get a roadie. But let me know if you want my help with the Reverend. And the union is still behind you--within reason."

The *within reason* caveat didn't make me feel very confident but at least Larry had given me some things to follow up on if I was going to take Tina's advice and become my own detective.

The *Funny Guy in a Hat* had a phone directory but there was no listing for Lauren Herbert. So I decided to tackle the Reverend Nagle first.

I was wheezing and blowing by the time I got to the top of Sylvan and coasted the rest of the way to the cute 1940s home where Nagle lived.

I had to ride past Sean's house to get there. The yellow police tape draped over the grounds made it look like Sean had been the victim of a teenaged toilet paper raid but my stomach clenched at the sight and threatened to lose the few swallows of coffee I'd managed to absorb.

I'd gotten so caught up in my own problems that I hadn't really thought about the real victims. Fred and Sean might not have been the cream of society, but they'd been people. Nobody, no matter how bad they were, deserved to be chopped up the way those two had.

I told myself that clearing myself wasn't completely selfish. If I was convicted, the real killer would walk free.

I couldn't tell whether I was justifying or if I really believed it, but thinking that way made me feel a little better.

I braked in front of the Reverend's place, locked my bike to a tree, and knocked.

He took his time getting to the door, but I finally saw his eyeball through the security peephole.

"Reverend Nagle, I need to talk to you."

"You don't normally deliver the mail this early."

"This isn't a mail delivery. Can I come in?"

He opened the door reluctantly, then stepped back and showed me into a formal parlor that looked designed to make his guests uncomfortable and in a hurry to leave.

"What's this about, Ms., uh," his eyes rolled back while he searched for a name, "Ms. Walsh, isn't it?"

"Right. Kimberly Walsh. Why don't you call me Kimberly? Everybody does."

He shook his head slowly, the full head of wavy white hair bobbing. "I'm from another generation. One that treats people formally and reserves first names for special friendships."

Which showed me where I fit. Being a Gen-Y'er, calling people by last names reminded me more of Jane Austen than polite formality.

"Well, I appreciate you taking the time to see me, Reverend Nagle."

"I heard about your afflictions on the radio," Nagle admitted. He patted me lightly on the hand, then drew back quickly as if concerned that those *afflictions* might be catchy. "You aren't a member of my congregation, but the church's door is always open to those who are troubled. And remember, the Lord can forgive you, no matter what terrible thing you have done. He understands anger, especially against those who serve the devil like Sean Herbert and Fred Turley. But you do have to ask for forgiveness with an open heart."

I told him I'd keep that in mind but admitted that wasn't why I'd sought him out.

He looked nonplussed. "Really? Why else would you come to me?"

I'd been thinking about this while I'd biked up the hill. If I just came out and told Rev. Nagle I wondered if he'd done the killing, he wasn't likely to be forthcoming.

"I'm talking to all of Mr. Herbert's neighbors," I explained. "Trying to see if anyone saw anything."

Nagle shook his head slowly. "And you just happened to come to me first? Somehow I don't think that's likely, Ms. Walsh."

"Help me out, here, Reverend. Everyone knows that you were watching Sean. You were always calling the cops on him, trying to catch him dealing so you could clean up the neighborhood. If anyone was likely to see something, it was you."

The Reverend hadn't spent decades counseling congregation members without being able to read between the lines. "You think *I* killed him when my protests went nowhere?" He pulled a white handkerchief from his pocket and wiped his forehead. "If you were a regular churchgoer, you would know how impossible that is. The Lord is responsible for death and punishment. Ordinary people who take judgment into their own hands risk becoming what they hate most."

He was right about my religious habits. I hadn't darkened a church door since I'd left home for college, but I knew plenty of people who called themselves good Christians who wouldn't at all mind helping out the Lord with the whole judgment thing, what with his backlog and all. I took Nagle's *good Christian* line with a grain of salt.

"Why don't we just forget about all of that?" I took my notepad from my backpack, quickly flipped past my one-name list of suspects, hoping that the Reverend couldn't see it through his bifocals, and licked the pencil. "Let's start with day before yesterday. The cops think the murder took place around midday. So, starting first thing in the morning, did you see anyone coming or going from Sean's house?"

Chapter 4

An hour spent questioning the Reverend got me just about nothing.

He's seen a few people coming and going from Sean's house, but Sean was a businessman and people were always coming and going. He agreed that Sean had once had a woman living with him but couldn't remember when that had stopped. He certainly didn't confess to any criminal actions himself, or even act nervous. If I hadn't been a complete cynic, I might have even believed his expressed sorrow that Sean had been killed before he had accepted the mercy of the Lord.

My stomach gave a couple of complaints as I biked back home, but they were easy enough to ignore. I could catch up on my eating when I was in prison.

When I got back to the trailer park, I knocked on Tina's door.

"I'm trying to detect," I told her when she opened it.

"Okay."

"Sean Herbert had a wife, I think named Lauren. Far as I know, the cops haven't talked to her yet, aren't looking for her, don't know about her. But the ex should always be a suspect, from what I know."

She nodded. "Makes sense."

"So, I need some hacking help tracking her down."

"And you thought of me."

"You are a computer geek."

She sighed. "All right, come in."

I had to shoo a chicken off her spare chair--incredibly enough, Tina kept the things as pets.

She got to work with some search engines I wasn't familiar with, then printed off a couple of pictures, a credit report, and an address.

From the pictures, Lauren was quite the babe. From the address and the dates on the credit report, it looked like she'd moved out to Allen, a neighborhood about three suburbs north of Dallas.

Since I lived in the south part of Dallas, this meant a long haul.

There aren't many times when I mind not having a car. I certainly don't miss the monthly payment. But having to load my bike onto light rail, take it to the end of the line and then ride another fifteen miles out through rows of McMansions made me wish for the days I'd just been able to jump in my BMW and go anywhere without even thinking about it.

Thinking about visiting Allen also gave me a bit of a retro chill. Back in my telecom days, I'd lived about two miles from where Lauren lived now. Back then, when we were all working eighty hour weeks and going to get rich on the IPO, I'd owned an over-leveraged McMansion, my Beemer, been in debt to my eyeballs, and trapped in the whole *living large* nightmare. When I'd lost my job, my mortgage and credit card minimum payments got impossible. The bank had repossessed the house and car, and was still dunning me for what they hadn't got when they'd auctioned them. They'd even got the Postal Service to hold back a quarter of my paycheck every two weeks to pay off those debts.

"So," Tina suggested brightly. "Want me to come along when you look her up?"

Going back to that neighborhood would dig through enough failures without sharing them with someone else.

I gestured to the pictures. "I can't imagine she's dangerous. She'd be worried about breaking a fingernail."

Tina shook her head. "Maybe. But you were the one who suggested the ex might be involved."

"Maybe she knows something. I'll let you know if I need help."

Sure I would.

I turned down her offer of lunch, suspecting she didn't have more in her refrigerator than I had in mine and went back to my trailer.

I caught myself waffling, checking through my notes, trying to figure something else to do. Procrastinating. There was only one way to deal with this. I had to confront the fear.

I dialed the landline number Tina had found for Lauren and got a breathy "hello?"

I hung up. Lauren was at home. I didn't want to give her any warning or time to get her story straight so I had to confront her in person.

I got on my bike and headed for the train station.

Dallas isn't like New York or Chicago with their fancy subways and abundant mass transportation. It's a city created around cars. Even after the gas crisis, it has far more SUVs and trucks than pedestrians, bicyclists and smaller autos, combined. But we did have a light rail train, which snaked through the city and out into the northern suburbs.

I got the day pass for three bucks, carried my bike into the train with me, and settled down.

It was past noon and the lunchtime crowd was heading back to their downtown offices. Once I got to Cityplace, though, I had the entire car to myself.

It takes almost an hour for the train to rush in from south Dallas, creep through downtown, then accelerate north alongside U.S. 75 through North Dallas, Richardson, and finally Plano where it ends in a fancy large and under-used terminal.

The trip gave me plenty of time to think about additional suspects, possible motives, and next steps.

It turned out that an extra hour of thinking time didn't help much. It did give me the chance to realize that Larry had given me one useful idea I hadn't followed up on. Although the Dallas Police Department wasn't going to give me any help, Lindner had ordered the Postal Police to get involved. I didn't have friends in DPD, but maybe my new buddy Preston Rolin could help find whether there was any evidence of blackmail going on with Fred Turley, the No-Tell Motel operator.

I called Buddy, had him track down Preston's number, and dialed it on my cell.

"Hi, this is Preston Rolin."

"Oh, hi Preston. This is--"

"I can't come to the phone right now, probably because I'm out working on a case. Press one if you'd like to leave a message. Press two if you'd like to page me."

I pressed two, then entered my own cell number.

We were pulling into the final stop on Parker Road, a modern-looking concrete and glass terminal, when my cell rang.

I pressed the phone to my ear, picked up my bike, and pushed the door-open button.

"This is Officer Preston Rolin. I'm returning a page."

"Hi Preston. This is Kimberly Walsh. I--"

"I'm sorry, I can't hear you. Could you speak directly into the phone?"

"Just a second."

The door slammed shut on my bike but I managed to pull it out, dropping the cell on the ground at the same time.

When I finally picked it up, Preston sounded a bit pissed.

"Sorry, Preston. It's Kimberly Walsh."

"Oh?" My name didn't make him any happier. "I really shouldn't be talking to you."

"I understand that the Postal Police have been asked to support the D.P.D. investigation into the murders on my route."

"That's why I shouldn't talk to you."

"I didn't do it, all right? I just need to know some things."

He sighed. "What sort of things, Walsh?"

"I have a theory on the Fred Turley murder. Running a business like his, it would be easy to snap pictures of some of the more affluent clients and blackmail them later."

He considered that. "I suppose."

"Which would give us another whole group of suspects."

"You know, you might have a point." His voice got more enthusiastic as he went on. "Getting you off would be good for the Post Office's reputation. And finding the real killer would be great for the P.O. Police rep."

I didn't believe he cared as much about the Postal Department reputation as he did about his own, but he was going my way so I agreed with him.

"Yeah, no kidding. I'm completely sick of D.P.D. treating me like a second-class citizen. What a crock."

"I wish Mr. Lindner had your attitude."

"You know suits."

Boy did I.

Vito would probably head Preston off before he got far, but I'd take whatever help I could get. "Do you think you could find out if the Rock Hill No-Tell was wired? If there were cameras in the rooms, that would be pretty good evidence that my theory has legs."

"Good thinking, Kimmy. I'm betting I can get the D.P.D. reports if I whine and grovel a little. And maybe I'll just do a bit of snooping around the ol' No-Tell myself."

I hated being called Kimmy but I gritted my teeth and didn't complain about it. The man was helping me, which was something not many people were doing.

"Thanks, Preston." Another train roared in, the squeal of its brakes momentarily overwhelming Preston's voice.

"Sorry, Preston," I said when the train pulled out. "If you said anything just now, I couldn't hear over the noise."

"I thought I heard something. Where are you, anyway?"

"I'm up in Plano, at the Light Rail Station."

A momentary pause. "You aren't running away, are you, Kimmy? Because--"

"Give me a break, Preston. It's not like DART is going to let me escape."

"It's out of Dallas County."

"I'll be back."

His chuckle sounded only halfway convinced. "I guess so. Say, I was thinking of something else."

"Yeah?"

"Has anyone offered to help you? You know, been too interested in the case."

"I wish. Why?"

"You know what they say. With this kind of serial killer crime, sometimes the perps like to get involved."

He paused and I didn't say anything but I was thinking about Buddy. He'd never actually been friendly before but he'd collected the dog and then come out to the crime scene the previous day. And then there was Larry. Sure the union angle made sense, but doesn't the union generally wait for workers to ask for its help?

"Hey, it was just a thought," Preston said. "Probably crazy."

"Maybe. But I'll think about it."

"Hey, no. I mean, I feel bad. Jeez, the last thing you need is to think your friends are stabbing you in the back. I'm probably just paranoid because of my academy training. I mean, how likely is it that we've got a serial killer in the Dallas Post Office?"

According to the Dallas Police, it was very likely. But now I was completely confused. And despite Preston's quick shift into reverse, he had a point.

Anyone interested, even if they said they wanted to help, had to be a suspect. I'd have to research both Larry and Buddy to see if they might have some connection to the victims. One obvious thing, I'd gotten back from vacation the day I'd found Sean's body. Larry had worked my route the previous week. He would have seen Sean and Fred. He could have seen something, done something, triggered something that left me holding the bag.

"Let me know what you find out about the Rock Hill No-Tell, I told Preston.

"I'll do what I can. I mean, you are still the primary suspect. I can't promise anything. Hey, now that I think about it, you're involving yourself in the case. That might support the D.P.D. argument that you're the killer."

"They've labeled me as a suspect," I reminded him. "That means they involved me, not that I involved myself."

"I take your point. I'm not sure they'll agree, though."

I was mad enough to throw the phone against the concrete wall of the train depot, but I restrained myself. Preston was right and he was doing his job. The cops couldn't just let the suspect know how close they were getting, what evidence they had found. At least not until they had exhausted their investigation.

I hung up the phone, checked my bike tires to make sure I hadn't picked up a flat, stuck on my helmet, and headed north.

* * * *

A couple of generations earlier, this part of Texas had been cotton country. The Great Depression had ended that, and North Texas hadn't recovered until the 1980s when telecom and high-tech had brought industry to the area. The 1990s had been the huge growth spurt, with highrises pushing through hayfields, and huge brick mini-mansions springing up in the ruined black earth of ancient cotton fields. Telecom had receded, and the housing bust had hit hard, but there was still wealth, still even some construction.

I passed a couple of kids on skateboards, but other than that, the only sign of life I saw were surprised faces behind SUV steering wheels. Out here, people didn't think there was such a thing as grownup transportation that weighed less than two tons.

Lauren's place looked exactly the same as four other houses on her street. I think they had three designs that they mixed and matched. Hers was a red brick two-story traditional with exactly one scraggly tree in the front yard.

I locked my bike to the faux-pillar outside her front door and rang the doorbell.

The doorbell played the first notes from Dixie.

I waited a good minute, then rang again.

A Hispanic-looking woman finally opened the front door. "Yes?"

"I'm looking for Lauren Herbert."

"What business, please."

"I'd like to discuss her husband's death."

"Always the police." The woman shook her head. "You wait here. I see if

32

she is up to visitors."

In my case, 'here' referred to the front porch. She wasn't going to invite me in without the say-so of her boss. I couldn't really blame her. I was drippy-wet from the August heat, had a serious case of helmet hair, and probably didn't smell as fresh as I could have.

Lauren Herbert took her time coming to the door. The photos hadn't done her justice. She was a knockout, with artfully applied makeup, an expensive streaking job, and green eyes that enhanced her already striking looks. If a woman like her had to settle for some drug lord, my chances for finding a reasonable date pretty much sucked.

She looked down her nose at me. "You aren't the police."

This wasn't news to me but I nodded. "You're right. But I'd still like to talk with you regarding your late ex-husband's murder."

"Late *husband*."

"I beg your pardon."

"We were separated, not divorced. I'm a widow and the police are treating me like some sort of whore."

I knew the feeling. I decided to try a little female bonding. "I've noticed the police jump to conclusions. That's one of the reasons I wanted to talk to you."

Lauren's eyes widened, then she blinked suddenly when a lens threatened to pop out. She rubbed it back into place, and then put her hands over her abundant breasts. "You're her, aren't you? The killer. Have you come to kill me as well?"

Lauren's overacting didn't persuade me of anything. "I don't want to kill you but we do need to talk. Can I come in?"

She rolled an overly plump lip over one of her canines and pouted--a look most men probably found hopelessly sexy but that was wasted on me.

I stared back at her.

Finally she looked away. "Very well, we can sit in the kitchen."

I couldn't blame her for not wanting me to drip sweat over her nice furniture. I followed her through the house into a kitchen roughly the size of my entire trailer. Huge copper pots hung from the ceiling, chrome electrical appliances lined the counter space, but I couldn't see a sign that any of it had ever been used. It was a Potemkin kitchen. I recognized it because I'd had one just like it when I'd been in telecom and lived in the neighborhood.

Lauren draped towels over a wooden chair before finally inviting me to sit. "What do we need to talk about?"

I couldn't think of any clever way to say it so I blurted it out. "I didn't kill Sean but the police are trying to pin it on me. If they can't get me, they'll try to pin it on you since you're the wife. I imagine you're also his primary heir."

She waved a hand, as if she could make that whole unpleasantness go away. "Sean always gave me plenty of money. I wouldn't have to kill him just to inherit."

Lauren looked high-maintenance. What if Sean had decided to put her on an allowance? From Lauren's perspective, the golden goose's entire nest might be a lot more appetizing than wishing for the occasional egg.

"I doubt that the police will see it that way. And they have been here, already, haven't they. Your housekeeper indicated that."

"Carmine thought you were a cop. They've been talking about adding bicycle patrols in Allen. Ridiculous, isn't it? How could they ever catch a speeder?"

"I know the police went over this with you, Lauren, but if you could run through your schedule for the past few days, it would help. We've got to be sure we're both in the clear."

I was playing the us-against-the-world card as hard as I could because it was the only approach I could think of other than accusing her--which wasn't likely to create a cooperative attitude.

She looked away from me. "I was shopping at Collin Creek Mall the entire day Sean was killed."

"Great." I tried to be enthusiastic for her even though this could just mean I'd eliminated a suspect. "Your receipts will have times on them. When you show them to the cops, they'll recognize that you're in the clear."

Lauren got up from the table, opened the refrigerator, pulled out a bottle of wine, and brought it, along with a half-pound package of Oreo cookies to the table.

Oreo cookies were one of my weaknesses.

"You don't look so good," she said. "When was the last time you ate?"

"I eat plenty."

"I'm not going to talk to you any more if I don't see you eating."

I selected a cookie from the package and brought it to the vicinity of my lips. "You do keep your receipts, right?

She shook her head. "I'm not that gullible. Don't wave your food, eat it. I'm watching."

I decided I could manage a cookie. I had been for a long bike ride and breakfast had been a long time before that. I tried not to think about how many calories had been in that Jack in the Box breakfast meal I'd ordered. Larry had eaten some of it but I was convinced I was responsible for the full couple thousand calories.

"Okay. Uh, thanks." I bit a hunk out of the cookie and chewed, putting the remaining bit down on the little plate Lauren had gotten me.

She waited until I swallowed. "Finish it."

"I'm pretty full."

"Do you really think I don't recognize an eating disorder when I see one? I used to be a model. I've seen them all, had them all. Eat the damned cookie."

I stuffed the rest of it into my mouth, wondering if I looked like Larry doing his snake act while Lauren poured a couple of big tumblers full of wine.

"Drink."

"I don't--"

"Would you shut up about this? I'm going to tell you everything I know. The least you can do is humor me."

34

I took a sip of the wine. It was better than anything I could afford. Still, I couldn't help thinking about the calories.

"Eat another," she told me.

I ignored that. "So, anyway, if you kept your receipts, you're off the hook. If you didn't, you can get Visa to send you copies of your credit card slips. They record the time they cleared them, and that should be within a couple of minutes of when you made the purchase." I knew this from my own run-in with credit card companies and overdue payments.

Lauren took a deep slug from her wineglass. "I said I went shopping, not that I'd bought anything."

Sorry, no. I didn't believe that. If *this* woman went shopping, she would have bought something.

"I told the cops they could show my picture around the mall. Someone would recognize me, let them know I'd been there. They took my picture, but I don't think they were going to do anything."

Some street cop would probably pin it up inside his locker and pretend he had a girlfriend as pretty as Lauren.

I couldn't blame them for ignoring her detecting advice. Sure, some mall workers would recognize Lauren--she probably shopped there all the time. But they wouldn't be able to establish that she was there during specific hours on a specific day.

"What about yesterday morning, early?"

"Eat another cookie."

"Huh?"

"That's the deal. One question, one cookie."

Since she was providing both the answers and the cookies, it didn't sound like much of a bargain for her. Since each cookie was fifty-three calories, it wasn't much of a deal for me, either. I couldn't understand why a woman with a figure like Lauren would want to turn me back into a blimp--it wasn't like I was competition.

Explaining that got me nowhere. I couldn't make her answer the questions without following her rules, so I took another cookie, bit off a hunk, then dropped the rest into my lap when I thought Lauren wasn't watching.

"Five second rule," she said. "Finish it."

My face burned. "Can I have some water?"

"No. Drink your goddammed wine and eat your cookie."

I was starting to see why Sean hadn't kept her around. This woman might be a babe to look at, but she had some seriously bossy habits.

"Yesterday morning?" I repeated once I'd swallowed down the cookie. "Tell me what you were doing then."

I tried not to think about how long I'd have to spend bicycling around the neighborhood to burn off these calories.

"Yesterday? I was in bed."

"Alone?"

"I am a married woman."

She was a non-grieving widow who'd been separated from her husband for I had no idea how long.

"Don't evade."

"All right, then. I was in bed alone. I have no alibi. But I didn't kill Sean. And I didn't kill that other guy in that motel." She picked up one of the Oreos, looked at it warily, then screwed off the top layer and scraped the white filling off with her sharp, perfectly white, teeth.

Talk about people with eating disorders. She had to be projecting her stuff onto me. No way I had a problem with my eating. Not any more. Back in the old days, I'd been a pig. I'd been miserable, and food was my comfort. As soon as I'd escaped from telecom, I'd dropped seventy pounds--seventy pounds of solid lard.

"If you didn't kill them and I didn't kill them, then who did? Who would have a motive? You know Sean. He's got to have enemies. Maybe other drug dealers. Maybe a pissed-off customer."

She gestured to the cookie bowl. "That's another question. Eat."

I pulled my sweat-soggy notepad from my pack and jotted down what she'd told me so far then, under her implacable glare, ate another cookie.

* * * *

Three hours later I was drunk, stuffed with cookies, and hadn't learned much. Lauren claimed complete ignorance of Sean's customers, enemies, girlfriends, or connections with Fred Turley at the No-Tell Motel.

One thing she did say was that Sean didn't deal in the normal street drugs--crack or heroine or marijuana. He specialized in illegal steroids, amphetamines, a bit of recreational cocaine, Valium, Vicodin, and performance-affecting drugs for athletes.

I wasn't sure whether to believe her or not, but if she was telling the truth, that made it less likely that he would have been killed by some addict desperate for his fix. People who were doping to make it into the pros wanted to have a steady source, and generally had the money to pay for it.

"That's how I met him," she explained. "I used to be a model but I liked to eat. So I used amphetamines to keep my weight down. Of course I don't do that any more."

Okay, that connected another dot.

I knew I should push harder, get aggressive with her non-alibi for the time Sean was murdered. She could have told me and the police that she'd been home watching television or something. Instead, she'd made up an obvious lie. But I was afraid that the alcohol in my system would keep me from picking up on any subtle signals. Besides, if she really was the killer, did I want her to know I was suspicious when I was in such a weakened position?

I pushed my chair back from her kitchen table.

"Look, I've got to go. I can't afford to ask you any more questions. Besides, you're out of Oreos." I couldn't believe two people had gone through an entire half-pound of cookies.

She shook her head firmly. "It's getting dark and it's not safe for you to be on the roads at night around here. People don't expect to see a bike and they'll run right over you."

"But--"

"So you'll spend the night. It isn't as if I don't have plenty of room. We can brainstorm who else might be behind the killers and get pizza delivered and eat ice cream and drink another bottle of wine. It'll be like we were in junior high again."

I'd never done anything like that, even without the wine, when I'd been in junior high school. Instead, I'd always been studying, working on the science fair, or doing homework for one of the cute guys I thought I could make like me.

Having a girls' night out might be somebody's idea of fun, but if Lauren had already killed two strong men, she certainly was capable of killing me when I was drunk and sleepy.

I couldn't get Preston's warning out of my mind. Lauren was the third person in two days who'd gone out of her way to be helpful, insinuated herself into the investigation. If Lauren was the killer, spending the night with her could just be the last mistake I ever made.

"I don't think so," I said. "I'd better go before the sun sets completely."

I stood, but too quickly. My blood all rushed out of my head and I sat down, missed my chair, and my butt hit the floor, hard.

"That had to hurt." Lauren gave me a hand up.

She barely yanked and I found myself launched back to my feet. This woman was strong. She'd said she'd been a model and I could see how she would be. She had to be five foot eight, maybe five ten. And she had the muscled look of an Olympic beach volleyball star. A woman that strong could stab a man--kill a man. Especially considering that any man who swung for the straight team would be so distracted by her looks that they wouldn't even see a knife coming.

I knew it was late for this but I realized I needed to reset our ground rules.

"The postal police know I was coming out here."

She wrinkled her nose at me in a silent query before making the connection--and bursting out into laughter. "Do you think I'd spend hours talking to you, feeding you, getting you drunk, if I was just going to kill you? I doubt you weigh eighty pounds. I could pick you up and break you over my knee. I don't need to get you helpless."

"I weigh more than that." I didn't argue with her about the knee thing. If I argued she couldn't do the knee thing, I suspected she'd feel compelled to demonstrate--and I didn't need that pain.

"I want to help you, Kimberly," she said. She put a hand on my arm and squeezed. "And I want to know who killed my husband. I don't think you did it, but the cops aren't going to look any further than the two of us. If we don't find out who killed Sean, who will?"

I rubbed my arm where she'd squeezed it. Who indeed?

"I'm not eating ice cream," I told her.

"It's Rocky Road."

I shook my head firmly. "I was a blimp before I lost my telecom job. I'm not going to turn back into that other person. And besides, counting calories isn't an eating disorder, it's common sense."

"You're in severe denial."

"You're almost a foot taller than me. You don't understand how little my body needed to keep going."

"Complete denial. Anyway, let's lay out the scenario. I know the neighbors. Have you thought about the crazy preacher next door. Reverend Nagle? He hates Sean." She stopped and got a funny look in her eyes. "Hated Sean."

That look almost made me cry. Either Lauren was a great actress or she was innocent.

Chapter 5

I woke up the next morning with a hangover, a bloated stomach, and the realization that Lauren hadn't killed me during the night.

Given my throbbing head, I almost wished she had.

I dragged myself to Lauren's perfectly clean and probably never used guest bathroom, stood under the shower for long enough to wash some of the cobwebs out of my brain. Cold showers burn calories and I needed all the help I could get.

After my body started wrinkling, I rubbed myself dry, pinched my stomach to see how far it was sticking out, and finally dressed myself in yesterday's cycling clothes.

Yuck.

Cycling clothes dry out quickly so I didn't squosh when I walked but they could have done with a wash.

I borrowed some of Lauren's deodorant and went downstairs.

Lauren sat on her white leather couch dressed in a pair of black jeans that could have been painted onto her butt, a black scoop-necked t-shirt cut high to show off her pierced navel, and a pair of black converse sneakers.

"*Honey West*," I guessed. I couldn't help it, during my down-cycle after my telecom layoff, I'd spent three months watching ancient reruns.

"Huh?"

"I guess models don't watch old television."

"I don't know--"

"You look like a really old TV show, that's all. Why the all-black look? Today isn't Sean's funeral, is it?"

She shook her head. "You don't get it, Kim. We're partners now. We're going sleuthing."

Was sleuth a verb? I needed to look that up. "I don't know, Lauren. It's pretty dangerous."

"Eat your breakfast and we'll talk about it afterwards."

The table was covered with fruit, five different flavors of breakfast cereal, and a pitcher of Bloody Marys.

I snagged a wedge of cantaloupe and worked on that while Lauren wolfed down a bowl of cereal, a banana, a whole stem of grapes, and two Bloody Marys.

"You'd better eat more," she told me when I finished my melon slice.

"I'm fine."

She sighed. "I don't have the energy to fight with you right now. We'd better get going. You can throw your bike into the back of my Celica."

A part of me wanted to go along. After all, she hadn't killed me during the night. But I couldn't help remembering Preston's warning about helpful people. Lauren was becoming way too involved, just like Preston had suggested that the real killer would. And a model is a sort of actress, isn't she?

I put on my stern face. "Lauren, I know you lied to me about shopping in Collin Creek Mall. How can I trust you, partner with you, if you're holding out on me?"

If I'd expected her to look guilty, I'd been kidding myself. She came back on counter-attack.

"That goes two ways, Kim. How can I know that you aren't the real killer? The police suspect you more than me."

Come to think of it, Preston's warning *could* apply to me. I was looking into the case, interfering where the police didn't want me. *I* knew I was innocent, but that didn't make my activities any less suspicious. No wonder Preston had been unenthusiastic about my trip north.

"Maybe not. But I haven't lied to you," I reminded her. "That sort of puts the ball in your court."

Lauren studied my face for long enough to make me wish I had a mirror.

"I'll tell you in the car," she finally decided. "Let's get out of here."

I gathered up my stuff, put it in my backpack, unlocked my bike from where I'd left it all night, and dropped it into the back of Lauren's cute little Toyota.

Lauren cranked up the air conditioner a notch but this was Texas. We were still baking.

"I *had* to lie," she when we got to 75.

"Huh?"

"I didn't go to Collin Creek Mall. I was down in Oak Cliff that day. I, uh, went to see Sean."

All of a sudden the air conditioner seemed too cold. "What are you trying to tell me, Lauren?"

"Oh, I didn't kill him." She laughed nervously. "I wouldn't have done that. But I was there in his house. I saw his body all cut up and mangled. If I'd called the police, they would have assumed it was me so I just left."

"You've got to tell the cops, Lauren."

Her laughter was harsh. "That would be great for *you*, wouldn't it, Kim. They drop you as a suspect and slobber all over me. But you know they won't give me a fair shake. They're going to pick a suspect and do their best to prove that case rather than look at the evidence objectively. That's why I'm not telling them anything."

"So, what's the point of--"

"I believe you, though, when you said you're looking for the real killer. I'll help you with that because it'll help me, too. Besides, you don't want Sean's real killer to get away with murder, do you?"

I cared less about Sean and his real killer than I did about getting sentenced to a lethal injection myself.

I considered going to the police with what she'd told me. Unfortunately, they'd probably decide I was lying. Even if they found evidence Lauren had been there, that wouldn't mean anything--she'd lived there. It was either take her deal or go back to where I'd been before I'd visited her--nowhere.

I'd take the deal, but I wouldn't stop watching her. Lauren was still number one on my suspect list, although I couldn't figure out why she would have admitted to being in the house if she'd been guilty. After all, just because I hadn't figured it out didn't mean it wasn't true.

"Okay," I finally agreed.

She stuck out a hand. "Partners."

I was being blackmailed and we both knew it, but I didn't see any choice. "Partners." If I had to break my promise, I'd claim I'd made it under duress.

"So, where do we start?"

* * * *

Where we started was lunch.

Lauren had lived in Seth's Oak Cliff neighborhood before they'd separated, so she drove straight to the neighborhood diner, Norma's.

"We just ate," I reminded her.

"I ate. You played with a melon. Besides, we want to find out if Sean had any enemies besides Nagle. If Pam doesn't know, who would?

Pam was the manager of Norma's and she knew everyone. I wasn't sure she knew everyone's business, though, and told Lauren that.

"Pam knows everything," Lauren assured me.

Pam certainly knew Lauren and, although I'd only eaten there a few times, she recognized me as well.

"We came to talk about Sean," I told her.

"Order up. I'll come sit with you when your food gets here."

I hadn't intended on eating anything but I could hardly tell her that when I planned on picking her brain. When the waitress arrived, I ordered a cup of soup and a diet coke.

Lauren looked at me funny, then ordered the chicken fried steak dinner with corn, green beans, and mashed potatoes. "Extra gravy," she said. "And plenty of rolls and cornbread."

"I guess you can afford the calories," I said.

"You don't get it, do you, Kim. You still see yourself as the overweight slob you were years ago. At some subconscious level, you probably decided to become fat because you were tired of the male engineers treating you like a sexual object rather than another professional. But since then you've overcompensated the other way. You're too skinny. I'm surprised you're even able to finish your route with the way you've cut into your muscle mass."

Pam's arrival spared me from more unwanted analysis although I recognized that I'd opened the door to that discussion.

Still, a part of me wondered how Lauren knew so much about me. Had I even mentioned telecom? Had I told her about being fat? Or had she been researching me, looking for the perfect sucker to set up for the murders?

Pam stared at me. "You look like you've been sick, Kimberly. A couple of good Norma's meals will take some of the gauntness out of you. So I brought you some of our peanut butter-chocolate meringue pie."

"Thanks." Being rude and ungrateful to people you planned to ask for a favor wasn't smart. But I was reminded of why I ate in impersonal chain restaurants. Nobody at the Funny Guy in a Hat ever commented on my weight or suggested I eat more because I was too skinny.

"We're trying to figure out who hated Sean enough to kill him," Lauren said between bites of the breaded meat. "The cops think it's one of us."

Pam screwed up her face in thought. "You already know about Steve, I guess. He hated Sean."

"Reverend Nagle." Lauren had her own notepad out and ticked off his name. "Yeah. He was the first person either Kim or I thought of."

"Then there's Fred. 'Course he's dead now too."

"Fred Turley?" My ears perked up at that. "I didn't know there was a connection between the two of them. I thought Fred barely ever came out of his motel."

Pam shook her head. "Huh-un. Fred used to deal for Sean. The motel was a great place to distribute because Fred could leave stuff in the room, collect a little extra when he rented the room out for an hour, and the cops would never see the actual handover. Since Fred only took cash, the whole thing was pretty easy to arrange. Plus he could launder his money using his business."

I had to admit that Lauren had been right. Pam did seem to know everything.

"But that makes it sound like they were partners, not enemies," Lauren said.

"Right. Until Sean cut Fred off. Fred was dealing too much coke. Sean said he was putting both of them in danger and decided to go another route. Not sure who he was using instead."

I made a note of that. Someone might have killed both Sean and Fred to eliminate the competition. As far as I knew, Dallas had never had a major drug war the way some of the big organized cities back east did, but that didn't mean there wasn't violence. Where there was money to be made, people would fight, even kill, to get it.

"So who's going to take over the business that Fred and Sean won't be serving any more?"

Pam looked worried. "Nobody is talking."

She described another couple of incidents when Rev. Nagle had stalked Sean, including having the city turn off his water and the months where he'd had his congregation members going through Sean's trash looking for evidence to connect him to the drug dealing everyone knew he was doing. She didn't have anything we could use, anything actionable, but it was definitely suspicious.

Lauren beat me to the bill so I left the tip. As we were walking out, Pam joined us outside the diner.

"I heard about you getting bit," she told me sympathetically. "Are you all right?"

I shook my head. "I'm sorry, Pam. I don't know what you're talking about."

She looked confused. "I must have heard from three people about how Andrew the Dalmatian got his teeth into the postal carrier and took a good hunk of leg off."

"It wasn't me," I reported. "If it happened last week, I was on vacation." She didn't need to know I'd spent my vacation playing video games with Tina Anderson.

"Oh. My mistake. I guess I just assumed it was you because that's your route."

I nodded. "Makes sense. Well, thanks for lunch, Pam. And for the pie. It was great."

"Even if you only took one bite?"

"Lauren has been stuffing me with so much I don't have any room left. But it was really good."

"Okay. Well, y'all come back soon."

We promised we would and loaded back in the Toyota. "So," Lauren said, picking up on Pam's bombshell. "Who worked your route last week? If a postal worker got bit, they just might try to make things even--and that just might have been what killed my husband."

"Look, Lauren." I shook my head. "Sure there were a couple of incidents where postal workers flipped out, but we're mostly just ordinary people. Nobody is going to kill someone just because they got bit by a dog." Especially not someone as laid-back as Larry.

"*Somebody* killed my husband," Lauren reminded me. "It's better to follow weak leads than no leads at all. Unless you want to tackle the Reverend again, first."

* * * *

Rev. Nagle was at his church doing a wedding.

Lauren wanted to bust in and question him in front of his congregation so we could make sure he was telling the truth, but I'd spent too much of my adolescence dreaming of fantasy weddings--and wedding disasters--to be willing to do that to some innocent bride.

We peeked in, though.

Rev. Nagle stood in front of the wedding party looking like an *Old Testament* prophet of doom. His wife squealed out the wedding processional on an old organ and the groom stood watching, his eyes flitting from face to face as if seeking some escape.

What was it about weddings? My vision blurred and I swiped away a tear or two, hoping Lauren wouldn't notice.

"Sean and I had to get married in the courthouse," Lauren whispered. "Five minutes, fifty bucks and we were done."

If I were ever to get married, I'd want the whole deal, white dress, flowers, attendants, a whole day of it.

Which got me thinking--always dangerous.

"You know, the wedding is just starting. And I'll bet Nagle gives one of those long sermons before he goes through with it."

Lauren tugged me away from the church door. "Are you thinking what I'm thinking?"

"I read somewhere that everyone brings something to a crime scene and takes something away. Let's check out and see if we can find what Nagle took away."

We parked Lauren's Toyota half a block down from Nagle's house just in case any neighbor got curious and made the hike.

"Told you I was going to need the burglar suit," Lauren whispered loudly.

"Yeah. Just in case none of the neighbors were suspicious when we break down Nagle's door you make it obvious for them."

She stopped dead on the sidewalk, glaring at me. Then she giggled. "You are so funny, Kimberly. It's Oak Cliff. Lots of people wear black--but you had me for a second."

I walked up to Nagle's front door, trying to look like maybe a *Bible* saleswoman who'd been invited.

To my surprise, though, the door was locked. "He said his door was always open."

"Speaking metaphorically, obviously," Lauren said. "Not literally. How are your lockpicking skills?"

"Non-existent. How about--"

"Mine aren't any better. Let's check the back."

I got on my cell and called Tina while Lauren and I tromped around back.

"You want me to help you break into Reverend Nagle's house?" she demanded when I explained our predicament.

"We're not going to take anything. We're just looking for clues. You were the one who said I'd have to prove my innocence, and the only way to do that is to find the real killer."

"You're a menace. And don't blame this on me."

"So you'll help us?"

"I guess."

Nagle's house was a fort. Each of his four doors was equipped with three substantial deadbolts. The doors themselves were, as Tina assured us once she'd arrived in her ancient yellow Geo Storm, steel-core so they'd stand up to a police battering ram.

Unfortunately for Nagle, managing a trailer complex had taught Tina some tricks. She handed each of us a pair of latex gloves and then, in about two seconds, she popped one of Nagle's sliding glass doors out of its casing.

"You don't have to come in," I told her. "If you're--"

"I've come this far."

I hadn't made it past Nagle's sitting room, but the rest of the house looked to be the same--stuffy, and hung with cheap prints of that particular brand of religious painting that emphasizes suffering and death.

"I'll check his computer," Tina volunteered. "Why don't you two go through his laundry?"

"Eeew." Lauren and I both let out the same disgusted sound.

"Why," Lauren demanded, "would we want--"

But then I figured it out. "Sean and Larry were both killed with knives. It would be almost impossible to kill like that without getting blood on yourself. Maybe Nagle changed in between, and maybe he's already done his laundry, but--"

"We're looking for bloodstains," Lauren concluded. "Your buddy Tina is pretty smart."

She hadn't been my buddy until I was accused of murder, which seemed like a strange foundation for friendship. Then again, I hadn't even known Lauren and we were turning into buddies as well.

If we all ended up in jail for breaking and entering, maybe we could form a prison girl gang. The idea wasn't especially reassuring.

Also not reassuring was Nagle's laundry.

The good news was, it didn't look like he'd had his laundry done in more than a week. The bad news was--well, we had more than a week's worth of dirty male laundry to look through.

It took ten minutes go through his things. I learned about what he'd had for breakfast (blueberry syrup), and discovered strange stains in strange places. The only blood we found was a few spots on a hand towel.

Lauren packed it in her handbag. "He might have cut himself shaving. But what would it hurt to compare blood types?"

"You know how to do that?"

"I have a vague memory from high school biology. I'll Google it."

"How would you know if it's Nagle's type? We'd need a sample."

"I know Sean's type. If there's a match, we'll--"

"But you don't know Larry's."

"Look, I'm doing the best I can."

I nodded, but an uneasy idea hit me. "If I'd killed someone and had blood all over my clothes, I wouldn't just stuff them in the laundry hamper. I'm betting Nagle is a conservative guy who makes his wife do the washing up. But would he want her to see all that blood?"

"Hey guys," Tina's whisper sounded loud. "I think I found something."

We trooped into Nagle's office where Tina had his computer running.

A series of unsigned notes promised damnation to whomever they'd been sent.

"There aren't any names," I observed.

"But he mentions drugs and pornography." Lauren jabbed a sculpted fingernail into Nagle's monitor. "That's got to mean Sean and Larry."

It made sense to me. Unfortunately, I didn't think the police would agree.

"He'd deleted these files, emptied the recycle bin, even defragged his computer so they wouldn't show." Tina started the computer shutdown process. "But he didn't know *Word* sometimes leaves TMP files behind. What about you guys? Did you turn anything up?"

"Dirty laundry," I admitted. "A towel with a little blood. I think if he had something really bloody, he wouldn't put it with the rest of his clothes."

"We'll have to search the entire--" Lauren cut herself off. "What was that?"

"Oh, shit," Tina said. The rattling of keys in a series of deadbolts was unmistakable.

I grabbed both women by the arms and dragged them down the stairs. "Come on," I whispered.

"We're going to get caught," Lauren moaned. "We're going to…"

"Shut up."

We made it down the stairs just as the front door opened.

"Stephen. I think there's someone inside."

I shoved Tina and Lauren out the back, through the sliding glass door still hanging off its frame, into the alley running behind Nagle's home and finally through back yard of the one house on the other side of the alley without a substantial privacy fence.

"They'll find our cars," Tina said. "They'll know it was us."

I shoved my gloves into a green garbage bin. "They probably didn't see us. We'll just walk around and pick up our cars now."

"You're crazy."

"Kimberly is right," Lauren said. "The longer we wait, the more likely the cops are to check them out."

We tried to look like three women out for exercise, dropped Tina off at her car, then Lauren and I got into hers and drove away.

I glanced at Nagle's house as we turned the corner--and met his glare.

"I think he knows who did it," I whispered.

"He can't prove it."

"Do you think that makes me feel any better? He couldn't prove that Sean was dealing drugs, so he dealt with it in a different way. I'd just as soon not have him cut my throat if it's all the same to you."

"But maybe," Lauren said, "he didn't do it. Writing threatening letters isn't the same as murder."

"That isn't as reassuring as you think it is."

Chapter 6

Lauren made noises about stopping and eating again--how did that woman stay slim with what seemed like fifteen meals a day? Instead, I suggested we track down Larry Mueller. He was still on my suspect list and with his questionable grasp on reality, he might even provide us with an alibi if Rev. Nagle called the cops on us.

Considering how helpful he'd been the last couple of times we'd met, he didn't seem all that glad to see me when I caught him at the end of what should have been my route. Still, he perked up with Lauren suggested we stop by Cafe Brazil in the Bishop Arts district for a fancy coffee, and then talk to him at home. She winked at him when she mentioned his home and Larry practically drooled.

Lauren took Larry's order, ignored my request for a black coffee, and returned with three frozen whipped-cream-topped drinks that probably weighed in at five hundred calories a pop.

We then followed Larry, who drove a surprisingly recent-model Audi, to his place, a bungalow in Cockrell Hill.

Larry made Lauren sit on a lumpy-looking couch, and crowded close to her. Rather than squeeze in, I grabbed a kitchen chair.

When I got back, Larry was playing with his food. "I love whipped cream, know what I mean?" He scooped a mound of whipped cream on his straw and licked it off so slowly I wondered if he'd lost a few brain synapses somewhere.

After a few seconds of incredulous watching I realized that he was trying to be sensual--making an effort to impress Lauren.

Lauren acted impressed. She giggled, touched Larry on the arm, and generally went into full flirt mode.

I tried not to gag. It wasn't just that Larry wasn't my type, it was that I didn't think Larry could be *anyone's* type. His long hair wouldn't have bothered me if he'd kept it clean, but he seemed to eat things out of it and that couldn't be a good sign. Plus his hygiene problems.

"When Kimberly told me you'd offered to help," Lauren cooed, "I thought, great. Because she was out of town all last week and I figured you might have seen something."

As explanations went, it wasn't much, but it did serve to remind Larry that he'd promised his help.

"Of course I'd like to help Kimberly." Larry's eyes never left Lauren's scoop neck and I could practically feel his psychic demand that her top slip just a bit lower, show a tiny bit more. "She is a member of the union, after all."

"Fabulous." Lauren made Larry's wish come true by bending toward him, giving him a slightly better angle.

"Ah, yeah. But what can I do for the pair of--I mean the two of you?"

"We just wondered if you could tell us how Sean looked when you delivered his mail last week. Did he seem upset about anything? Was he expecting anything in particular in the mail? Did he get any strange packages? You know, that sort of stuff."

"Oh. Sure." Larry leaned back for a moment, realized that he'd worsened his view of Lauren's boobs, and abruptly leaned forward again. "I don't remember anything out of the ordinary."

Lauren pulled away and straightened her top, punishing him for the wrong answer. Dang, the woman was good.

"Are you sure, Larry? Let's go through the days. Kimberly was gone for six working days, right? Monday through Saturday? Try to think which days you actually saw Sean."

She pulled back her shoulders a bit, let her breasts stick out just a little more.

I decided she didn't need my help with her questions and that it was time for me to do some exploring.

"I, uh, have to go to the bathroom."

"Sure, Kimmy." Larry's eyes never left Lauren's chest. "It's down the hall."

* * * *

I walked down the hall, stepping carefully to avoid piles of what I hoped was laundry but that might have been science experiments.

Dust puffed up every time I moved, and I had to pinch my nose to keep from sneezing.

I wasn't obsessive about filth, but it was lucky I didn't really need to use the facilities. There was no way I'd put my clean butt on Larry's disgusting toilet.

I closed the door, turned on the faucet, and went through his medicine cabinet.

I found toothpaste, aspirin, *Neosporin*, something for acme, and an unopened bottle of cologne. I wasn't surprised that I didn't find any deodorant.

His sink didn't have a cabinet underneath, but he had a storage box above the toilet.

The toilet looked like it could use a flush even though I hadn't used it, so I cranked the lever and used the noise to cover the sound of me opening the box.

Inside, I found what I'd expected--maybe a kilo of marijuana. What I hadn't expected, though, was a couple of rolls gauze for bandages.

Larry had been limping. He claimed Andrew had bitten him, but maybe his victims had fought back.

The marijuana gave Larry a possible link to Sean. Sure, Lauren had claimed her husband only did performance-enhancing drugs, but he might have told her that to make himself seem less like scum.

So, Larry did it.

A couple of hours earlier, I'd been certain Rev. Nagle did it and it wasn't likely, considering their differences, that Nagle and Larry had teamed. But who knew. The world had seen stranger alliances.

I spent a couple of minutes scrubbing my hands and wishing I could wash the rest of my body, then headed down the hall away from where Lauren was still distracting Larry with her questions and her body, and into his bedroom.

Sure enough, the laundry there was even thicker than in the hallway. Who would have guessed that a guy I'd never seen out of uniform had so many clothes.

I grabbed what looked like a bloody t-shirt from near the top of one of the piles and stuffed it under my top.

It was disgusting--but I planned on taking a long shower that night anyway, and I didn't think Larry would glance at me for long enough to notice I had something under my shirt.

"You okay, Kimmy" Larry shouted.

I faked a smile as I reclaimed my chair. "Much better, thanks."

"You doing the bulimia thing?" he demanded.

"No, Larry. Although, if you don't mind, I won't go into details on what I was doing in your bathroom."

"No problem." He turned his attention back to Lauren's boobs.

Okay, I'd seen it before, but I couldn't help wondering if somebody had skipped a few steps when they'd assembled the Y chromosome. I like a nicely shaped male butt, but I wouldn't stare at one for hours at a time. Guys, though, seemed to find gazing at female breasts to be continual fascination--as if maybe they'd hop out and do a Can-Can.

"Tell Kimberly what you were saying about Sean," Lauren urged.

Larry nodded. "I saw Sean just about every day because he's always getting packages he needs to sign for."

"For his eBay business," Lauren explained.

"Yeah, I guess. It seems like it was Tuesday when he also got a big Express Mail pack--"

"How big?" I interrupted. "Do you know what was in it?"

Larry scratched. "He seemed surprised to see it."

Lauren leaned closer, straightened an errant strand of his hair. "You didn't tell me about that. Did you see who it was from?"

"I don't pay any attention to that kind of thing."

The post office would have records, though. And if Sean was getting the mail for his eBay business, it probably had tracking codes. *I* couldn't get into the post office computers, but I could ask Buddy to do it.

"What else did he get?"

"Mostly, he got the same junk mail as everyone else."

"But he seemed calm. Not worried about anything?"

"Far as I could tell. Not that I was paying a lot of attention to him."

Lauren was practically sitting in Larry's lap now and ran a sculpted fingernail down his thigh. "So, how did he seem when Andrew bit you? Or didn't you think that was anything out of the ordinary."

Larry's head snapped back like she'd connected with a punch. "How did you, I mean," he stuttered for several seconds before pushing back his chair. "You'd better go. I've got an early day tomorrow."

"He's hiding something," Lauren said after Larry physically shoved the two of us out of his house, then locked his door.

We got into Lauren's car and she drove to a convenience store where she parked.

"There are two things I'm wondering about," she observed.

"Yeah?"

"First, what are you hiding under your top? And second, why would Larry hide getting bit?"

I pulled out the bloody t-shirt. "You can add this to Nagle's towel when you figure out how to do blood testing."

"Maybe he used it on the dog bite."

"Or maybe it isn't a dog bite at all. Maybe killing Sean and Fred the pervert wasn't easy and they fought back. Maybe if we looked, we wouldn't find a dog bite at all. Of course, if Andrew really did bite him, that gives him a motive, too."

"So, you're liking Larry as Sean's killer?"

I stared out the window. "Tina told me I had to be a detective, but I pretty much suck at this. When I think about Nagle, I think he did it. When I think about Larry, I'm sure he's the one. They both have motives, sort of. To me, both motives feel weak."

"At least they have motives. I'd think the cops would be happy to hear them--they don't have any motive on you."

I considered it. But throwing Larry to the wolves didn't feel right and I didn't think it would get me off the hook. I was still the woman who'd found the bodies.

"We need more, and something more definite."

"You have something specific in mind."

"I found a decent stash of dope in Larry's bathroom. If he was buying from Sean or Fred, there's another connection."

"Sean didn't do marijuana."

I took her hand. "I hate to break this to you, Lauren, but he was a drug dealer. When he told you he only did performance-enhancing chemicals, he was probably lying. Dope dealers lie all the time."

She pulled away. "I don't think so."

"I'll bet we can find out, though."

"How?"

"You've got to know some of Sean's contacts in the drug world--who supplied him, that kind of thing. We can talk to them."

Lauren cranked her engine. "You know, that's not a bad idea. Let's go."

Uh-oh. What had I just agreed to?

"There were a couple of narcs always trying to flip Sean," Lauren told me as she headed south. "I didn't get involved with Sean's business but I know enough to be sure that wherever there are drugs and money, the D.E.A. is around. They might even know who killed Sean. This wouldn't be the first time they let an innocent person be convicted to protect their sources."

She drove us to a combination Chinese Super-buffet and donut shop near Wynnewood Village. This neighborhood, a diverse mix of upscale apartments, public housing projects, and some funky shops including Dallas's only surviving independent bookstore, was way off my mail route but I came there to shop sometimes. I'd never tried the donut shop, though. I'd had my last donut the day I'd been laid off in telecom and wasn't even tempted any more.

Hardly.

It seemed like too much the cliché, but sure enough, there were a couple of chubby white guys sitting at the counter eating donuts when we walked in.

"Is this a joke?" I whispered. "Cops in a donut shop."

"What do you think? That they actually work," she whispered back. "They're always here."

The older of the two nudged his partner. "We got company."

The partner had looked half asleep, a black baseball-style cap with D.E.A. stenciled on the front pulled down over his eyes but he had his gun out and was in a shooting crouch before I could breath.

He looked around, his pale eyes squinting as he flicked his aim from me to Lauren, and then back. "Shit, Pete. You made me spill my coffee."

Pete got a good laugh out of that. "Maybe you need to cut down on the caffeine, huh, Clark."

"Aren't you two the kings of comedy?" Lauren observed. "We came by to talk about Sean."

"Ancient history." Clark tucked his automatic back in a shoulder holster only partially obscured by his overlarge suit jacket and waved his empty coffee cup at the Asian waitress. "Drug business in Dallas is always changing and Sean made the final change."

The man was seriously wide, but in a flat and muscled way. Like a professional football player, his head didn't end in a neck, it just sort of sloped into massive shoulders.

"Sean's dead," Pete agreed. "If you wanted to rat him out, you missed your chance."

"That's cold, man," Clark observed.

It was cold. I couldn't believe they would talk that way to a woman who had just lost her husband, albeit a husband she was separated from.

"We're wondering who's taking over Sean's territory," I said.

Clark took a bite from a custard-filled chocolate éclair, leaving Pete to do the talking.

"There's always another scumbag waiting. The good news is, most of them aren't as hard to roll as Sean was. Hate to say it in front of his wife and all, but Sean getting killed is a nice bit of cleanup for Dallas and a good thing for the war on drugs."

He squinted at me, then took a pair of oversized plastic-rimmed glasses from his suit pocket. "Hey, I recognize you from your picture in the paper.

You're the one who did him. I'd like to shake your hand."

He held out a powdered sugar and sprinkles decorated paw.

"I didn't kill anyone." I ignored his hand.

If I shook it, I could count on Pete testifying that I'd admitted to the murder. D.E.A. agents weren't responsible for local crime, but they needed cooperation from the local cops. Bringing in a murder suspect couldn't hurt them, and it might let them one-up the FBI.

Pete winked at me. "Hey, guess you've got to stick with that story. But I didn't know Sean's ex was involved with Sean's killer. Sort of gives a love triangle spin to the whole murder thing, don't you think, Clark?"

Pete nudged his partner in the ribs just as Clark was taking a sip of coffee.

The scalding liquid went everywhere. "Damn it, Pete. You do that one more time and I swear the Dallas cops are going to have another murder to solve."

"I'm surprised that you guys are just sitting here." Lauren interrupted the good-ole-boy moment even though she'd as good as told me they never left. "With Fred Turley dead, why aren't you out pounding the streets trying to line up another informant?"

"They want to talk," Clark said, "they know where to find us."

I wanted to get my notepad out and write that down but I managed to resist. The narcs probably didn't even realize they'd blown cover on one of their informants--even if he was dead. Lauren had been pretty sure Fred was involved with the narcs, but she couldn't have been positive.

"Must have pissed you off that you couldn't get Fred to roll over on Sean, though," Lauren went on. "That's the usual way you do things, isn't it? Get evidence on someone low, then roll uphill from there."

"You know it is," Pete admitted. "You try your angles. One don't work, there's always another."

I suspected that was true. Most people don't go into drug dealing because of their desire to help others. And it certainly isn't because of the company they get to keep.

"With drug pushers getting killed everywhere, though, I'd think you might be running out of angles," I offered.

"Like Clark said..." Pete grabbed the coffee pot from the waitress and poured his own coffee, "...there are always more scumbags."

Clark leered at Lauren. "'Course, those new scumbags aren't about to support your ritzy style, are they?"

"I don't know what you're getting at." For the first time since I'd met her, Lauren sounded flustered.

"Fancy house up in Allen... mortgage payments got to set you back some. Then there's the shopping lifestyle. When was the last time you cleared a paycheck of your own?"

"I'll get by."

"You're getting a bit old for the modeling gig. Guess you could go back to stripping."

"I was never..."

"Sure you weren't."

Lauren looked close to tears so I decided on a distraction. "Lay off of her." I rammed a thumb into Clark's midsection. It felt a lot harder than it looked. "She's had a loss and she doesn't need--"

"Had a loss. That's a laugh." Clark grabbed my thumb and twisted it so hard I thought he might yank it off. "Maybe you can give her your lease in the trailer park--seeing as how you're going to be on death row before long."

My arm felt like it might be permanently dislocated, but Lauren got the few seconds she needed to suck it up. "Back off on Kimberly, guys. Yeah, I'm going to have a hard time--what of it. Lots of people are having a hard time with the economy in the pits."

"Except drug dealers," Pete observed. "They always seem to do okay."

A lightbulb went off in my head. These guys weren't harassing Lauren, they were going through a script. I got a glimmer of where they might be going with their little act and decided to play along.

"I'd be lying if I said we couldn't use some money."

Clark shook his head almost sorrowfully, but he let go of my thumb. "Like I said, if you could have sold out Sean, we would have paid for that--killing him, not so much. No 'dead or alive' in the DEA."

"But..." I let my voice trail off, turning the word into a question.

"On the other hand," Clark said, "there's a vacuum in the drug market now. Some slimeball is going to step in, going to take over the market Sean developed.

"Bastards," Pete agreed happily. "Worst comes to worst, we might have to go out there, break a few heads, spend some effort developing a new network of informants. And Lil here wouldn't like that, would you, hon." He grabbed at the waitress's butt but she sidestepped and left him grasping empty air.

"Looks like she could survive." I should have kept my mouth shut, but sometimes I couldn't help myself.

"Nah. She'd wither away from missing us. Which, it seems to me, you've already done." Clark poked me in my stomach. "You trying to turn into Mary Kate Olson or something? Because believe me, you don't have the face even if you got the figure."

"I don't know what you're talking about."

"You guys are trying to say something," Lauren said. "Lay it on us."

Clark poked at me a second time but this time I saw him coming and jumped away. "Here's the thing, ladies. Somebody's going to take over Sean's network. It would be easier for someone with access to his sources and who's got the confidence of his dealers and customers. Now, we could let the market work itself out, but why not give it a nudge?"

"You're suggesting I take over Sean's business?"

Pete shook his head. "We can't suggest anything like that--that would be illegal. Just, if someone we knew, someone we trusted, were to take over the business, we could back off a bit, especially if she was, shall we say, cooperative.

"Wouldn't be much of a business," I observed, "if we spent our lives testifying against our suppliers and customers." I wasn't really thinking about going into the drug business, but I could see some advantages to starting a rumor that we were. Because I couldn't believe two drug dealers had been murdered without some drug angle being involved. Nagle's religious objection was one possibility. Larry's high-volume using another. But murder isn't exactly rare in the drug world--their deaths could have come from inside the business.

Lauren sidled closer to the two men, trying the same sexy trick that had worked so well on Larry.

I wanted to let her know that it wasn't going to work. Those two were more interested in donuts with jelly filling than they were in the female of the species.

"Tell you what, boys," she said. "Let me know who's trying to take over Sean's territory and I'll be cooperative."

Clark laughed, spraying powdered sugar all over me. "Send a thief to catch a thief, send a drug dealer to kill a drug dealer. Sounds sweet."

"Sweet as sugar." Lauren gave Clark a smile. "But I'm not a drug dealer. Not yet."

"Sweet for you," Pete growled. "Come on, Lauren. You come in here with the lead suspect in a murder case and you expect us to believe that you're only thinking about taking over Sean's business. That's bullshit and you know it. You're working this angle. Mary-Kate there may look like a sissy but she's killed two dealers already. I think Clark was damned brave messing with her."

Clark's smile faded. "Hey, I hadn't thought about that."

"Think about keeping your coffee in the mug rather than on the floor," Pete told him. "We aren't going to tell you girls anything. We're on track to do a major bust and the last thing we need is for a couple of amateurs to be wandering around mucking up the scene."

If Clark knew about any major bust, his expression didn't show it. "Uh, yeah. We've got a lot on our plates." He set down his donut and wiped his hands off with a napkin. "When do we start?"

"Shut up, Clark."

"But--"

"Now get the hell out of here," Pete growled at the two of us. "We're working and you're going to keep anyone from coming in here."

"Want a donut to go?" Lil the Asian waitress asked, in case we'd missed Pete's hint.

"No thanks," I told her.

Lauren practically danced back to her car. "Pete did it. Either he did it himself, or he set up one of his pet pushers to kill Sean. My husband wouldn't go along with them, wouldn't split his take, wouldn't rat out his sources. Killing Sean means that their C.I. will run the trade and Pete will get a big cut of Dallas's drug money. That has to be why they backed off when I asked them for his identity. They've already got a deal going with him and didn't want to jeopardize that."

I walked around to the back of her Celica. "Open up the hatchback,

Lauren. It's time for me to get my bike and go home."

Lauren laughed at me. "Home? Don't be a quitter, Kim. We're on a roll. We know for sure Fred was a C.I. We confirmed that Sean wouldn't play ball. We have good reason to believe that the local D.E.A. agents are involved in the trade and the murder. Now's the time for us to push."

I didn't doubt that Pete and Clark would let morals hold them back from murder. But why would they kill Fred, given that he was one of their own confidential informants? And I wasn't buying the theory that the two deaths were unconnected.

"In the past couple of days, two people I knew were killed," I said. "I have a really bad feeling that the count is going to go up if I keep pushing. You've managed to piss off Larry, Nagle and now the two D.E.A. agents. If any of them are the killer, what do you think they'll do? Don't' stretch your brain because I'll tell you. If they think we've got evidence, they'll come gunning for us."

The reality of the situation had taken a while to hit home. It would be terrible to be falsely convicted of a crime and sent to one of the Texas death rows. But from what I'd read in the newspaper, you can live for years on death row while your appeals play themselves out. It wouldn't be much of a life, but it would be a better life than being gunned down by a mad postal worker or D.E.A. agent."

Lauren nodded. "You're right, Kim. We're taking chances. And maybe I've been too pushy. But nobody else is going to find the evidence we need to clear your name--and my name. We've got to keep on going. And pushing is the only way I know how."

I sighed. I wasn't going to be able to get rid of her. Besides, if I did manage to dump her and she ended up the next victim, I'd feel responsible. "Right. But we've been working it dumb. I don't just want to find Sean's real killer, I want to stay alive while we're doing it."

Lauren gave me the same smile she'd used on Larry and the Narcs. "That's why we're a team, Kim. I'm pretty and I'm go-go-go, but nobody ever thought about nominating me for class brain. If you think we've got enough for you to put your engineering brain to work, I'm all for it."

Chapter 7

Lauren insisted that we go grocery shopping before heading back to my trailer. She loaded up on healthy stuff so I couldn't object too much, but I had never had so much food in the trailer at one time and didn't know where we were going to put it.

Once we got to the trailer, Lauren mau-maued a couple of local males to carry the stuff in and then went into complete domesticity mode unpacking the groceries, putting things away, straightening up the books I had lying around and generally turning my trailer into a downscale version of her own minimansion.

Just when the work was over and Lauren had settled down with a beer, Tina stopped by to let us know she'd been tracking her police scanner. Since she had her pet chicken on her shoulder again, it took me a minute to focus on what she was saying. When I go there, we didn't have a lot more to go on. Nagle had bent the ear of every cop he could find but, from what Tina could tell, he hadn't mentioned any names. Either he hadn't gotten a good look at us or he was planning on taking care of us--the same way he'd taken care of Sean and Fred.

Watching Tina and Lauren take over my trailer intimidated the hell out of me. For the first time, I felt a bit of sympathy for some of the engineers I'd known back in telecom who'd taken a girl out on a date and had her moving in before they knew what hit them.

"We've got to open things up a bit," she explained when I caught Lauren shoving my recliner into a corner. "If this is going to be where we collect evidence and plot our next move, we need room to move around in."

"Plus," Tina added, "you need a place for your witnesses to sit while you put your brain to work."

Talk about my great brain made me feel like a bit of a faker. My high school class had named me 'woman most likely to be an egg-head,' and I did have an engineering degree, but I'd been running around every bit as ditzy as Lauren-- who admitted to being a ditz and had the looks to pull it off.

I was supposed to be the thinker, but I'd let her ride over me roughshod for the past two days. It was time for me to start pulling my weight, even if Lauren thought my weight was way under what it needed to be.

Tina and Lauren did a bit more arranging, then Lauren disappeared into the kitchen and started making domestic noises while Tina discovered a chicken disaster, wiped it up, and disappeared with her pet chicken--Charlaine.

It seemed like the first time in ages I could actually think. I pulled out my notebook and started organizing.

Ten minutes later, Lauren peered at me from my trailer's tiny kitchen. "Here. Try this."

"Wha--"

She stuffed something cheesy into my mouth before I could finish talking, so I was left waving my notebook for a few seconds while I chewed and swallowed. Pretty good but I could practically feel the calories attaching themselves to my tummy. I really needed to get back to my exercise.

"I'm trying to bring my notes up to date," I explained. "We've got to keep track of what we've been doing, and we've got to start planning. From now on, I want to be ahead of the people we're talking to rather than just flailing away. I want to know the questions we're going to ask and the answers we expect. I want to be aware of any hot buttons we're going to push rather than just sending the guys into hormone shock and then pissing them off."

She nodded slowly. "Okay. I guess that makes sense."

I put my head into my notes and tried to remember exactly what Larry had said before Lauren had asked him about the dog bite. And why had he been so upset about that?

Lauren was silent for a good minute. Then she couldn't stand it any longer. "If you're doing that, what can I do to help?"

I remembered tagging along after my brothers when they worked on souping up their cars, trying to persuade them to let me install the supercharger or help chop the top for a lower profile. They'd both been more than a decade older than me and hadn't wanted anything to do with a seven-year old girl, but I'd gotten the drive to become an engineer from that. I didn't want to discourage Lauren the way my brothers had me, so I thought about what she could do that might help.

"Can you make a list of everyone Sean was associated with? Group them into logical categories. Like social enemies, friends, drug customers, drug suppliers. That kind of stuff. And when you're done with that, make the same list for Fred."

"I didn't know Fred much."

"I didn't know him at all, except that he subscribed to magazines about girls with big butts and wanted to show them to me."

She giggled. "I'll show you mine if you show me yours. Guys never get over being five. Sean always kept a stack of magazines that--"

I held up a hand. "Too much information, Lauren. Unless you think one of his magazines climbed down from his closet and paper-cut him to death."

"Given what he did to them, they might have been tempted to." She pursed her lips. "Okay, can I borrow a notepad?"

I equipped her and went back to my own list. We still had the Rev. Nagle and Larry to worry about. Maybe the union thing had gone to Larry's head and he'd gone after Sean because of the dog bite and Fred because he'd harassed me. They weren't much as far as motives went, but they were better than what I had on Buddy, which was nothing. I added Buddy to my list anyway, based on Preston's reminder that anyone who tried to be too helpful might be suspicious. If the murders were some drug gangland thing, we had nothing to go on, so I just labeled a couple of pages Drugs and D.E.A., leaving the contents blank for the moment.

I flipped to the next page and studied Lauren surreptitiously as she sat at my table doodling on her notepad. I felt guilty about adding Lauren to my suspect list but I did it anyway. She had motive, at least for Sean. And she'd had the opportunity. When it came to Fred, it wouldn't be hard to come up with a motive.

I had a feeling I was missing something, but that wasn't unusual. When I'd been a kid, I'd gotten fascinated by mazes. I'd finally learned to make a plan and keep working on it. Exactly what plan doesn't matter so much--it's the sticking to it that pays off. Wander around with no plan, or changing the plan every couple of minutes and I could be stuck forever.

This whole murder thing was a new kind of maze. The only problem was, we weren't allowed to decide it was just too hard and give up. If we didn't find the real killer, one of us was most likely to be the one sent to jail.

I decided to follow through. I would pick a plan and stick with it.

I glanced at Lauren again to see how she was doing.

She had that scrunched-up forehead look going and was painfully printing names for her list, stopping and licking the tip of the pencil after almost every letter.

"I'm not much of a writer," she admitted when she caught me watching her.

"Maybe. But you can flirt the heck out of anything in pants."

"Oh, yeah. Like that's a big deal."

I put down my writing and walked over to her. "Mood-swing warning, Lauren. What's going on with you?"

She threw her pencil at the wall--and put a dent in the thin aluminum. "I suck this. I thought I could help you but it's obvious that I'm just causing problems. I ran Larry off after he'd bent over backwards to help you. And I pissed off the D.E.A. guys."

I felt guilty about it, but learning that Lauren had her feelings of inadequacy made me feel a little better. At least she wasn't perfect.

"You did great, Lauren. You're upset because your husband got killed and I'm upset because I'm a suspect. That doesn't mean we're not both decent people. So, let's pull it together."

"Yeah? How?"

That was the question, all right. I put my engineering hat on. "It seems to me that we have three different motives. First, it could be that the killer is connected to the drug business. That would explain why two drug dealers were killed within a relatively short amount of time and distance. Second, there could be a connection to the post office. That could explain Larry's sudden interest in backing me up, and Buddy's coming out to the crime scene or collecting Andrew the dog. Third, it might be someone who hated Sean and Fred for what they were doing to the neighborhood."

"I get that."

"For each of these motives, we have one or more suspect."

Lauren looked at me like I'd grown an extra head. "But so what? Seems like an organized way of saying we don't know anything."

"So far," I agreed. "But think about it. If we can eliminate one of the motives, we can eliminate all of the suspects that fall into it. For example, if the drug connection is a ruse, then the D.E.A. guys, whoever replaced Sean, everyone connected that way is off the hook. Likewise, if we learn, say that the clean-up-the-neighborhood angle is the motive, we'd be down to the short list of Rev. Nagle and some of his more rabid parishioners."

I didn't really expect Lauren to break out into applause, but I would have liked at least a friendly nod or 'that makes sense.'

Instead she shook her head. "I can't see how that helps at all. If we could figure out what motive was behind it, we would already have had to figure out who killed Sean. How are we supposed to eliminate any of these possibilities?"

I wasn't sure she was wrong, but at least I was ready for that question. "It seems to me that we'd have different results, different evidence, depending on the motive. There should be a way to tell the difference."

She didn't look convinced. "Like how?"

I wracked my brain. I knew I was right on this, but how would I know what kind of evidence to look for? Finally, the hint of an idea poked up. "Bear with me for a second," I urged. "Let's suppose that the motive is that someone wanted to take over Sean's business. Right?"

Lauren shrugged. "Okay."

"They'd probably want to do more than just kill him. I mean, you're the expert on Sean but if it was me, I'd want information about his customers and his sources, as well as any contacts who might come after me for revenge. And think about this--whoever killed Sean killed Fred too. So, if they were just looking to take over the business, why would they kill one of the customers?"

"I'll bite. Why?"

I shrugged. "I have no idea, which maybe means that I'm missing something but maybe it means that we can rule out the motive. If we found out Sean's house wasn't ransacked, between that and Fred getting murdered, we could rule out the entire taking over the drug business motive. We wouldn't know the killer but the list would be shorter. A lot shorter since our list now includes about half of the Dallas population."

"Hey, I get it. But those D.E.A. guys know something. I'm not ready to let them off the hook."

"But first, let's start by finding out whether Sean's house was ransacked." I grabbed my cell. "I'll call Preston Rolin with the Post Office Police. So far, anyway, he's been willing to share at least a little information with me. He, along with my supervisor, seem to be about the only people who realize it would be better for the post office if we can show that I didn't do it."

Lauren nodded firmly. "Do you want *me* to talk to this Preston guy?"

I considered. She could get guys to talk, but she also had the knack of pissing them off. "Maybe later, if we need to crank up the heat. But so far, he's been at least slightly forthcoming just because it's his job."

I dialed Preston, left my number on his pager, and waited for his return call.

In the meantime, Lauren wandered into my kitchen and embarrassed me by asking hard questions like *do you have a saucepan* and *where do you keep your spaghetti sauce.*

* * * *

Lauren was serving dinner, chicken pasta, Caesar salad, a huge loaf of Italian bread, and a bottle of Chianti when Preston finally returned my call.

"I'm glad to hear you're okay," he told me before I could say anything.

"Why shouldn't I be?"

"You told me you were heading out to Allen to visit Herbert's ex-wife. The Dallas Police Department sent a request that Allen police pick her up and send her down for questioning but she hasn't been seen all day. If she's the killer, she wouldn't hesitate to kill you, too."

I swallowed. "Well I'm fine." If I told him Lauren was with me, he would feel obligated to turn her over to the D.P.D. and we'd have more troubles. "I have a question, Preston. Did it look like anyone went through Sean's house looking for anything?"

His voice sounded suspicious. "What angle are you working, Kimberly?"

I couldn't think of any reason to keep my thinking from him. Who knew? Maybe he could persuade the D.P.D. to start a more logical investigation.

"We know Sean was involved in the drug trade. If someone killed him to take over his business, they'd want his stash and any contact information. If he was killed by a personal enemy, there might be different kinds of physical evidence. This could help us narrow down the suspect list."

"What suspect list? I didn't know the cops had narrowed it down to anyone. Except--" his voice trailed off in mid-sentence.

Well, duh. He wasn't going to rub my nose in the fact that I was the lead suspect.

"We've got some ideas, Preston. But we need help."

His pause was just long enough for me to realize I'd made a terrible slip. "Who's this *we?*"

"Larry Mueller has been helping me," I improvised. "He says it's part of the union's support for its members. You know how intent he is on getting reelected next year."

"Yeah? Maybe." Despite the doubt in his words, I thought I'd persuaded Preston not to follow up on the 'we' angle.

"I'm just not so sure about that union thing," he said. "Be careful of Larry, Kimberly. I already warned you about people who seem too interested in your case."

"I'll be careful," I promised. "But let me know what you find out about

Going Postal

Sean's place. Nothing looked too disturbed in his living room, but I didn't bother checking out the rest of the house."

"I'll look into it."

* * * *

Fat engineer girls don't get asked out on many dates. Although I'd lost weight since becoming a postal carrier, I still wasn't Ms. Popularity. And the few times I'd let a date progress to the logical conclusion, he had left immediately afterwards.

All of which meant I wasn't used to actually sleeping with anyone.

Sharing my tiny trailer meant sharing a bed. At least Lauren didn't snore. She did squeeze her arms around me like an octopus after its prey.

I unwrapped her for maybe the fifteenth time and checked my clock.

Five o'clock. That was when I normally got up. Since I was still on leave from the Post Office, I could have slept in, but I didn't see that happening. Inviting Lauren to spend the night had been logical. Both of us were at risk. Two women working together were more formidable than one woman alone, and I just didn't believe that Lauren was going to kill me in my sleep. I hadn't considered that she might maul me. Unlike me, she seemed used to cuddling.

Well, I'd survived the night. Despite Preston's friendly warning, I hadn't suffered anything worse than an arm around my shoulders.

I got up and took my shower.

I'd just wrapped a towel around myself when Lauren stepped into my tiny bathroom. "Hey."

Should I remind her about knocking? I decided not to bother. "Morning."

"You didn't hear anything back from your cop friend?" She yanked off the t-shirt she'd slept in and stepped into the shower.

"Uh-un." I wasn't running, exactly, but my trailer was definitely not big enough for two women.

"I had an idea." She had to shout over the shower spray.

"What?"

Her drowned face peeked from around the shower curtain. "Why don't *we* go and look."

As with most of Lauren's ideas, it was terrible. Also as with most of her ideas, we did it anyway.

After breakfast, we loaded up in Lauren's Toyota and headed the few miles over to Sean's place.

It was all perfectly legal, Lauren assured me as she pulled into his driveway. She had a key. She was Sean's heir. What could the cops do if she just wanted to visit her own house?

I didn't know the answer, and I didn't want to find out.

Lauren hit the garage remote control and drove into it, getting her car off the street.

Unfortunately, the garage was almost completely blocked by overturned boxes, meaning we couldn't hide the car inside.

"It's Sean's eBay stuff," Lauren said.

61

"He leaves it in a wreck like this?"

She laughed. "Are you kidding? Sean is a neatness freak." She paused, the smile fading from her face like a mirage. "He *was* a neatness freak, I mean. God, I hate saying that, hate thinking that he's gone." She glared at me like it was my fault. "Screw it. Anyway, with Sean, everything was organized and arranged. Either the killer went through his things or the cops did. No way *he* left this mess."

She left her car hanging halfway out of the garage, walked around to the back door to Sean's house, and peered in through the window. "I can't go in there."

I watched her carefully. Was she wigging out? Maybe she really was the killer. I'd read that returning a killer to the scene of the crime can cause flashbacks, breakdowns, admissions of guilt.

"What are you trying to say, Lauren?" I asked.

"It's a wreck. I'll have to hire a cleaning crew before I can do anything with it."

I pushed forward until my nose was pressed against the wall. Sure enough, there was junk tossed everywhere. Cheerios littered the floor, a pyramid of what looked like sugar decorated the kitchen counter, and every drawer in the room had been yanked from their rollers and tossed into a big pile in front of the door.

"I think I can squeeze in," I decided.

"You're crazy."

I wasn't going to argue with her about that. "See how far you can get the door open."

We shoved the door in as far as it would go, which wasn't nearly far enough, and I started shoving my way through the opening.

"Don't ever try to make me eat again," I growled as the latch tore a big hole in my shirt.

"If you were bigger, we could have shoved the door open further."

That didn't help.

It took me a couple of minutes, but I finally managed to squeeze in. Once inside, clearing away enough of the drawers to let Lauren join me only took a few seconds.

"Do you think the cops did this?" she asked.

I was clueless and told her so. "I didn't make it this far back when I found Sean."

"Me neither," she admitted. "I wish I had looked."

Well, that made two of us.

Sean's body was gone, of course, but the cops hadn't done a great cleanup job. I carefully skirted the crusted borders from where the cops had sort of cleaned up Sean's blood Sean had left, and we headed upstairs.

Lauren led me directly into Sean's office.

"Looks like a repeat of the kitchen, but without the Cheerios," Lauren observed.

62

"Yeah, but a lot more paper."

We didn't have to squeeze our way in, but we did have to step carefully. The floor was literally covered with receipts, printouts, and the miscellaneous detritus of an eBay career.

From the skid marks, a computer had once graced Sean's desk but it was gone--whether taken by cops or by the killer, I didn't know.

"Do you know if he kept customer lists or anything like that?" I asked.

"He had a Rolodex," she admitted. "One of those compact things with names of his customers and what they shopped for. I know enough about a few of the customers to figure out his code, but I don't' see the Rolodex yet."

"Let's see what we do have." I picked up a handful of paperwork and studied them.

Everything looked normal--what an eBay expert would have.

After a minute, Lauren squatted by me, sorting through paperwork at least as quickly as I was.

I didn't know how to ask her, so I just blurted it out. "Did you do business with any of Sean's drug contacts?"

She studied me for a good twenty seconds before shaking her head. "I knew he was dealing, but Sean never shared." She flipped through another couple of papers, then froze.

If I hadn't been looking, I wouldn't have noticed the way she stuffed a paper under her shirt.

"What is it, Lauren?"

"What's what?"

"Come on. What did you find?"

"It's really nothing. Nothing to do with Sean's drug business at all."

"In that case you won't mind me looking, right."

"It isn't what it looks like," she insisted.

"You know, until I know what it looks like, that doesn't give me a lot of information."

The muscles on her cheeks twitched, as if her whole body was revved up for fight-or-flight. Finally, though, she passed over the legal-length papers she'd snagged.

I blinked, but the forms didn't change. "Oh, shit, Lauren. He was divorcing you."

She shook her head. "He wouldn't have gone through with it. He always threatened, but he never would have actually done it. We were going to get back together once he got out of the drug business."

"Sure, Lauren." If the cops had spotted that, they weren't just looking for Lauren because her alibi sucked, they had a motive in spades.

She stood up abruptly. "I think we'd better get out of here."

"I'm not done looking."

"I think we are. I see flashing lights outside."

We piled down the stairs, out to Sean's garage, and took off down his alley. Cops pulled up to the front of the house as we drove out the back way.

That was too close.

"So we've got proof positive that his house was ransacked," she commented when she was finally convinced that no one was following us.

"Unless the cops made that mess." From what I'd seen of the Dallas Police Department, cleaning up after themselves wasn't high on their lists.

She shook her head. "It's got to be the killer. This confirms your drug-connection theory. Looks like the Reverend is off the hook."

"The cops would have taken pictures," I said. "We need to get a look at the photos from the crime scene guys. The police should share those with--"

Lauren pulled over and stared at me, her green eyes cold. "Unless the killers were also cops. Don't forget our friends in the D.E.A. We're going to have to hit your boyfriend at the Post Office Police up for some serious help here."

Boyfriend? I almost laughed. Preston Rolin was definitely not my boyfriend. He was just a cop trying to do his job and doing his best to keep the Post Office's nose clean. If getting me busted would make the Post Office look better than clearing my name, I didn't think he'd care.

"I'll see what I can get out of him."

Lauren pulled by a dumpster and stopped her car, got out, and methodically shredded the divorce paperwork, tossing the minute scraps into the dumpster and then picking up a stick and stirring the remains into the rest of the garbage.

She said nothing until she finally climbed back in her car. "Okay, here's the deal. I'm wearing the same underwear I wore yesterday and it's grossing me out. Let's go to my place, pick up some things, and then eat. Once we get our blood sugar up to a reasonable level, we can figure out our next steps."

Something told me this was another bad idea, but I'd been having that bad idea feeling so much lately that it was getting easy to ignore. Still, I was supposed to be the planner. How come I wasn't coming up with the ideas?

As we were heading north, through Dallas, my cell rang. Buddy told me that the cops had found out about my old harassment case against Fred. It gave them the motive they were looking for.

"You were on the investigative panel," I reminded him. "What else could I have done?"

I could almost hear his feet shuffling. I'd followed procedure and he knew it. That didn't mean I was off the hook.

"The cops say you neglected to tell them about your motive."

"I don't have a motive. The guy was a jerk. If I killed all the jerks in Texas, we'd lose half our electoral votes."

"Come on, Kimberly. Play nice."

"Just be logical, Buddy. I wouldn't have reported Fred if I was planning on killing him. My so-called motive should clear me, not put me in trouble."

The shuffle was even louder now. "You don't have to persuade *me*, Kimberly." The pause was almost indiscernible, just long enough for someone to whisper instructions. "I think you should call the cops, Kimberly. Come clean on this." Another pause. Then, "Where are you, anyway?"

"Gotta go, Buddy. Talk to you later."

I'd spent long enough in telecom to know that a cell is always talking to the cellsite controllers, passing information about its location so it would know what radio signals to use. Rather than let the cops trace me using my own technology, I popped open the back and yanked out the battery. Try to trace me now.

Lauren negotiated past a fender-bender and glanced my way. "Bad news?"

"The cops think I killed Fred because he was a pervert."

"You could kill them one a minute, twenty-four hours a day without putting much of a dent in the pervert supply."

"That's what I said. If they prosecute me, I'll put you in the witness chair."

I was busy feeling sorry for myself and worrying about what I was going to do and what prison felt like so we didn't talk much on the rest of the way out to Allen.

The rows of almost identical minimansions were even scarier by car than they had been by bicycle. Scariest of all was my realization that, if it hadn't been for the recession, I'd probably own one of these and have a mortgage for twice as much as the house was worth. I much preferred riding my bike, spending my days walking around real neighborhoods, and making people's days with the delivery of birthday cards, presents, eBay purchases, and Social Security checks. Of course, it didn't look like I'd have my job long. With Larry as union representative, I couldn't really count on their competence to make sure I stayed employed.

I almost laughed when Lauren had to read the house numbers to recognize her own house. Depressing.

"Come on in and have a drink while I throw some things in a suitcase," Lauren said as she opened her car door. Somehow she'd invited herself to move in with me. She had the mansion and yet we were going to be squeezed together in a trailer? Go figure.

The instant she put her key in the door, every siren in Allen went off.

For a few seconds, I thought maybe she'd inadvertently set off her burglar alarm. But the harsh sound of cop radio and the flashing red lights finally penetrated my skull. The cops had been staking out Lauren's house and we'd stumbled into their trap.

"We haven't done anything wrong," I reminded Lauren quickly. They can't have anything on us because we didn't do it."

"Right." She was agreeing, but I could see her heart wasn't in it.

Chapter 8

Cops with drawn automatics, shotguns slung across their arms, and even gas masks, swarmed out of Lauren's closets, her neighbors' garages, and the nondescript cars and vans parked along her street.

They separated us almost instantly.

Although Allen has its own police force, the Dallas Police Department had at least as many patrol cars on site as Allen did. Detectives Poll and Sarno hustled me into an unmarked Crown Victoria that was parked in a neighbor's driveway blocking access to their garage.

Obviously I hadn't disconnected my cell quickly enough. Equally obviously, they'd been staking out Lauren's house before I called. There was no way all those D.P.D. cops could have beat us there.

"You're in big trouble now, Ms. Walsh," Sarno told me. "One lie we might put down to a mistake. Two lies is over the top."

"I haven't told you any lies." I knew my protest would be useless but I had to make it.

"You misled us about your motives for killing Fred Turley." Sarno ticked that off as number one, then held up a second finger. "In our earlier interview, you denied any knowledge about Lauren Herbert. But you've spent the past two days with her. That's two."

Poll glared at me. As if I'd personally let him down.

Sarno opened a battered, fake leather briefcase and flipped through a mound of papers, finally pulling out one that was disfigured by a large chocolate stain. "Let's start by talking about your motive to kill Fred Turley."

"I didn't have a motive to kill Turley."

Poll slammed a fist into the car upholstery about an inch from my head. "Did I tell you to open your mouth? We're conducting a murder investigation and you've been interfering with it the whole time."

When fists get slammed near my head, I can be a fast learner. I kept my mouth shut.

"Your boss, Mr. Vito Lindner, released your employment records to us. He's been most cooperative, unlike yourself."

Sarno glared at me, daring me to say anything, but that wasn't going to happen. Not even when I knew Lindner had broken a bunch of rules to hand over my employment files.

"According to your records," Sarno said, "you reported Mr. Turley for sexual harassment and creating an unpleasant working environment. But Mr. Turley didn't stop bothering you even after he'd been visited by a Post Office representative, did he? He kept on showing you those dirty magazines."

Sarno slid closer to me and lowered his voice. "Disgusting magazines, weren't they, Ms. Walsh? Pictures of large-breasted women, of spanking and bondage, of girls way to young to have their pictures taken naked like that. Turley plumbed the whole gamut of human perversion, didn't he, Ms. Walsh? I can certainly understand why you were offended."

He was getting into it, exciting himself by his own descriptions.

And I was in a no-win situation. If I didn't answer Sarno, he would get pissed. If I opened my mouth, Poll might put a fist in it. I compromised on a small nod. Yeah, I had been offended. Turley had bothered me a lot and some of those pictures had been disgusting, although I'd never seen any of the underage girls he was talking about. I wouldn't have reported those as harassment, I would have called in the Feds for child pornography.

Poll didn't look happy with my nod, but he didn't hit me.

"It's perfectly natural that you'd flip out when Turley continued to harass you, continued to create an unpleasant workplace environment, even after being repeatedly warned by a supervisor and even threatened with a lawsuit by the Post Office attorneys," Sarno continued.

That wasn't a question and I didn't answer it. Of course it would have been natural for me to be angry with Turley, and I had been. But I still hadn't killed him.

"Do you want to tell me about it?"

A glanced at Poll.

His glare back wasn't reassuring.

Instead of answering Sarno, I shook my head. No talking, no telling.

Sarno gazed at me sadly. "We're going to have to take you in, then."

* * * *

They let me stew in a tiny holding cell in the main Dallas police station for about six hours before getting around to letting me make my phone call.

I didn't have a lawyer so I called Larry. I figured that with the supposed motive relating to my delivery work, the union should back me up on this one.

Larry promised to get on it, but no lawyer had shown up three hours later when I got dragged out of the cell and into an interview room that looked like something out of the Middle Ages.

The Dallas Police Department had a beautiful new building just east of downtown. Huge windows provided light and attractive color coordinated cubicle dividers made the entire building look like something that could have been an engineering center rather than a cop hangout.

The architects must have hated it when they'd had to mess up their beautiful design with such an ugly interview room.

Large rust-colored stains discolored its institutional-green paint, and a sizable, fist-sized dent decorated into one wall. The table was a solid hardwood, but my chair was a flimsy plastic thing that was barely big enough for my butt.

If I'd still been at telecom fighting weight, I suspected it would have collapsed under me.

Sarno and Poll looked as ragged as I felt. Neither had shaved in at least twenty-four hours and at least one of them suffered from deodorant failure. There was way too much of that going around, but it was Dallas in summer.

"We've been talking to your partner," Poll growled. "She's flipped on you, telling everything. She's making you out to be the ringleader, the brains behind the operation. If you're going to have any play at all, you need to open up wide."

I smiled.

He sighed. "You can talk now. So, spill."

"I didn't kill Fred Turley and I don't know who did. I didn't kill Sean Herbert and I don't know who did. I never met Lauren Herbert before yesterday, after both murders had taken place, but I don't think she killed anyone." That last, I wasn't so sure about. Now that I thought about it, she hadn't really seemed surprised by the divorce papers--she just hadn't wanted *me* to see them. And she was Sean's heir. She had one heck of a motive.

Poll laughed. "Never met her before but now you're sleeping with her. Pretty fast work."

"I don't know what you're talking about."

Sarno grabbed me by my t-shirt and pulled me up against him. Okay, he was the source of the deodorant failure. There'd been a mouthwash failure too, so the proximity was painful.

"Listen, girly. You're in trouble. We know you and Ms. Herbert were planning to take over Sean Herbert's drug operation. We've got physical evidence. A list with both of your fingerprints on it details the major drug suppliers in south Dallas. We've got enough to take it to the D.A. Motive and opportunity. It's all there."

"I want a lawyer." From what I'd seen on T.V., that was supposed to end questioning right there.

It appeared that Sarno and Poll didn't watch those same shows.

Sarno pushed me back down on my chair.

"You're going to need more than a lawyer," Poll said. "You need a miracle."

He reached out a hand and clicked the stop button on the video recorder.

He leaned across the table toward me. "Listen, Ms. Walsh. We want to help you. It's obvious to us that Ms. Herbert is the brains behind this whole plan. She suckered you into her scheme to become a drug lord by promising you a way to get your revenge against that pervert, Turley. The two murders look to be connected, but we both know that you've got the motive against Turley and Lauren has the motive against Herbert."

I looked at him. Sure he was putting on the buddy act, but if I agreed to this ridiculous story, they'd have both Lauren and me fitted for a lethal injection in no time.

"Hey, come on, Kimberly. Neither one is a great loss to the world, but we can't have drug wars in Dallas. Tell you what. Help us nail Lauren Herbert and things could go a lot easier on you."

He put a thumb on the red button on the video recorder. "Want to retract your request for a lawyer and spill?"

I didn't think they were allowed to ask me to retract my request for a lawyer. On the other hand, Dallas wasn't known as a city that bent over backwards to protect civil liberties. We were into law and order but the emphasis was definitely on the order side.

"I have nothing more to say."

"Your next girlfriend may not be as good looking as Lauren Herbert," Poll warned.

I said nothing. I wasn't sure about Larry's innocence, but I trusted him to contact the union. He wouldn't get a single vote in the next union election if word got out that he'd let a member down after lying to her. Sooner or later, I'd have a lawyer to help me cut through some of the police lies. Whether I'd be able to post bail was another question.

* * * *

"You are to have nothing to do with the case. You are to mention it to no one. You are definitely not to associate with Lauren Herbert or anyone else connected with the case. Do you understand me?"

It had taken two days, but Larry had finally come through. The police had moved me around, trying to keep me ahead of the union attorney but eventually lawyer Shantell Hirte had tracked me down, helped arrange my bail, and given me a thorough lecture on the wheels of justice.

"They haven't accused you of murder, yet, and I think the obstruction of justice case will fall apart pretty quickly, but not if you don't back off."

"I understand."

Shantell didn't look over twenty and had a figure that put even Lauren's to shame. Her honey-brown skin glowed wherever it was exposed to the atmosphere and, with her short skirt and sleeveless top, she exposed plenty. But she was smart, had whipsawed the young assistant D.A. assigned to the case and gotten me bailed out in exchange for signing over the title to my trailer to Big Bob, the bail bondsman.

"If you violate the terms of your bond, you'll lose your house and you'll end up back in jail."

"I understand."

"All right." She didn't look like she believed me, but she'd done her job. She dragged me to her little BMW, and whipped me out to my trailer.

"Call me if the police so much as sneeze in your direction," she handed me another copy of her business card as I got out of her car. "Don't go anywhere without your cell."

I nodded, reminding myself to put the batteries back in. That ploy hadn't fooled anybody.

"I'm going to ask the court to fund an investigator but I don't think my chances of getting anything approved are very good," Shantell told me. "So, be thinking about what you can sell to raise some money. The union isn't going to cover this."

"Great." It had taken me three years to dig out of the hole my overspending and overeating had left me in and now it looked like I was going to end up even deeper. I got out of Shantell's Beemer thinking that *I* might lose everything but that my lawyer was doing fine.

She grabbed my arm just before I could pull it out of her reach. "Remember, don't talk to anyone. Nobody."

"I won't forget what you told me." If she chose to hear that as a promise, that wasn't my problem, was it?

She drove away and I opened my front door.

My house looked a lot like Sean's had. Stuff was dumped everywhere. It looked to me like my underwear drawer had been gone through especially thoroughly. If I'd been flush, I might have tossed the whole lot and bought new. As it was, I gathered all of my clothes into pillowcases and headed for the Laundromat.

I pumped quarters into the machine optimistically named 'triples' and sat down with a new spiral notebook--the cops had taken all of my notes from the case and I was going to have to recreate them. I understood Shantell's position and knew the police would go non-linear if they learned I was still investigating, but my lawyer had as good as told me she wasn't getting the money for an independent investigator. If I didn't investigate, nobody was going to.

Ten minutes after I'd sat down, Lauren walked into the Laundromat. Tina must have told her where I was heading.

She gave me a disapproving look. "You look like you lost even more weight in jail, babe."

Who wouldn't lose weight if the only so-called food around was baloney sandwiches on moldy bread? "The cops told me you admitted everything, told them I was the one responsible."

She nodded. "They told me that about you. I figured they were lying."

I was almost convinced, but not completely. She'd lied about everything else.

"My lawyer ordered me not to have anything to do with you."

Lauren gave me a big grin showing teeth bleached within an inch of their lives. If she hadn't been so enthusiastic and so wanting to be my friend, I could hate this woman. "Hey, mine too. And I'm supposed to stop investigating and let the cops run the show."

It sounded too familiar. "Our lawyers are reading from the same script."

Lauren peeked into my washing machine, then headed over to the vending machine and fed change into a slot. "I noticed your sheets were pretty scratchy. Let's splurge and use fabric softener. It isn't too late to add it and it'll make them smell better too."

Which meant she was going to be moving back in with me and she thought I smelled up the place. Perfect. When the cops found out we were sharing a bed, they'd think all of their fantasies had come true.

Going Postal

"At least I did learn one thing while I was in jail." She poured the sweet-smelling fabric softener into one of the rubber doors on top of the washing machine.

"Yeah? I guess that puts you one ahead of me. I didn't learn squat."

"I got them to admit Sean's house was already torn apart by the time the cops got there. And nobody spotted the Rolodex. It looks to me like the drug scenario moves into the lead."

"Okay. That angle makes more sense than the others, anyway. Given that we have two dead drug dealers."

She sat down next to me and grabbed the notebook I'd been scribbling in. My pen left a stripe down my leg before I could adjust.

"Looks like you're trying to recreate what we did the other day. Did the cops steal your notes?"

I nodded.

She was quiet for a moment, studying what I'd done. "I can't think of anything major you left off."

"Thanks."

She made a *tsking* noise with her tongue. "Hey, don't blame me for getting us arrested. I was just as surprised and just as unhappy about it as you were. And I didn't even get my clean underwear. Gross."

I wasn't being fair to her and I knew it. I gritted my teeth and apologized.

She nodded, happy again. "Okay, then. Now that we're back on track, let's see how we can update this given that we know the murders are related to drug dealing."

She drew a line through Reverend Nagle's name. "He wouldn't bother searching Sean's house. It's not like he'd want to take over the business, and once Sean was dead, he didn't need proof he was involved in dealing."

"Probably." I still felt like the Reverend was hiding something, but I couldn't disagree with her logic.

"Then there are the post office people." She carefully drew a line through Larry's name and through Buddy's.

"I'm sorry I doubted your strategy, Kim," she said. "But this is great. We've already narrowed down our list to the two D.E.A. guys. Now all we need to do is figure out how to get an angle on them."

She was leaving out a lot of possibilities. Even if they'd been involved, Pete and Clark wouldn't have killed Sean and Fred directly. They had access to a host of confidential informants--admitted criminals who worked for the D.E.A. in exchange for payoffs, drugs, or immunity from prosecution. I would have been shocked if they couldn't find, somewhere on their C.I. list, someone who would kill for a couple of hundred bucks. Worse, I still didn't have names for any of the dozens of drug dealers who could have killed Sean and Fred simply to reduce competition. The drug angle was one I had hoped to eliminate, not settle on. Of all the motives available, this was the one that would be hardest to investigate and most challenging to get any proof at all.

I got my notebook back from Lauren and stared at it for a while.

71

No lightbulbs went off.

Meanwhile, Lauren bundled my stuff from the washing machine into one of the huge driers at the Laundromat and cranked up the heat.

"Don't blame your landlady for ratting you out," Lauren said. "I figured you'd be here because the cops pawed through my underwear too. I threw everything out and bought new stuff for myself. I knew you'd be too cheap to do that, though."

"Not cheap, broke."

"Right. Just like you don't have an eating disorder."

"I'm fine."

She shook her head.

* * * *

When we finished my laundry, I gathered everything up, stuffed it in pillowcases, and prepared to leg it back to my trailer.

"Come on," I told Lauren. "Let's head back and we can plan. Maybe we can get some help from Tina and--"

"Your trailer." She laughed. "There are probably five different law enforcement agencies listening in there."

"But where--"

"We need to eat," she reminded me.

Okay, I'd been here before. Nothing was going to happen until Lauren got me to pretend to stuff my face.

"I'll take you to Gloria's," I volunteered. Back when I really had stuffed my face, the El Salvadorian restaurant had been a favorite of mine with its plantains, and spicy pork and chicken dishes. Now, I figured it figured to be a good place to fake stuffing.

Lauren ordered for both of us, insisted that we get El Salvadorian beer, and ate an entire basket of chips with dip before slowing down enough to talk. "Good stuff. I thought I was going to starve on what they fed us in jail. Can you believe that macaroni and cheese? I had to ask a guard what it was supposed to be."

I'd figured out a clever way of making it look like I was drinking my beer. I sipped a bit, then pretended to wipe my mouth and spit it out. It was gross but it let me pretend to keep her company. I couldn't help it Lauren thought everyone had her metabolism. On me, a single chip turned into lard before I'd finished chewing it.

She shook the empty chip basket at a waiter, waited until he'd brought a replacement, then leaned toward me from across the table. Lowering her voice, she whispered, "Okay, so what's the plan?"

I'd known this was coming. Since I'd wanted to be the brains of this outfit, it was up to me to deliver.

"Since we're going with the conclusion that the murders are drug-related, we've got to figure out whether Clark and Pete were involved," I said. "If they weren't, we can try to get them to help us. With their contacts and resources, we should be able to figure out who is the winner in the fallout from Sean's murder. And they'd be real interested in getting their hands on Sean's Rolodex."

Lauren took a slug of her beer and smiled. "Now I've been doing some thinking about that and talked to a couple of users in jail. The guy who's set to move in on Sean's territory is Manuel Stefano. He always wanted Sean's business. They were friends, sort of, but they were rivals all the same."

She took in my shorts and ragged t-shirt. "You'll like Manuel. But you might want to dress up a bit before you meet him."

"Do you think Clark and Pete know about him?"

She didn't even have to consider. "Of course they do. They're idiots, but they've been working the area for a couple of years. They could roll up the entire trade if they wanted to, instead of just taking their cut. Not that it would do any good. A new crew would take over within a week even if they arrested everyone."

That wasn't a very positive attitude about our War on Drugs, but then again, she'd been married to a drug dealer. What did I expect?

"Okay, how's this. We meet with this Manuel. Tell him we've got Sean's Rolodex and we're thinking about taking over Sean's market but we want to do it in partnership with him. The only thing is, we're worried that whoever killed Sean will come after us. Then we watch his reaction."

Lauren put down her fork and clapped her hands. "That's a great plan."

* * * *

I wasn't as enthusiastic about the plan as Lauren. For one thing, it seemed like the kind of thing she would suggest--heading half-cocked into danger. I wished we knew whether we could count on the D.E.A. agents as allies or enemies.

Lauren wanted to just drop over at the real estate office that Manuel used as a front for his drug business, but I persuaded her to set up a meeting in a hopefully neutral location--the food court at Southwest Center Mall. If the cops had bugged my trailer, I was certain they, or the D.E.A. would have bugged Manuel's office.

Fortunately, real estate people are anxious to meet with prospective clients. When I told him I wanted to buy a house, Manuel agreed to join me right away.

I don't know what I was expecting. Maybe someone like the Mexican bandit in a cheap Western. But Manuel looked like a movie star, tall, well built, with dark bedroom eyes that smoldered when he saw the two of us waiting outside the McDonalds. His gray suit had to be a Ralph Lauren and it hugged his sexy body like a starlet over a film producer. The jacket seemed to have just a little extra give, though. Enough room for a weapon, I thought.

He kissed Lauren on both cheeks, took a long, appraising look at me, then extended a hand. "I don't know you."

I shook his hand, pleased that he gave me a firm grip without trying to crush me. "I'm Kimberly Walsh. Thanks for agreeing to meet with us."

"I'm in the people business. I'm always ready to get out and meet with prospective clients. Are the two of you interested in looking at something around here?"

It made sense that he didn't trust us. Still, if we were going to be speaking in code, we could be at this all day and not learn anything.

"Let's cut to the chase, Mr. Stefano. We want to talk about business. And not the real estate business."

He grinned at me. "But real estate *is* my business, Ms. Walsh. And please call me Manuel."

"We're considering taking over my husband's enterprises." Lauren stroked Manuel's arm in an intimate gesture that promised everything. "But we don't want to get into trouble. Since you were always Sean's friend, I thought we could come to you, get your advice on next steps, maybe divide some of the customers since I don't know that we really want to operate on the same scale."

Manuel's eyes narrowed. "Sean's business was dangerous. It's not the type of thing two little ladies like you should involve yourself in."

"Spare us the sexism," Lauren said. "We know it's dangerous. Somebody killed Sean. What I want to know is, are you interested in going partners with us, or are you going to try to hoard the entire supply chain yourself?"

Manuel considered Lauren. "What do you have to offer?"

"We've got Sean's Rolodex," I said. "We know the customers, what they like, how they pay, which ones can be given credit and which ones need to pay cash. We have his list of agents so we'll be able to start supplying them and collecting on what he already provided them. It would take you months before you could develop that level of information. In the meantime, someone else might push in, give you competition you didn't want."

He nodded, sharing a pearly smile with me. "Possible. But why should I help you become that competition?"

"We don't want to compete with you," I put in. "We bring the customers, you bring the supply. There's enough money for all of us."

"Ms. Herbert brings the dealers and customers," Manuel observed. "What, exactly do *you* bring to the table, Ms. Walsh? Besides the suspicion that you murdered my friend Sean."

"Everyone knows that I'm a pushover." Lauren was extemporizing now. "We both know that you have to be tough to survive in this business. Sean was the tough one in our relationship. Now that he's gone, I need Kim to be the tough guy--to say no. The fact that she's got the reputation as my husband's killer, as Fred Turley's killer, makes me look stronger. Who would mess with her?"

Manuel considered that for a moment--long enough for me to believe he'd go for it.

I tried to look as tough as Lauren made me out, like I might just murder a guy because he showed me dirty pictures or was a bit slow to come up with the money he owed us for his drugs.

My Clint Eastwood glare must not have worked. Manuel's deadpan expression split open and he let out an annoying guffaw.

"This is too amusing, Lauren, dear. Your dear friend, Ms. No, looks like she'd loose a wrestling match against an overgrown cockroach."

He snagged one of the French fries Lauren had been trying to force down my throat before Manuel had appeared and bit into it.

"McDonalds has the best fries, don't you think?" He paused and chewed. "But let's speak seriously now. You wouldn't have approached me if you weren't looking for something. Your drug sales scheme is a pathetic fabrication--I hope you haven't tried it on anyone else because the two of you just aren't believable as dealers. Since I'm here, and since I was Sean's friend, I'll provide what help I can. The police think you're the killers but I can't believe that. I'm guessing that you are looking for an alternative suspect to offer the police. Someone like, let's all admit it, me. Do I have it?"

I just stared at him. We were the ones who were supposed to be learning things, not him.

He helped himself to another of my fries. "Did you get ketchup for that?"

Lauren tossed him a couple of packets.

I tried to catch her eye, to get some sense on where we should go from here. She neatly avoided my gaze.

Since Lauren had extemporized and wasn't helping, I figured I could do the same. I just had to hope things wouldn't backfire as badly on me as they had when she'd tried it.

"You're right, Manuel. We're in trouble with the police and we don't have enough money to pay for the investigators our lawyers say we need. Lauren figured we could sell you Sean's Rolodex. But I suggested it might be worth more if we threatened to use it to go into business ourselves. That way, you'd be buying not only the information but two less competitors."

"Clever. Very clever," Manuel observed.

"We're not looking to rob anyone," I said. "Those names have got to be worth tens of thousands. You'd be able to pick up where Sean left off with no gap at all. Lauren will even handle introductions if any of them are worried."

I knew I had a tendency to run on, to undersell myself after I'd closed the deal. This time, I brought myself up short. "What do you think?"

I watched him carefully. We didn't have Sean's Rolodex, of course, although Lauren remembered enough to fake it a bit if Manuel pushed. The only way Manuel would know we didn't have the Rolodex was if he had helped himself to the files after he'd finished Sean off--if he, himself, was our killer.

If he was willing to pay for the Rolodex, that would mean he hadn't stolen it from Sean's house. For Manuel, the theoretical customer listing should have had substantial value. If he wasn't willing to pay for it, that could mean only one thing--he had found it when he'd murdered Sean.

He stared back at me, his dark eyes devoid of expression.

"Got it," he announced. "You are trying to put me into the frame. Is my agreement to purchase it supposed to mean something, or are the cops waiting to search me when they leave?" His dark eyes seemed to burrow through my forehead. "Or am I supposed to turn it down?" He paused for another moment, still processing. "Did someone steal Sean's Rolodex? Is that what this is about?"

I would have bluffed it out but Lauren hotted up. "Somebody killed my husband, Manuel. And we're going to track him down and make him pay. If it's you, you'd better start running. If it isn't you, you'd better get ready to help us because anyone standing in the way is likely to get hurt."

I'd thought Manuel's eyes were emotionless. That was before I saw what he looked like when he got mad.

His entire face froze and eyes narrowed just a bit and went cold as dry ice. "Sean and I were friends, Lauren. Neither of us would hurt the other. Neither of us would ever threaten the other. Think about that before you even consider threatening me."

"Did it sound to you like I was making a threat?" Lauren demanded. "Because it wasn't. It was a promise."

Chapter 9

"That went well," Lauren announced. She had traded her probably bugged Celica in on a rented minivan with tinted windows and we were headed back toward my place, bags of laundry in the back and the weight of half a McDonalds hamburger sitting heavy in my stomach.

"Oh, dear, look at that sign." I gestured out the window. "We're in a no sarcasm zone."

"Very funny. But I was being serious. We know Manuel wanted Sean's business. If he didn't already have it, he would have gone for Sean's Rolodex. As it was, he didn't even try to negotiate. Manuel did it."

It made sense, but it didn't feel right to me. Manuel had been too smart, had seen through our scheme. "I don't think so."

"Don't let his sexy smile get to you, Kim. Manuel is a drug dealer. That means he's a lying, cheating, bottom-feeding parasite. He might have a great body and a five-thousand-dollar smile, but that's just camouflage."

She was getting a little hot, but I felt my blood chill. This was a serious emotional outburst from a woman whose late husband was also a drug dealer. A woman who didn't have an alibi for the time her husband had been killed.

"He didn't buy the list because he deduced we didn't have it," I said. "We didn't learn anything we didn't already know." Except that Dallas had some hunky drug dealers running around. Come to think of it, Sean had been some kind of good-looking as well.

"Suppose we turn him over to Clark and Pete." Lauren was ignoring my negativity. "They'll sweat him until he breaks. The D.E.A. doesn't bother with Miranda or any of that civil rights stuff. They just start seizing property and dare you to try to get it back."

"Why would they do that for us?" I wondered. "Especially since they're already getting a cut out of Manuel."

"Good point," she admitted.

She looked worried for about five seconds, then her smile came back. "We'll come back to that plan once we get more information. In the meantime, what's our next step, captain?"

I opened my mouth to tell her I was completely out of plans, but an idea popped into my mind. It was about time, but I didn't reprimand my brain for being late. I wanted to encourage the idea's little sisters and brothers to come out of hiding too.

"Remember when we were talking about Preston Rolin and you said you'd use your sexy act on him to get him to help us?"

From the blank look on Lauren's face, I could tell she didn't remember anything of the kind.

"The Postal Policeman," I reminded her. "The one who was going to find out if Fred had been running cameras through the Rock Cliff No-Tell Motel."

"Oh, yeah. I guess."

"Since I got arrested, he's been less supportive. Which brings you in."

"I'm not following."

"I thought you could vamp him a bit. Stir him up with your dumb blonde bit and see if we can learn anything else about what the police are up to."

"What dumb--"

"Very funny. I know you fake that. We've been working this from Sean's angle for a while and keep running into dead ends. So, maybe we should switch back to Fred, work on that end of the string to see if we can untie any knots."

I stopped at a 7-11 and dialed Preston's number.

For a miracle, I didn't get the machine.

"Rolin."

"Hi Preston, it's Kimberly Walsh. I was wondering if you had some time to meet with me."

"You know I can't do that, Kimmy. You've been arrested and charged with obstruction of justice. If Mr. Lindner hears that we've even been talking, he'll ream me a fresh one."

I couldn't argue with him there. Lindner didn't care about the truth, justice, or anything other than making himself look good.

"We've come up with some evidence we think will help clear us," I lied. "But we need some official help to make sure we're not missing anything."

His pause was long enough for me to wonder if he'd hung up on me.

"Don't you have any contacts in the D.P.D.?" he finally demanded. "They're lead on this case, not the Post Office Police."

"Come on, Preston. Think what a hero you'll be if you solve this case and clear the Post Office's name."

"I don't want to be a hero, I want to keep my job."

His words were still saying no, but something told me that I'd have him if I just pushed a bit harder. "Mr. Lindner would never have to know unless you cracked the whole case, in which case he'd pretty much have to give you a commendation. We could meet somewhere private."

Another pause. "Oh, hell. Why not? But if you tell anyone about this meeting, I'll say you're lying--and I'll never help you again."

"Deal, Preston."

We settled on an eight o'clock rendezvous at Kidd Springs Park on Tyler Street just up the hill from my trailer park.

"If you can tell me a little about what you've learned, I can do some research before I leave the office," Preston offered.

"Just be there," I said. "You'll be satisfied."

Going Postal

Kidd Springs Park was a pleasant urban oasis with ducks, a small lake, and ice cream vendors who wheeled little pushcarts down the tree-shaded paths.

Lauren bought both of us chocolate coated drumsticks and happily munched on hers as we waited for Preston's arrival.

"Want to tell me about him?" she asked.

"He's just a cop. Dark hair, pretty good build. I'd guess he works out."

"If I'm going to blonde on him, I need more."

I wracked my brain but came up empty. "Just another guy around the post office."

"That narrows it down."

Preston was a few minutes late but he spotted us at the picnic table we'd claimed and clomped over.

I decided he was trying to look undercover in a sleeveless t-shirt with the neck ripped out, a pair of baggy jeans, and clunky looking sneakers with no laces.

"You're looking good, Preston," I told him. He was even better built than I remembered, with cut muscles and a deep tan. He didn't do much for me, but I could almost smell Lauren going into vamp mode.

He inspected me. "You on a hunger strike or something?"

I ignored that. "This is Lauren Herbert. Lauren, Preston Rolin is the Post Office cop assigned to work with the D.P.D. in investigating the murders."

"Just one of many," Preston said.

Lauren brushed a long hunk of blonde-streaked hair out of her face and gave Preston a traffic-stopping smile. "I doubt that you're 'just' anything, Preston. It's nice to meet you. Kimberly says that you've been very helpful."

He actually looked around to make sure no one was listening. "Not *too* helpful," he said. "You'll get me fired."

Lauren leaned closer, brushing against his muscular arm. "Kim said you were looking into Fred's motel, trying to find out if he might have been in the blackmail business. Did you learn anything?"

He slapped his forehead--using the arm Lauren wasn't touching. I noticed he didn't move that one at all. "Sorry. I was going to get back to you on that one, Kimmy, but then you got arrested and it didn't exactly seem like a good idea."

"That's all right, Preston." Lauren edged even closer to him, let one of her breasts *accidentally* brush against him. "But you did learn something? Was Kimberly right about the motel?"

He looked completely bemused. "Huh? Oh, right. Well, that motel had more wires running through it than cockroaches." He gave a high-pitched snicker. "Fred had thousands of photos stored on his computer. Some of Dallas's most upstanding citizens in fragrant delicate, as they say."

Fragrant delicate? That sounded like a perfume shop to me.

"Sounds like reasonable doubt material."

Preston shook his head. "Don't count on it, Kimmy. Between when the cops were looking at it at the motel and when it arrived at the evidence room, Fred's hard drive got wiped. No pictures, no evidence, nothing."

"How the Hell could that happen?"

"Nobody let me look at the pictures," Preston admitted. I just heard about it second hand. But I have a theory there were just a few too many cops in those pictures. I can't prove it, and I certainly wouldn't want to guess whether it was orders from the Chief's office or just a uniformed officer who didn't want to make the front page of the *Morning News*. One way or the other, it's written up as a sad accident. For my money, it's one hell of a convenient accident."

"At least we know there was another motive." Lauren brushed the back of her hand down Preston's arm, rewarding him for being so forthcoming.

"I don't see how the blackmail angle could connect to your ex-husband, though," Preston said. "And the cops aren't going to buy any story that the two killings aren't connected. The M.O.'s are too similar."

"There's a connection, all right," Lauren said.

"Hey, that's right. You've been pumping me like there's no tomorrow, but you got me here because you were supposed to have some evidence of your own, right?" Preston glanced at me, but then turned his gaze back to Lauren. "So, what's the deal? I've spilled what I know. Your turn."

"We're working the drug angle," Lauren said. She and I had agreed to remain vague. I didn't trust Preston not to run to the cops with whatever we told him. He'd even had time to get a wire if he wanted. I hadn't killed either man and I was almost convinced that Lauren hadn't either, but that didn't mean the cops couldn't take anything we said out of context when the D.A. played it for a jury. "The two were both involved. Fred had been one of Sean's dealers for a long time before they had a falling out."

"Makes sense," Preston admitted. "Not exactly evidence, though. And you've got to remember that Sean got killed first. If Fred killed Sean, who killed Fred? And if it was about drugs, why murder a wholesaler and a retailer? Two different levels, generally two different motives."

"Whoever killed Sean ransacked his house," Lauren said. "They stole Sean's records. That would have included Fred. Killing him would pressure the other dealers to go along with the new regime."

Preston rubbed his eyes. "Say you've convinced me. I'm the easy guy in this. After all, no matter how off-target Mr. Lindner can get, it's still good for the Post Office if we find a way to get Kimmy off the hook. The problem is, I'm not the guy you've got to convince. The D.P.D. thinks they have their killers--and it's the two of you working together. You're going to have to give me more than this if I'm going to persuade anyone of anything. As it is, Lindner is already telling me to get back to purely postal things. If I'm going to help, I need information, not speculation."

"Do you have any links into the D.E.A.?" Lauren ran an acrylic fingernail along the outer seam of Preston's jeans. "We think the two local agents, Clark Study and Pete Treloar, may be involved. And we're suspicious of a drug dealer named Manuel Stefano."

Whatever Lauren was doing to Preston's libido, it wasn't enough.

He ignored Lauren and glared at me. "First you want me to give you inside scoop from the Dallas Police and now you want me to violate my orders to investigate Feds? Are you crazy? I won't just lose my job over this, I'll go to jail."

"Come on, Preston. Don't you want to be a hero?" Lauren gave him an *I already think you're a hero* gaze.

"What I want is to get out of this madhouse while I still have my own sanity." He pushed himself away from the picnic table, stalked away, then turned when he was well out of our reach.

"If I find anything that might clear you, Kimmy, I'll forward it through D.P.D. channels. But don't try to contact me again without hard evidence. And even then, let's meet by phone. The two of you are poison."

* * * *

Lauren wouldn't leave our picnic table until she had spent five minutes studying her face and hair in a little compact mirror.

"If I was five years younger, he never would have walked away," she assured me. "I could walk into a bar and the band would stop playing and stumble over each other."

If I'd walked into a bar five years before, everyone would have snickered about whether whales were in season. "He's under a lot of pressure at his job," I reminded her. "And he wasn't blowing you off, he was blowing *me* off."

"It shouldn't matter." She touched up her powder, considered her lipstick, then wiped it off and replaced it with a darker shade, and tugged her shirt so it clung just a bit more tightly to her body. "Maybe he is gay."

"Wouldn't surprise me." I didn't think so, but she needed encouragement, not reality.

"Well I know Nagle isn't gay. Let's hit him up at church."

"Why bother? He can't be connected to the drugs?"

The cops had confiscated our bloody rags, so we couldn't run Lauren's tests, but they hadn't accused us of having either victim's blood so I figured that lead had come up empty.

"He watched Sean all the time. Think of him as a witness, not a suspect."

"But what about--"

"If he'd recognized us, he would have reported us and the cops would have added that to our list of crimes."

I nodded and headed for the minivan. Lauren had thought talking to Nagle was a waste of time earlier. Now that she needed reassurance about her impact on the male of the species, she'd changed her plan.

* * * *

It was nine o'clock on a Wednesday night and Nagle's church was just letting out.

The beige clapboard church didn't have the impressiveness of the many brick churches in the neighborhood, but the congregation seemed large, enthused, and energized as they stepped into their foreign sedans and high-end

SUVs.

Although I looked, I didn't spot a single African-American or Hispanic face among the crowd pushing through the double door and heading for home. In this neighborhood, that was a bit skewed.

"Looks like an upscale group," I commented.

"Yeah. Worried about their property values." Lauren gestured to the letterboard outside the church. *MAKING YOURS A GOD-FEARING NEIGHBORHOOD* it read. "They go around killing people, for sure their neighbors are going to be filled with fear."

I didn't remind her that we'd cleared Nagle. She knew that.

We caught the minister just as the choir members, stripped of their golden robes, trooped out the church door.

He sighed when he saw me and frowned when he noticed Lauren beside me. "Is this something we need to deal with tonight?"

"It's important," I said.

"Important to you doesn't mean important to me."

I shouldn't have gotten mad. First, I wanted his help. Second, he was a minister. And third, I've learned that I say things when I get mad that I regret later. Even thought I knew this at the time, it didn't help.

"How big a congregation do you think you'll have if word gets around that you might've killed someone? That isn't exactly turning the other cheek, is it?"

"Don't you dare quote scripture at me."

"How about I paint you a picture, then? You've been on a neighborhood cleanup campaign for years and your next-door neighbor was interfering. Poof, now he's dead. Down the street, Fred Turley ran a hooker motel and managed a little blackmail scheme at the same time. Can't be good for property values. Zap, he's dead too. Did you kill him because you wanted to clean up the neighborhood? Or was it, maybe, that he had some pictures you didn't want made public? More than one minister had his career shortened because he was spending the offerings on getting his rocks off."

Nagle swelled up like a disturbed puffer-fish. "These are the most ridiculous accusations I've ever heard. If you don't leave now, I'm going to call the police."

Lauren had been nudging me since I started spouting. Since that hadn't worked, she stomped on my foot.

"Come on, Reverend," she said. "You had your problems with Sean, but you and I always got along fine. We're hoping you'll do the generous thing and help us out."

Nagle's face had turned purple when he'd been shouting at me but gradually faded to something more like a person and less like an eggplant when Lauren interposed herself between us. "I don't know what you expect me to do to help you, Mrs. Herbert. I didn't kill your husband. And I'm certain that no one in my congregation did, either."

Except he didn't sound certain. Not at all.

"Let's go into your office and have a cup of coffee," Lauren suggested. "If we put our heads together, I'm sure we can find a way to work things out."

"But she--" he gestured my way.

"Kimberly gets overly excited sometimes," Lauren admitted.

She doing the same touch thing she'd tried on Preston but on Nagle, it worked like a charm.

"But she means well." Lauren was purring now, happy again now that her magic was working. "Believe me, Steve, we're all in this together."

He muttered something that didn't sound like a prayer, but he led us through his church and into a small office at the back.

The church coffee tasted like it had been made the previous Sunday and left to condense over a heating element for the three days in between. It was a jet-black sludge that only turned to a dark gray shade when I diluted it liberally with creamer.

Nagle didn't seem to mind the biohazardic taste, though, and gave an appreciative sigh as he took his first sip. "I'm always anxious to help a neighbor in trouble," he advised Lauren. "But I really don't--"

"Oh, good." Lauren pulled her chair around the desk so she was sitting next to Nagle. "We really appreciate your help. Kim has been trying to figure how Sean spent his last day. You know, who might have visited him, whether he left the house, whether he did something special."

"I'm quite busy, you know. I don't keep track of everything my neighbors do."

"Don't you?" Lauren dropped a bit of the saccharine sweetness. "I think you kept a twenty-four hour watch on my house. Lord knows, I never felt safe trying to get a tan in the back yard."

Nagle tried to bluster, but his blush gave away the lie. "I wasn't trying to look at you. I'm not a peeping Tom."

Lauren smiled at him. "Of course you're not. You weren't trying to watch me in my bikini. You were keeping track of Sean, trying to find out what he was up to so you could plan a way to get rid of him. Like your sign outside says, you wanted to create a God-fearing neighborhood. Sean wasn't the right type."

"I know he was your husband, Mrs. Herbert. Your support for him is a testament to the power of the great sacrament of marriage. But I wouldn't be honest if I didn't tell you that Sean was a blot on humanity. Before I founded my church, I worked in a central city ministry. I spent my life with the victims of drug abuse and addiction. I met women who had sold their children for a crack rock, men who pimped their mothers and sold their own bodies to be used as sex-toys by the evil and jaded. Don't tell me that drugs are a victimless crime. I saw the victims and I didn't like what I saw."

"Seeing Sean sitting there in a luxurious house in an improving neighborhood must have really rubbed you the wrong way," I suggested.

Lauren's glare almost matched Nagle's. "Sean didn't deal in crack or heroin," she said. "He was more into amphetamines, steroids, performance-improving agents."

Nagle only snorted. "He was in the business of ruining people's lives for money. I pray for his soul but I don't find myself regretting that he is no longer able to spread his poisons."

"Right. So, you *were* watching him. You can help us with his schedule and with anyone who called on him. Let's have the list." Lauren ran a hand over Nagle's bald head, leaving her fingers resting on his shoulder and bringing her body close enough to his that I was sure he could feel her heat.

"But--"

"Even if eliminating Sean did the world some good, murder is against the law," Lauren reminded him. "Didn't you tell me there was a commandment against it?"

"Yes, but--"

"Kimberly and I don't think it was one of your parishioners, if that's what you're worried about."

"I would never think that." From his tone, I knew that was exactly what he was worried about. If he wasn't worried that we'd put *him* in the frame.

He sighed, then took another sip of coffee. "All right, what do you want to know?"

It turned out that Sean had been a busy beaver during the days leading up to his death. Nagle had seen five women and twelve men enter Sean's house during that period. On closer questioning, one of the 'women' turned out to be Larry Mueller. His waist-length hair had confused the minister.

Unfortunately, Nagle generally refused to wear the glasses he needed and his descriptions were vague. The fat guy could have been Fred, but Nagle wasn't sure. From the description, he might have been Buddy instead. The curvy blonde woman was definitely Lauren--the time matched when she'd admitted she'd been there.

"One fat guy, one curvy girl, and a long-haired postal worker. Everyone else was just a blob? Come on, Reverend. Give us more."

Nagle was already sweating but he took another sip of his steaming coffee-sludge. "I wish I could help you, Lauren."

"How old?" I asked. "You can tell that from the way they walk, even if you can't make out the facial features."

He creased his forehead in concentration. "One of them--no, forget it."

"We won't accuse anyone without real evidence, Reverend," I assured him. "We just need some kind of break."

"All right. But you've got to remember that I don't see that well and that it was pretty late."

"We'll keep that in mind."

"Well, it looked to me like one of the guys had sort of a military look to him. You know, the way he marched to the door. And he was carrying something when he left. A carton of some kind, it looked like."

"How long did he stay in the house?" Lauren asked.

"A while. Maybe an hour."

"When was he there?" I looked at the notes I'd taken.

"He was the second to last. The one before the curvy woman."

Going Postal

Bingo. Who says that when you go to church, your prayers aren't answered?

Chapter 10

"It's got to be Clark Study," Lauren said as she drove us back to my trailer. "Did you get a good look at him? With that short hair and poker up his ass, he has a definite military look. And he and Pete would just love to get their hands on Sean's records."

"I don't know. Manuel has sort of a military look too," I reminded her. "He's got a really erect posture."

"Yeah. I saw you looking at his erect posture."

I felt my face get red but I didn't argue with her. Maybe I *had* noticed the way he filled out his slacks. There wasn't any law against noticing.

"We know Sean was dead when I got there," Lauren said. "The odds say, the one before me did the killing. Otherwise, why wouldn't whoever found him have called 9-1-1?"

Maybe for the same reason she hadn't--they knew they'd be suspected. And I only had Lauren's word for it that Sean had been dead when she'd gotten there. Still, I wasn't going to get anywhere by accusing her. And if I was going to trust her, her theory seemed as good a place to start as anywhere. Besides, if we could track down the military-type, we'd either clear Lauren or put her in the spot.

Identifying a man when our entire description was a vaguely military look wasn't going to be easy, though.

Still, we were ahead of where we had been. So far, we had two data points. Based on the way that the house was ransacked, we knew the killing was drug-related. And based on Nagle's evidence, including the alleged carton--which could have held the Rolodex as well as Sean's most valuable drugs--and Lauren's assurance that Sean had already been dead, we could hypothesize that the killer was a male with a military build. I didn't want to assume that Dallas wasn't full of ex-military drug dealers and narcs, but of the suspects we'd identified so far, Clark Study and Manuel Stefano seemed to fit the evidence better than anyone else. Both warranted more study.

"We've got to get some sleep before we tackle Clark," Lauren said. "And even before that, let's eat. I'm starving."

Cesar's Taco Stand is open twenty-four hours and serves some of the best and freshest food in the city. It also doesn't charge much and serves small portions. One of the things my lawyer had given me was a notice from the Post Office that I'd been suspended without pay pending the results of the investigation, so money was a larger issue.

I ordered a taco and a diet coke.

Going Postal

Lauren ordered two of the number three specials and proceeded to force-feed me.

"I'm a big girl," I told her. "I don't need a mommy to make me eat."

"You're starving yourself," she said. "And I need you healthy if we're going to figure out who killed Sean."

I ate half my taco and then I made myself to eat a little of what Lauren had bought. She didn't seem to mind leaving some of her food untouched, obviously didn't have the 'clean your plate' compulsion that I had been brought up with. Which might explain why she had perfect curves and I had only recently left my blimp status behind me.

It was nearly midnight when we finished eating and headed back toward my trailer. "Do you think it's Clark, or Manuel?" Lauren was so tired she slipped a yawn into the middle of her question.

I shrugged. "Clark seemed too stupid and Manuel too smart to kill Sean. If you think about it, though, I'll bet it's easier to fake stupid than fake smart. So I'm voting for Clark."

She patted me on the leg. "I never did like those D.E.A. guys."

"We'll worry about it tomorrow," I promised. "First, we need some sleep."

* * * *

Needing sleep and actually *getting* sleep are not the same thing. For once, though, I fell asleep with no problem at all. Even the softly breathing person in the bed next to me didn't really bother me.

A jolt to the head at two in the morning bothered me a lot, though.

"Hey!"

I was just recovering, from an elbow in my skull, suddenly awake enough to wonder what was going on, when Lauren's hard shove knocked me right out of my double bed and onto the floor.

A trailer floor has a bit of give to it--not like the hard concrete foundation of, say, Lauren's minimansion, but it still hurt.

"What the heck--"

I cut off my complaint. Lauren thrashed around on the bed like she was being attacked by fire ants. If she hadn't rolled me out ahead of the worst of the attack, I would have been seriously bruised.

"Lauren, wake up. You're having a nightmare." I tried to shake her awake. Mistake. She grabbed me and yanked me to her.

"Come on. Quit it."

She opened a single bloodshot eye. "Go away."

"If you let me loose, I might be able to do that."

She released me, then pressed a shaking hand against her forehead. "I feel like shit."

I didn't answer until I'd backed well out of range. "Do you feel sick? Should I take you to the emergency room?"

Her laughter wouldn't have convinced anyone. "We were going to meet with Manuel later today anyway, weren't we?"

I shrugged, then saw her eyes weren't tracking. "I guess. So?"

"So, call him. Get him. Now. Tell him I need some shit."

Shit was right. Lauren was suffering from withdrawal symptoms right in the middle of my bed. If I did nothing, she might die. If I called Manuel like she wanted, they'd add drug charges to my murder rap. In Texas, juries automatically assume that druggies did it, so I could kiss my already slim chances of being exonerated goodbye.

"Hurry, Kim."

She rolled over, cracked her head against the metal wall to my trailer, got halfway out of the bed, then collapsed into it.

Drops of sweat collected on her face and her breath rattled inside her lungs. "Tie me up before I hurt myself."

I wasn't into that kind of action but this was looking serious.

I found some old pantyhose I hadn't used since my engineering days and used them to spread-eagle her over the bed. Then I called Manuel.

He wasn't happy to hear from me.

Not a big surprise. I wasn't happy to be calling him.

"Lauren is in trouble," I assured him. "She needs help from you. Help only you can provide." I was talking in code but I figured Manuel would understand.

"Shit." He understood, all right.

Lauren had lied to me again. She'd assured me that she didn't use drugs, that she'd left Sean because of his drug dealing. The truth seemed different. Maybe he'd kicked her out because of her addiction.

I liked Lauren, but I wasn't sure I could be her friend. I'd always be wondering what secret she had waiting to sneak out and bite me.

I called Tina and we spent the thirty minutes Manuel took to get to my place trying to calm Lauren, keep her from screaming and waking up the neighbors, and trying not to panic. It wasn't easy.

I almost flew to the door when I finally heard the knock.

Manuel had been hot in his suit, all dressed up like a real estate agent. In a pair of jeans and a white t-shirt, he sizzled.

He pushed past me. "Where is she?"

I led him to my bed.

He studied her spread-eagled figure. Lauren was wearing a lace camisole and a pair of panties and nothing else. Her breasts pressed against the thin camisole fabric with every inhalation and her sweat glued it to her, exposing every curve to his view. "Kinky. I like it."

What a bastard.

"She's hurting. Can you help her?"

He glanced around the trailer. "Is it safe to talk?"

I shook my head, not even daring to answer his question out loud.

"Right. Well, I'm not a doctor but it seems to me that the first thing is to get the fever under control. Why don't you fill a plastic bag with ice cubes and I'll see if I can get her to drink some water. She's been sweating out her fluids big-time."

I followed his instructions partly because they made sense but mostly because I knew he wanted to do something he didn't want me to see-- something I didn't want me to see, either.

I took a bit of extra time making the icepack, then wrapped it in a towel.

When I returned to my bedroom, Manuel was bent over Lauren speaking to her in Spanish but in such soothing tones I instantly felt a bit better myself. Not too much better, though. And Lauren still looked like Hell.

Tina took a look at Manuel and mouthed something to me.

I shrugged.

She walked over and whispered in my ear, "you going to be okay?"

"Don't know."

"Call me if you need me."

"I will."

Manuel followed Tina to the door. "I'll step out for a moment. Run the ice pack over her entire body. She should start feeling better soon."

Sure enough, by the time I had melted half the ice with her body heat, she had stopped thrashing.

"Well? Are you going to untie me? This is just a bit humiliating, don't you think?"

Untying knotted pantyhose was not a happening thing. I had to go into my kitchen to get a pair of scissors.

Manuel was brewing a pot of coffee. "I'd be remiss if I didn't compliment you on the look as well," he said.

Here I thought he'd only noticed Lauren. For half a second, I allowed myself to fantasize that he was serious, that he actually thought I looked good.

Then I looked at myself. Reality can be a bitch.

I wore a faded University of Texas at Dallas t-shirt that had fit me when I'd been a beached whale and that now could have contained three of me. It hung down almost to my knees. The only thing sexy about it was that it had been through the washing machine so many times that the fabric had thinned out.

The best counter to a sarcastic bastard is an attack. "I don't approve of your business." I grabbed the scissors from a drawer.

"I don't suppose it matters to you that if I didn't do my job, someone else would. Someone who might not answer a two o'clock call for help."

"Is that how you live with yourself? Boy, I wouldn't settle for such a pathetic excuse."

He shook his head. "Uh, would you mind pointing those scissors some other direction? Given what happened to Fred and Sean, sharp blades make me a hair uncomfortable."

His t-shirt was snug enough to his body that I knew he wasn't hiding any weapons, but I still doubted that he was really intimidated by a five-foot tall woman with a pair of scissors.

Manuel moved like a cat, watched everything around him like a hawk, and stared at me with the cold eyes of a killer. The worst part was, I couldn't help getting a little turned on when I watched him. What did that say about me?

"Why don't you pour coffee for the three of us?" I suggested. "I'll set

Lauren loose, put on some clothes, then we can talk."

When a woman threatens 'talk,' most guys head out. Manuel simply nodded.

"Took you long enough." Lauren looked completely recovered but she was still grouchy.

Well, I was grouchy, too. After all, I'd been the one kicked out of bed--and it was my bed.

"Manuel is waiting to talk with us. Shut up, put on some clothes, and let's go out and see him."

I opened my closet to see if I could find something to wear other than a ratty t-shirt or a postal uniform. I pulled out a little tank top I'd hardly ever worn because I couldn't wear a bra with it but Lauren stopped me. "Wear this."

This, freshly pulled from her suitcase, was a tiny sundress that tied behind the neck, not covering any of the back and even less of my legs than my ratty t-shirt had done.

"No way this fits you," I said.

"I bought it for you. I looked through your closet. Everything is either cruddy or fat-girl."

I had a couple of nice looking bicycle jerseys for long rides, but I didn't argue with her. I knew I wasn't a fashion plate. "Thanks."

Lauren insisted on putting on her makeup before leaving the bedroom even though Manuel had already seen her at her worst, writhing on the bed. It took a while. With every second of delay, I'd become more convinced Manuel would vanish.

He gave us a low wolf-whistle when we came out. "Don't the two of you pretty up?"

"Is that coffee?" Lauren headed straight for the line of mugs on my tiny table.

"Help yourself. The milk went bad but the sugar looks safe."

Lauren sucked down a cup, poured herself another, and drank it like water.

The inside of her mouth had to be burning but she didn't seem to notice. Manuel did. His hand jerked a little as if he was restraining himself from grabbing it from her for her own protection.

I took advantage of the distraction to gather up my notebook.

"We have a witness that can place you at Sean Herbert's place at around eleven fifteen on Friday night," I told him, pretending to be reading back something I'd written down. "Do you want to tell us about it?" For the first time, I felt a bit safer knowing that the cops were probably listening in.

He blinked. "I thought we were going to talk about Lauren's problem, not about some crazy story."

"You were wrong. Do you have any answer to our witness's account?"

He considered me for five seconds. "Outside."

Okay, that made sense. At least the cops listening in would be suspicious if we vanished.

We followed him outside.

"Well?"

"I have an answer. Your witness is a liar."

"Our witness is a minister," Lauren blurted. "Why would he lie?"

Uh-oh. Maybe Manuel didn't know which minister lived next door to Sean, but I doubted it. If something happened to Nagle, I would feel responsible-- even if his murder would be a pretty compelling argument that we'd found the right guy. Of course, if Manuel decided Nagle needed killing, he'd probably have to kill us first, which would mean I wouldn't have to feel guilty. The thought wasn't comforting.

"That one is easy," he said, answering Lauren's question. "Nagle has it in for drug dealers because of what happened to his daughter. He used to be an okay guy, worked the streets, helping people who were hurting. When his daughter got hooked, though, he went crazy. He hated anything to do with drugs. He'd frame me in a New York minute."

"There are lots of people besides you in the world," I said. "I doubt he'd single you out."

"Nagle wanted Sean eliminated--and guess what, he's dead. He wanted Fred eliminated--and he's dead too. He'd like me eliminated, next. So, he sets me up as the killer and gets a bonus. It wouldn't bother him at all that I was innocent. He'd let God sort it out."

"Maybe we should get out of here," Lauren suggested.

* * * *

Dawn was still a promise. In the distance, Dallas's skyscrapers glowed a green and purple haze. They provided enough light to obscure the stars but not enough to see by. I stumbled over one of Tina's pet chickens as I tried to follow the faint glow of Manuel's white t-shirt.

He led us to a Lincoln Navigator, dweeped his alarm system, and let us in.

Lauren scrambled in the back and Manuel took the drivers seat, leaving the passenger seat to me.

As I settled into the leather upholstery, I realized something scary.

Manuel hadn't asked me, or Lauren, what she was using, or to describe the withdrawal pangs she was fighting. That could mean that the symptoms for each drug withdrawal are completely different and that Manuel had come with a full pharmacy. But the more likely scenario was that he'd already known, that he'd been her supplier. Which meant that Lauren and Manuel just might be collaborators.

I definitely didn't need the cold blast from the air conditioner when Manuel started his car--my arms were already covered with goose bumps. I had an uncomfortable suspicion that I might be the killer's next victim. And that Manuel and Lauren were co-conspirators. Maybe she'd been in Sean's house after his death because Manuel had called her to clean up after him. Maybe he was the reason she and Sean were divorcing.

"I have my car scanned every morning by a technician I trust." Manuel shifted the car into gear and bumped over the rough asphalt of the trailer park. "It should be safe to talk now."

91

"So, talk." I hoped I was the only one who noticed the slight shake in my voice. As usual, my hopes were quickly frustrated.

"Are you cold, Kimberly?" Manuel glanced my way, then to the road as he swung out into a dark street. At four in the morning, there wasn't a lot of traffic in our part of Dallas.

"Don't worry about me."

"But I do worry about you. You've been accused of murder, advised by your lawyer to stay away from the case and let professional investigators take over, and you're running around trying to get yourself killed."

It sounded like a threat to me.

"You know no investigators are looking into the murders," Lauren said from the back seat. "So don't give Kim a hard time."

"How do you know what my lawyer told me?" I demanded.

Manuel got onto Polk Street, heading south. "I'm not trying to give Kimberly a hard time, Lauren. And all lawyers say the same thing. It's what they learn in law school. To cover their own asses first."

It sounded believable. But Manuel sold real estate when he wasn't selling drugs. Of course he could be convincing.

I bit my tongue to keep from spouting off. Instead, I looked out the window as we rolled further south into Oak Cliff, out of my neighborhood and into unknown territory.

Now and then, a car passed us, bright headlights splashing light into the darkness. Moving blue shadows from behind closed curtains said that a few night owls were up, watching the tube in the wee hours of the morning.

When I rode my bicycle, I often felt an attachment to the road, the neighborhoods I was passing through. A post office van is not too much farther removed. Manuel's big Lincoln SUV was almost like seeing the world on a big screen. Ordinary city sounds, dogs barking, chicken crowing, cars doplering by, none of this penetrated the eerie silence of the monstrous vehicle.

My screams wouldn't penetrate its soundproofed walls either, I realized. And even if someone out there happened to be awake, no curious eyes could see through the vehicle's reflective windows.

"What, exactly, did Nagle say?" Manuel's question broke the silence like an ax through kindling.

I was committed to this line and I stuck with it. "I already told you. I didn't say it was Nagle. But our witness saw you entering Sean's house at eleven on Friday night. You carried a box when you left."

"An interesting amount of detail, don't you think?"

Beating around the bush wasn't helping. I needed to appeal to Manuel's logic. "Look, Manuel. If I end up dead, you'll be the lead suspect. Your fingerprints are on the coffee cups in my trailer so the cops will know you were with us. And Reverend Nagle will tell the police about meeting us. They'll put one and one together and you'll be in jail quicker than you can spit."

Polk had turned into Tyler by now and we were in an increasingly rural neighborhood. Manuel jerked on the wheel, turning onto a little street that ran along a little creek.

I'd ridden my bike out here and I hadn't even noticed the street. Which meant it was pretty well hidden.

Here and there, mounds of trash stood out among the 'No Dumping' signs--signs that looked like they'd been ignored for fifty years.

If Manuel dumped my body here, it wouldn't be discovered before some futuristic archeologists dug it up.

I knew I was feeling sorry for myself, but I wondered who would miss me. Tina might miss my rent. Larry Mueller might wonder why I hadn't showed up to vote for him in the Union election. Big Bob, the bail bondsman might be pissed because I was a no-show for my court date. Other than that, my disappearance wouldn't create much of a ripple. It wasn't the kind of epitaph I'd want on my tombstone--*her bail bondsman is still looking for her.*

If I managed to survive this, I promised myself I'd turn over a new leaf, make friends, volunteer for stuff, maybe even find a church to belong to--although not the Reverend Nagle's.

Manuel pulled the car into the absolute darkness between two trees. The only light, from the faint glow of the Lincoln's navigational equipment, faded quickly when he switched off the engine. "Why would I kill you, Kimberly?"

I'd thought his voice was sexy. Now it was just scary. Cool, calm, almost kind. As if he were asking me about my favorite color or astrological sign.

"It's obvious that you and Lauren know more than you're saying, more about each other. Was it a love triangle, maybe? You, Sean, and Lauren? Were the drugs simply a bonus?"

"Me and Lauren?" He was amused by that.

"You've done worse, big guy," Lauren said from the back seat."

And Lauren had blown hot and cold about Manuel. She'd been the one who had brought him to my attention in the first place. But she'd tried to direct me away from Manuel, wanted us to put our attention on Clark Study. I wasn't a relationship expert, but this ambiguous feeling stuff made sense if she had something going on with Manuel.

"You convinced me." It was a feeble attempt, but I figured it was worth the go. At least nobody was killing me yet. "Obviously I was mistaken. You have nothing to do with Sean's murder. I got carried away by the coincidence of you knowing about whatever Lauren is addicted to."

"Let's go for a walk, Kimberly." Manuel opened his door and stepped out.

For an instant, I entertained the idea of escape, of dashing into the darkness and vanishing. I clutched at my door latch and yanked.

The thing didn't respond at all. Obviously, when Manuel had unlocked his door, he hadn't bothered with mine.

I fumbled for the lock, found it, then felt it twist in my hand from its electronic control.

Should I shove it back? My fingers were too slow and clumsy. Before I could act, Manuel had opened my door.

"Allow me."

I couldn't help my shiver when his strong hand tightened on my elbow.

"I'll wait here," Lauren chirped.

Had she waited in his car when he'd Sean? Nobody would be surprised to find Lauren's fingerprints all over Sean's house, after all.

I tried to jerk away from him, but he was stronger than me. Lots stronger.

Maybe Lauren was right. Maybe I needed to eat more, become strong enough to assert myself. Not that it mattered any more. My last meal looked to be the number three special from Cesar's Taco Stand. If I'd known it would be my last, I would have had the flan with it.

* * * *

Manuel led me down to a little path that ran along the creek. As we walked past them, tree frogs gave out their characteristic croaks--a sound close enough to a human scream to make anyone from the neighborhood ignore any real screams. Manuel had picked his location perfectly.

"Nice area," I observed. "It would be fun to come here for a picnic some time."

It was another feeble shot but I didn't feel capable of more. My legs were shaking so hard my knees kept slipping and I had to lean on Manuel to support me. If he let me go, I wouldn't run away--I'd simply drop to the ground.

Was this pathetic or what?

"Sit," he said. He guided my collapse onto a large rounded stone.

"Kill me and my ghost will come back and haunt you," I promised. I wasn't sure I believed in ghosts, but I certainly intended to do what I could to make his life uncomfortable.

"Sean and I had a longtime rivalry," he told me.

In the movies, the bad guy always seems to find the need to confess, or brag, about his crime before killing the hero. Of course in the movies, the hero then manages a daring escape. I wasn't much of a hero and I didn't see how I could possibly escape from a man who weighed twice as much as me, was stronger than five of me put together, and who was on his own ground.

"I don't want to know anything," I said. "I promise I won't tell anyone anything."

"Would you cut that out? I'm trying to tell you what's going on."

I screamed.

It was a good one, loud enough to make Manuel wince.

The reaction was instantaneous. From hundreds of yards around me, a million tree frogs responded, their own characteristic screams adding to the night noise.

Manuel's hand moved, just a hair, as if he was instinctively getting ready to clamp it over my mouth.

"Shut up, Kimberly."

"Do you expect me to just sit here and let you kill me?"

"Don't be ridiculous. I'm not going to kill you."

Chapter 11

"I'm not going to kill you." His words seemed to echo in my brain like a bullet's ricochet.

Logic said I should feel relief. Instead, I was pissed.

"You dragged me way out to the country, practically made me pee in my panties from fear, covered up some sort of drug dealing with Lauren, and this isn't about killing me? Are you into some sort of perverse sadism?"

"I told you Nagle was lying. I never said I was going to kill you. When I realized you thought I intended to hurt you, I stopped driving so we could talk. It seems to me that I should be the person who's angry here. It's not nice to falsely accuse people of murder."

"Oh, yeah. You've had a rough time of it."

"You seem like a pretty intelligent woman, Kimberly. But you're not very good at listening, are you?"

That was a low blow. "I do okay."

"Maybe you need practice. So listen to this. I did not kill Sean. I did not kill Fred. I do not intend to kill you, no matter how much you insist on tempting me."

Like he would warn me in advance. Still, I felt a bit reassured. And the little bit of emphasis he put on the word "tempted" sent a trickle of awareness through my body. *Sick, Kimberly. You're getting turned on by a drug pusher who might be a killer.*

"Let's say you didn't kill him. So why were you in Sean's house, then? Somebody killed him and the cops say he was killed right there where I found him."

"It wasn't me, Kimberly. Nagle was lying if he said I was."

He paused a moment, thinking. "But he didn't really say it was me, did he, Kimberly? Because if he had recognized me, he would have told the police and they would have been all over me. Nagle wouldn't have held that back from the cops."

"He couldn't put a name--"

"It seems to me like you're just making the whole thing up, trying to stir up trouble and find someone else to take the fall. Am I right?"

A faint glow of dawn started in the eastern sky--I still couldn't see enough to run, but at least the shapes of the trees, of the man in front of me came into view.

I decided to go with the truth. "Nagle said he saw someone with a military build. It wasn't a great stretch to realize it must be you but it might have been more of a stretch than the cops were willing to attempt."

I didn't tell him that they probably thought Nagle's description of Lauren was me, putting me on the scene just in time to do the killing.

"Maybe I'm supposed to be flattered that you think I'm the only guy in Dallas with decent posture."

I shook my head, momentarily forgetting that he couldn't see the gesture in the darkness. "Get real, Manuel. I know you have something going on with Lauren. She wasn't getting her drugs from Sean, was she? She was getting them from you."

"What goes on between Lauren and me is our business. But it has nothing to do with Sean's death."

"Why do I doubt that?"

"Because you have a suspicious mind?" He turned it into a question but it felt like a slam. Of course I was suspicious. I'd already found two bodies. I didn't want to be the next one to turn up. Or just go missing.

I considered, reminded myself that I was still alive when I thought I'd be dead, and decided to move forward with the investigation.

"You're claiming that you weren't the person who went into Sean's house around eleven, Friday night."

"That's my story."

"Do you have an alibi?"

He laughed. "Nobody the police would trust. Nobody you would trust, either, little Ms. Straight-Arrow."

"What about the following Monday, when Fred was killed?"

He shrugged--and it was finally light enough that I could actually see the gesture. "What time?"

"First thing in the morning."

"I sleep first thing in the morning. I work nights."

"Sleeping alone?" Maybe my motives for asking that question were a hair questionable.

"Definitely alone. You don't really think Lauren and I have something going, do you?"

I didn't know what to think about that. All I knew was that they had more of a relationship than either had admitted to the first time we'd gotten together.

"It sounds to me like you have nothing. No alibi, no convincing story about why it couldn't be you."

"Except it wasn't me. Besides, I liked Sean. I thought his attitude toward the D.E.A. guys showed more guts than sense, but I admired him for it. I've already got a sweet bit of business. Why would I murder Sean and put myself at risk?"

It wasn't a convincing argument. Few people think of success as a destination. No matter how much they get, they want more. I would be very surprised if Manuel were different from the rest of the human race.

"Who was Fred's supplier, then?"

Manuel had been brushing a fallen leaf off his shoulder when I asked, and it was just light enough for me to see the slight hitch in his gesture, to watch him open his mouth, decide against the first answer, and come up with a second.

"Why don't you think Sean supplied him?"

"Because Lauren told me that Sean didn't trust Fred."

"Lauren is a drug addict. She sometimes has an estranged relationship with the truth."

"Are you telling me that Sean was Fred's supplier, or are you just jerking with me?"

"Let's get back to the car. Lauren is probably getting worried."

Lauren wasn't worried, though. She was happy. She'd obviously found something in Manuel's car that agreed with her mood and taken more than was good for her.

Manuel studied her, rolled back her eyelid and shined a flashlight into her eye, and shook his head. "She needs to eat. Jump in and I'll treat the two of you to breakfast."

He took us to a little place in the Bishop Arts district where they serve one-dollar breakfast burritos and oatmeal with sweet milk and cinnamon. Then he made sure Lauren finished everything he put on her plate.

No wonder Lauren was always on me about eating, I realized. She was on something that would wring her out if she didn't consume calories by the thousand.

"Lauren was a model," Manuel explained. "She got started on amphetamines to help control her weight. People say amphetamines aren't addictive. They're wrong."

I ate a tiny spoonful of oatmeal and nodded. Of all the people I'd met on this case so far, Manuel and Lauren were the ones I liked best. He was a drug dealer and she was an addict. I was afraid that said more about me than I wanted to know.

Lauren ate what Manuel told her, smiled at the other restaurant-goers, and told hysterical stories of her days on the runway circuit and earlier as a teen beauty queen. The closest I'd ever come to being a model was when I'd applied for the "Teen Board" at a local department store. Due to a computer error I was sent an acceptance. When I showed up for the first fashion-show fitting, they'd sent me home with a five-dollar gift certificate.

Manuel made sure Lauren ate, ordering seconds and thirds on the breakfast burritos before he was finally satisfied.

"You should listen to your lawyer," he told me after he came back from paying the bill. "Stay away from this case. Someone has already killed twice. Sean carried and Fred was a gorilla. Do you really think whoever it is would stop just because an eighty pound midget was coming after them?"

I weighed more than eighty pounds and at five feet tall I wasn't a midget, but I understood Manuel's concerns. I'd felt them a couple of hours earlier when I'd been convinced that he was going to kill me.

That didn't mean I could take his advice.

"I'm supposed to let the cops railroad me into prison? I don't want to be involved, but I am. And if I don't find out what really happened, no one else will."

"We've got to go after Clark," Lauren agreed. "I told Kim yesterday that he was the one behind it. He has the military build, too. I knew it wasn't you all along, Manuel. It's Clark. He's the guy Nagle witnessed."

Manuel looked me up and down with a stare that would have intimidated me even if I hadn't already been intimidated. "You're a big one for jumping to conclusions, Kimberly, and Lauren is always happy to push. I hope your next jump doesn't get you killed. Clark Study looks like an idiot. For all I know, he *is* an idiot. But he's ruthless and he's tough. I wouldn't want to take him on myself without a backup and, frankly, I don't know how much help Lauren will be."

"Hey."

"Stay out of trouble. If you need me, pretend you don't remember my phone number, please. I've got work to do and I can't spend my life picking up after the two of you."

He walked out of the restaurant leaving us stranded a couple of miles from my trailer.

"Come on," I told Lauren. "We've got a walk ahead of us."

* * * *

By the time we got home, Lauren had blisters on both feet and was snapping mad.

"We could have taken a taxi," she argued as I opened my trailer door.

"In Dallas? We'd still be waiting. Now do you want to take your shower first, or shall I?"

By the time I'd finished my shower, she was eating again. But she looked up as I stepped into my kitchen area, a towel over my hair.

"We've got to go after the 'C' man." She made a listening gesture toward the walls. "If we can separate him from the 'P' man, we'll have a chance."

It wasn't fair. I felt like something the cat barfed up, and Lauren looked great and had more energy than any three people. Telling myself that it was a drug-induced façade didn't help.

After a couple of blank seconds, I decoded the 'C' man as Clark and the 'P' man as Pete. I wondered how long it would take the police to do the same.

"I have no idea how to separate the two of them. I thought they were Siamese twins."

"It's a witness thing," she explained. "The Feds seem to think that their men can't be corrupted if they have two together. It makes a certain amount of sense, but then they create teams who stay together all the time and get corrupt together. Now they have witnesses who are willing to swear they're not corrupt, even while they're both piling money in the bank."

I wasn't sure that was really the Feds' intent, but I couldn't prove she was wrong. Considering the pay-scales that cops and federal agents lived on, a pay-scale I was familiar with as a postal worker, and the lifestyles of the criminals they were responsible for tracking down and busting, it was no wonder that some of them decided they deserved a little something extra. Or a big something extra, for that matter.

"Let's head out to that Chinese donut place where the boys hang out and maybe we'll think of some way to separate them when we're out there," I suggested.

"I think I could eat a dozen donuts."

Okay. Not only did she have energy, she could eat a million calories a day without losing her figure. The whole thing wasn't fair.

* * * *

It could have been a time warp. Pete and Clark appeared to be wearing the same suits they'd had on when we'd visited them a week earlier. The same Asian waitress was serving up hot donuts right out of the fat, and the two D.E.A. agents perched on exactly the same stools where we'd left them. I wouldn't swear to it, but I thought Pete was telling Clark the same joke he'd been telling him when we'd walked in days before.

The cook pulled a tray of donuts out of the bubbling oil and poured a thick layer of glaze over them. The waitress forked three donuts each in two baskets and pushed these to the two D.E.A. guys without waiting for instructions.

"Well, I guess that's one rumor that was wrong," Pete observed when we approached.

"Huh?" Clark was being the straight-guy. Again.

"Looks like Stefano didn't kill the chicks after all."

"Oh, yeah." He brightened. "Hey, the day is still young."

"Last time we talked, I told you to get your butts out of here and stay out," Pete slid away from the bar and pushed his belly against me. "What's the matter? Did your drug habit erode your memories or something?"

Lauren and I had brainstormed twenty ideas for splitting them up when we'd been driving over. At the time, they'd sounded like good possibilities. Now that the time had come to put them into action, I realized they'd all been wishful fantasies.

"We know that Sean was killed because of his drug dealing," I said. "The two of you know everything going on with the drug scene. Since you haven't let the police in on what you know, we know you're holding out something for your own purposes. So, let's have it. Unless maybe what you're hiding is that you killed Sean yourselves."

"Same old tune," Clark observed. "You'd think they would give it a rest." He punctuated his words by taking a big bite out of one of his steaming donuts.

I grabbed the donut from his hand and tossed it into the trash. "We've got new evidence. Evidence that someone who looks uncomfortably like you, Clark, was seen at the scene of the murder that very night. Evidence that puts you in the frame."

"'That very night,'" Pete echoed. "And then 'in the frame.' I didn't know people still used expressions like that. Wouldn't you admit, though, that the 'very' is redundant."

"What I'd admit is that Clark has a lot of explaining to do," I countered.

Pete started to bluster something, but he must have noticed that Clark wasn't with him on this. Instead, his partner seemed to pale a bit.

"Tell them it's bullshit, Clark. You were with me Friday evening. Until about nine, when you said you wanted to get home early to check out the game."

"How was the game?" I demanded, pushing my luck. "Another big victory for the Rangers, right?"

"I had a stomachache and went to bed early instead," Clark said. "Ended up not watching the game."

"You went to bed alone?" Lauren demanded.

"Of course he went to bed alone," Pete answered for his partner. "Or did you think he had something going on with your husband?"

I tuned out Pete's bluster. Which was what he was doing. He was covering for Clark, trying to distract our attention while his partner pulled himself back together. He was being a good partner. But he was being a terrible law enforcement person.

Clark might not be the brightest bulb on the Christmas tree, but he wouldn't have made it as a field agent if he'd been a pushover. He'd rally soon enough.

I needed to push my advantage while he was still off balance.

"What did you plan to discuss with Sean that evening, Clark? Did you hope to get him to start paying your protection money? Or maybe it was something a bit more personal." I decided to play a hunch based on Pete's denial. "Sean was a good-looking guy, wasn't he, Clark. I always heard he swung both ways."

He'd been starting to get some color back, but it faded when I went on the attack. "It was nothing like that."

With conservatives running the law enforcement agencies, and the memory of J. Edgar Hoover on the upswing, even completely unfounded accusations of unorthodox sexual habits could get an agent in trouble.

"Really? What *was* it like, then, Clark? I want to believe you, but so far you and Pete have told us nothing but lies."

"All right, I'll tell you. I did go over to see Sean Herbert. I thought I'd push him around, just a bit. Pete doesn't like it when I do that so I don't always tell him. I might have bruised Herbert a bit, but I didn't kill him. And I sure didn't kiss him. He was fine when I left him and there's no way you can prove he wasn't."

"Maybe you meant to push him but he accidentally got his throat cut out," I suggested. "I'm prepared to believe it was an accident. Let's just talk about the details."

I was lying, of course. If Clark had killed Sean, he'd done exactly what he'd intended to do. But I read the occasional mystery novel, sometimes watched *NYPD Blue* reruns. The cops always pretend to be sympathetic, to believe they agree with the perp that the victim had it coming. Often, this gets the killer to admit everything.

"Now that is bullshit," Clark said. "When I saw him that night, he was fine.

He was alive when I left him and if he ended up dead, it had nothing to do with me."

I looked at Lauren. If Clark was telling the truth and Sean had been alive when he'd left, that meant only one person could be the killer. That one person was my partner, the woman who had been helping me this whole time.

I'd rather believe Lauren than Clark any day. The only problem was, Lauren had lied to me ever since we'd gotten together. So far, her record was worse than Clark's.

Then I remembered that Nagle had said the military-looking guy had taken something with him. Something like a box of papers.

I turned back to Clark. "So, you pushed him around and then you left. Got it. But what did you take with you when you headed out? And why did he let you?"

"You know, I don't have to answer your questions. Get the Hell out of here and stay out."

"Want some donuts to go?" the waitress asked.

We were in a time warp, but it seemed to me that we were spiraling toward some part of the truth.

If we survived long enough to get there.

* * * *

While Lauren drove back toward my trailer, I got Preston on the phone and told him we had a serious suspect for Sean's murder--Clark Study.

He perked up when I said suspect, but when I shared the evidence, he wasn't impressed. He ended up telling me not to call him again without something concrete.

I hung up the phone with my ear ringing. If I had to hear about how many men in Dallas have military posture again, I thought I'd scream.

Lauren wasn't impressed, either. "Hey, cool. Snow cones. Want one?" She ignored my rejection, pulled into a little standalone shack and brought back two neon-red frozen balls of ice.

After a few bites, the dye from the flavoring turned her mouth red too. She smiled at me and I was reminded of the cheap vampire movies I'd enjoyed when I'd been a kid. The ones where the vampires start out weak and pale but gradually gain strength and a rosy-red color as they suck blood from innocent virgins.

I was no innocent virgin, and Lauren hadn't been sucking my blood--yet, anyway--but that blood-red smile was still a little shiver-inducing.

I took a bite out of the snow cone she'd given me and got a brain-freeze.

"Sean and I used to get snow cones when we were going to get kinky. If you put a bit of the ice in your mouth and then take his--"

"Way too much information," I said. "I don't want to hear about your perversions."

"Sex between consenting adults is hardly a perversion, Kim."

Someone else had said almost those exact words to me. It took me a minute to remember whom and when I did, I could see why I'd suppressed that

101

memory. It had been Fred. He'd explained it to me when I'd told him I would sic the police on him if he didn't stop showing me sick pictures every time I came by to deliver the mail.

My brain gradually got over the frozen shock, but it didn't get over the thought of Fred and his lost blackmail pictures.

Fred kept his computer right behind the counter where he registered his guests. That was a pretty exposed location. If I'd been Fred, I would have worried about one of my victims snatching the computer and ending his blackmail career. No way I would leave the whole enterprise exposed like that. Not without backup.

"What do you say we go home and take a nap," I suggested. "We didn't get much sleep last night." Thanks to Lauren's adventures.

"I'm wide awake."

I could have guessed that from the perky way she was moving. Whatever Manuel had supplied her seemed to give her energy--and require a constant supply of food.

"Yeah? But are you going to be wide awake at two in the morning?"

She grinned at me. "You have a plan, don't you? Are we going to raid Clark's house? Because I know where it is."

"I think it's time to go back to Fred Turley," I explained. "He had to keep backup copies of his blackmail pictures somewhere."

"The cops would have found them."

"According to Preston, they didn't. Also according to Preston, they weren't especially interested in letting the world see all of those pictures. Maybe they didn't look real hard."

"Or maybe they found them and managed to lose them too."

"We'll just have to hope that's not the case."

"Okay. Let's go there now."

"Too many people around."

"Gotcha." She winked at me, slowly, then licked her lips with a bright-red tongue. "Let's you and me go to bed."

After what she'd said about consenting adults, I was pretty sure she was just razzing me.

But only pretty sure.

102

Chapter 12

My alarm went off at one thirty and I struggled into the shower.

I'd slept like the dead, exhausted emotionally as well as physically by the events of the past week.

"Can we eat first?" Lauren answered her question by heading to the kitchen and yanking peanut butter and jelly out of the refrigerator. "I'm starving."

I put on a pair of black jeans, a long-sleeved black t-shirt, and tossed a black bicycle hood to Lauren to cover her blond hair.

Her lip turned up as she examined it. "How come *you* don't have to wear an ugly hat?"

"Because I steer clear of peroxide," I reminded her.

"That wasn't very nice. Oh, I don't have any black jeans with me. But I've got a pair of black yoga pants. Those should work, right?"

Since Lauren was eight inches taller than me and proportionately larger in the hips, I didn't offer her any of my clothes. "That'll be okay. Unless you want to change your mind and stay here."

"No way."

The Rock Cliff No-Tel Motel had been one of the glorious motels of the heyday of American motoring. Its neon signs still promised massage beds, family rates, and fine dining--in a restaurant that had closed before I was born.

Its glory days might have been long-gone, but the motel had survived, after a fashion. Survived until someone drew a knife through Fred Turley's throat.

No one had turned off the neon lighting outside the motel, but the multiple low buildings themselves were dark, the parking lot empty.

We pulled the minivan into one of the little carports that were an affectation of a few motels built during those old times.

It barely fit--cars must have been smaller back in the old days, and I was glad I was as skinny when I squeezed out.

"These little carports are so cute. And lucky. Somebody would have to be looking to see the van in here," Lauren said.

Maybe. But we wouldn't be able to pull a getaway in any kind of hurry.

The motel office's main door had a modern lock. The door was the kind of safety glass that doesn't break easily and sticks together even if you hit it with a hammer--I knew this because it looked like someone had hit it with a hammer.

After a minute of poking at the lock with a couple of bobby pins, I realized we weren't going in that way. If my dreams of burglary weren't going to end abruptly, we needed another plan.

"There's a delivery door in the back," I said. "Let's check it."

The delivery door was sealed with a heavy padlock--again more than my locksmithing skills could handle. Before I could get discouraged, though, Lauren pointed out the way the latch was fastened--screwed into the wall with the screws exposed.

I attacked it with a screwdriver.

Ten minutes later, the back door hung open.

"Cool." Lauren beamed her flashlight around the corroding cardboard boxes that filled the storage room we found inside the door. "This would be a great place to hide blackmail pictures."

It turned out to be a great place to hide ancient Christmas ornaments, old cheesecake calendars, and empty gin bottles. After half an hour of searching, I realized we were going about this wrong.

"The good news is, it doesn't look like the police bothered to search here," I said. "The bad news is, they didn't have to. These cobwebs and this dust are way more than a week old. Fred would have to hide his backup photos pretty often. Which would mean we should be looking somewhere a bit, well, less dusty." I'd been about to say cleaner, but given the subject matter, that didn't make a lot of sense.

"Maybe. But take a look at this." Lauren pulled a pair of oversized feather-fans from one of the boxes. "They must have had strippers here, once. How cool is that?"

They'd still had strippers there as of a week before. Only they weren't stripping, they were moonlighting as hookers.

"Very nice, Lauren. But not what we came for."

"Yeah, okay. But wouldn't it be fun to run a place like this? We could fix it up so it'd be original, turn it into a bed and breakfast. They've still got the old restaurant, so we could upgrade and feed the guests breakfast. It probably has a decent kitchen too."

I didn't like it that so much of our history is being renovated out of existence, but I didn't think Lauren's idea was ever going to happen.

"I don't think they let you do things like that from jail," I reminded her. "Let's talk about future plans once we've figured out who really killed Fred and Sean."

She didn't look happy about it but she nodded. "Right, chief. So what's next?"

What was next was checking out Fred's office.

The cops might not have bothered with the storage room. They'd probably figured out that the cobwebs meant nothing there had anything to do with Fred's murder a lot quicker than I had. But they seemed to have gone through his office pretty completely.

Filing cabinets gaped open, but empty. A loose USB cable and a power strip were all that remained of Fred's computer system, and the last three months' worth of entries had been yanked from the motel sign-in book.

"Hey, maybe they're really trying to track down the murderer rather than just pinning it on us," Lauren said when she pointed out the missing registers.

"Yeah. And maybe the Easter Bunny will drop by and give us chocolate. But I'm not counting on either one."

"You're being negative, Kim."

"Lend me the hammer and I'll show you some positive."

The No-Tel hadn't been renovated in decades. Unfortunately for us, though, it had been built in an era when construction was supposed to last.

It took us an hour to yank the molding off the floor and ceiling, mangle the ceiling tiles that someone had installed to give the place a *modern* 1950s look, and knock all over the floor listening for a hollow spot.

I'd found eight mothballs, a dead mouse, three petrified jellybeans, and twelve cents in change. I pocketed the change. I hadn't seen a Mercury dime or Indian penny for ages. The jellybeans, I hid before Lauren could eat them.

"Hey, here's something interesting." Lauren had started looking in the linings of furniture but she'd given up a long time before and settled down to read something.

"Don't tell me: you discovered the original recipe for Coke?"

"Very funny, Kim. I'm trying to help, you know."

That made me feel like a complete heel. "Okay. So what do you have?"

She looked up from the remains of the registration book. "I just think it's odd that Fred never rents out unit seven. He rents out six and eight, and they're in the same building as seven. You'd think, if the roof leaked, he wouldn't be able to rent out any of them, wouldn't you. Even if it only leaked into one, the mold and smell would make the other ones unbearable. But he hasn't rented seven in a couple of years, at least."

I surveyed the mess I'd made. Without a jack-hammer, I wasn't going to go much deeper--and I was pretty sure Fred wouldn't have hidden his backups that carefully.

An unrented motel unit could have meant anything--that the room was damaged as Lauren had guessed, that Fred just liked to keep a space between guests, that he'd parked a girlfriend there, even that he had it reserved for the next time the President decided to visit. But it was worth checking out.

Unlike the office door, nobody had upgraded the motel room locks since Highway 80 had died. A credit card made the perfect tool for popping open the door. Lauren thought using a credit card for anything other than buying was close to sacrilege, but I didn't think they took plastic in the state pen. Besides, with my loss of income, I wasn't about to start running up the credit again.

* * * *

The room didn't look promising. The dingy mattress with thin blue pinstripes looked like an original from the 1930s. The ceiling had big wet stains and the carpet actually squished under my feet.

"What's that smell?" Lauren demanded.

I sniffed. "You were right about the mildew problem."

Dallas had been hit by something called black mold, which was also called *instant home ripout-and-replace if you have good insurance.* I didn't think Fred had had good insurance. "Try not to breath," I added.

"No kidding." She pointed upward. "I think that's asbestos hanging down from the ceiling."

"I think you're right. Maybe the bed and breakfast idea is a bit impractical after all."

Lauren ignored me and opened the bathroom door.

I expected more gross-out noises. I'd pretty much given up on finding anything and I just wanted to get out before I caught some disease.

"Ohmigod."

"Someone forget to flush the toilet a million years ago?"

"Huh-un. Paydirt."

She came out with a box overflowing with flimsy color printouts of consenting adults and a bunch of zip drives.

"Let's go home and check these out."

Unfortunately, it wasn't that easy. What had been a bathroom had been converted into a storage room with cardboard boxes lining every wall. Even the minivan couldn't carry everything, and I didn't want to spend a couple of hours lugging dirty pictures out to it.

Lauren's box was the only open one, but I insisted on going through each of the other ones.

Either Fred had been subscribing to dirty magazines since he'd been born or he had simply carried on a family tradition. The boxes were stuffed with pictures and magazines that celebrated every combination of the male member with inappropriate objects of desire that I could imagine and plenty that I had never imagined before and never wanted to think about again.

"We've got to go through these," I told her. "Figure out which ones might be evidence."

"*You* can go through them. I've never been interested in doing it with horses."

"He might have hid more pictures or zip drives in the boxes."

I had to promise her I'd take her out to breakfast when we finished before I could get her to agree to get to do anything else.

There had to be fifty boxes.

I flipped through each magazine, holding it upside down and shaking it to see if pictures or computer storage dropped out.

We added three writeable C.D.'s to our collection that way.

We were down to the last three boxes--from the very bottom of the last stack and the hint of dawn was shedding a pink glow through the dusty curtains of room seven. I was about to suggest heading out before anyone spotted us.

"You were right, Kim. We've hit the mother load."

The box was ancient, the cardboard crumbling whenever Lauren touched it, but the read-write DVDs looked pristine and new.

And the thick layer of cash underneath looked beautiful too, even if it wasn't quite as clean and neat as the DVDs.

"Guess we don't have to worry about our retirement," Lauren said as she riffled through a thick stack of hundred dollar bills. "There have to be thousands here. We're rich."

Just for a moment, I let the fantasy ride. Slurping fancy drinks on exotic tropical islands, all the dancing boys I could stand, no more bosses demanding that I accomplish the impossible and then whining when I didn't meet their impossible deadlines. Those were thick stacks of hundreds. We weren't talking about a couple of thousand dollars, we were talking hundreds of thousands of dollars.

I forced myself back to reality. "It isn't like it's our money."

Lauren glared at me. "You want to call the cops, tell them we broke into Fred's apartment and found a bunch of money? First, they'd arrest us for burglary. Second, they'd steal most of it themselves. And third, why *shouldn't* we keep this? It isn't like Fred will be needing it."

"It's evidence, Lauren."

"These are the guys who couldn't even move a computer the three miles from here to downtown without managing to erase the entire hard drive."

"We just can't keep the money. Trust me on this. This is going to clear us, you know. Now come on. It's getting light out. If we wait any longer, we'll get caught."

Finding a bunch of money should have made me happy. I'd known that Fred was a pornoholic, so it had been possible he'd taken the pictures for his personal use rather than for blackmail. The cardboard carton filled with cash and DVDs made it clear that he'd made profitable use of his information. This definitely created a motive for someone to kill him.

But what was I going to do with thousands of dollars in cash? Moving it to my trailer didn't seem smart, especially since the police had already checked through my place once and were likely to want to do so again.

Opening a safety deposit box at a bank would be a red flag for the police to get another search warrant and come looking. I doubted they'd accept my explanation of protecting the evidence.

Lauren's place wouldn't be any better.

"Let's leave the money and take the DVD's," I suggested.

"Are you crazy? I can use this money. What if someone breaks in and steals it?"

"It isn't ours. Sooner or later, it'll have to become evidence in the murders."

"Not if we're the only people who know about it. The cops had plenty of chances to search. Who knows how much money they found and pocketed? What would it hurt for us to make a little profit on this whole deal? Besides, if we take the zip disks and DVDs, we're already stealing."

She had a point, but I wasn't about to go driving around with a zillion dollars in cash. The cops would be sure I had a motive if they found out I'd made a fortune out of Fred's death. Killing for money made a lot more sense than killing because a guy insisted on showing me dirty pictures.

I glanced at my watch. It was already after six. The streets would be filled with people heading to work. The longer we waited, the more certain it was that someone would see us coming out of the deserted motel and wonder what we'd been up to--maybe to the point of calling the cops.

The turn out of the motel is a bit blind and Lauren was pissed because I hadn't let her keep the money. She barely missed sideswiping a sleepy commuter as she pulled out into traffic and headed for food.

* * * *

Lauren drove into downtown Dallas and pulled into a little diner that looked like time had forgotten it. The place was a converted gas station with three tables and a surly cook even Lauren couldn't charm.

Breakfast wasn't friendly. Lauren was mad because I'd made her leave *her* money. I was mad at myself because I should have planned for this and I hadn't. For that matter, we could have found a huge stash of drugs. Fred was a drug dealer, after all, in addition to being a blackmailer. Maybe if we'd checked out some of the other rooms, we would have found more money and more trouble.

My stomach was tied up in knots and I barely managed to choke down a half-slice of toast. Lauren didn't have the same problem. She attacked scrambled eggs, a thick slice of ham, hash brown potatoes, and some of the thickest biscuits I'd ever seen.

I almost missed her dropping a couple of small white tablets at the same time.

"Sooner or later, those drugs are going to get you in trouble."

She just looked at me. "Yeah? Like you're such a good example. *You* don't use drugs and they're sending you up for murder."

I'd overstepped the bounds of friendship and was turning into a mom. I needed to back off.

"Finish up and let's go back to my place. I want to look at these disks."

"I'm hungry."

I'm pretty sure she deliberately slowed down then, making sure she chewed each bite before swallowing and calling for a refill on her coffee.

She made me pay the bill, but since the diner's prices were stuck in the dark ages along with the décor, I got out for under five bucks. Pretty good.

When we got back to my place, we started going through the pictures. It was amazing what a lifetime obsession with photography and naked people could do. Amazing and humbling. Unlike most of the models in the magazines Fred had insisted on showing me, most of Dallas's step-out-for-sex crowd was overweight, aging, and unattractive.

We weren't worried about the police bugs as long as we didn't say anything.

The CDs and zip drives were bad enough. They contained thousands of pictures--all of them involving some combination of multiple people doing something. In addition to old-fashioned woman-on-man, there was man-on-man, woman-on-woman, threesomes, moresomes, and some particularly gross ones that could have featured in one of Fred's magazines, if only they'd hired more attractive models to play the roles.

My computer has a *Thumbnail* option that let us look at dozens of pictures at a time, fortunately. Still, even in tiny thumbnails, I recognized some of those people, had delivered mail for them. I didn't want to know that Eileen Smith was having an affair with her next-door neighbor while she was supposed to be at the Mary Kay convention. For sure, learning that one of Dallas's ex-mayors had a thing for overweight balding males was way too much information.

Unfortunately, the still shots weren't the worst of it. Fred must have recently upgraded his cameras because the DVDs were filled with videos.

Modern DVD burning software lets you create directories, label the movies so a viewer can quickly flip to an interesting scene. Fred hadn't bothered. Lauren and I had to sit through hours of watching couples do it in fast-forward.

"Shit. Stop. There's Sean. That son of a bitch."

I'd been fast-forwarding and had almost skipped past the brief scene. Now, though, I back-peddled and put the computer on normal speed.

I recognized Sean's voice instantly although I hadn't recognized his backside which was the part facing the camera.

Lauren had spent more time than me looking at his butt, which was how she'd recognized it even at maximum wiggle speed.

A few frames later, we got a good body-view of the dark-haired woman he was doing.

I couldn't make out her face at first, but she had a great figure and incredible flexibility. Still, I couldn't understand why Sean wanted to step out when he already had a wife as attractive as Lauren.

"He was always trying to get me to do that." Lauren jerked a shoulder in the direction of the video image of the woman. Her wrists and ankles were both handcuffed to the corners of the headboard leaving her wide open and fully exposed.

"Maybe you should have gone along."

"Oh, sure. Blame me for this, Kim. Oh, shit."

The brunette's face came into view.

"You know who she is?"

"Hell yes. That slimy dog always did have a thing for my sister. A couple of times he suggested doing a three-way with her. I mean, maybe I could do a threesome if I really liked the woman. I'd do it with you, Kim. But with my sister? Gag me."

"I'm sorry you had to see this, Lauren." If I ignored her comment about doing a three-way, maybe it would go away.

"Me too. That dirty bastard."

I pushed the fast forward button again. I wanted to get past Sean and to other people. But I had a horrible suspicion I had already seen too much.

Lauren had never fully explained what she'd been doing in her husband's house the night he was killed. Clark's story was that Sean had been alive when he'd left. Lauren's was that he'd been dead when she got there. Rev. Nagle's was that there hadn't been anyone in the house between them.

Clark could have been lying. I didn't think Nagle was, although it was remotely possible that someone had sneaked in under his radar scope. But

Lauren had the biggest motive and she'd lied just about every chance she had.

She'd acted surprised by Sean's betrayal with her sister, but she would have to do that, wouldn't she? She'd consistently gone on about how he was still her husband and she still loved him. If she loved him so much, why had she moved out in the first place?

Up until now, I'd convinced myself that Lauren couldn't be the killer because I knew the murders were connected and she had no motive to kill Fred.

But a video like this would have given Fred ideas--ideas like blackmailing Lauren. He'd know that she'd become suspect number one if he released that video to the cops, and that she'd pay plenty to have him keep his mouth shut. From what I knew of Fred, getting too greedy was likely to be a problem for him. The blackmail video gave Lauren the best of all possible reasons to kill Fred--staying away from Texas's notorious death row.

Nothing I had *proved* that Lauren had done it. But the story hung together too well.

When the cops found out Lauren had been in Sean's house that night, had a motive to kill him, and had a motive to kill Fred, they'd be all over her and I'd be off the hook. Especially when they heard Clark's testimony that he'd been there only a little while before Lauren had arrived and that Sean had still been alive when he left.

All I needed to do was betray a woman who'd become my friend. My troubles would be over, I'd get my job back at the post office, and maybe the union could get me paid for the time I'd been on involuntary unpaid leave.

I'd solved the mystery. I should feel great.

Instead, I felt like someone had taken a knife, stuck it inside my stomach, and rotated.

I looked at Lauren and tried to read her.

"What?"

"Nothing." I casually reached for my phone.

"But--" Lauren's eyes widened and slapped the phone from my hand. "You think I did it, don't you? That I killed Sean because he was porking my sister?"

Chapter 13

My hand stung where Lauren had connected with it when she'd knocked my phone away. Obviously I wasn't a good enough poker-face to fake my new number one suspect out.

I thought again about Preston's advice--his warning that the killer just might want to seem helpful and get involved in the case. At the time, I'd thought of Buddy and Larry because I hadn't even met Lauren back then. And I still wasn't sure that they hadn't seemed to be a bit too interested.

But a couple of visits from my co-workers hardly compared with the way Lauren had literally moved in with me. Who knew I'd be so desperate for a friend? How pathetic was that?

Considering the way Lauren was glaring at me, I didn't think anything I said could convince her to back off but it was either that or become victim number three in her murder spree.

"If we can find some pictures of Clark or Pete in Fred's collection, I think we'd really be onto something," I said. "Those two would murder to avoid getting blackmailed faster than they'd spit."

"Huh-un. You can't just ignore the elephant in the room, Kim. You've decided I'm the killer and don't try to deny it."

"But--"

"Don't you think we need to talk about this?"

Letting a crazed killer know the evidence I had against her didn't seem like the smartest plan. On the other hand, refusing to talk to her about it wasn't going to work either.

"Don't worry about me," I temporized. "I'm your friend and I believe in you. I'm just thinking about what the cops are going to suspect once they find out what we've learned. The video of your husband and your sister bonking like monkeys gives you a motive to kill him. And since Fred is a blackmailer, the cops will instantly realize, uh, I mean falsely believe, that he was blackmailing you and you killed him to keep him quiet."

"That's ridiculous." Lauren's eyes glistened just a little. If I hadn't already known what an actor she could be, my heart would have gone out to her. Hell, my heart did go out to her. She might be a ruthless killer, but she had stuck with me when everyone else I knew had moved away from me like I was a plague bearer.

"Of course it's ridiculous. But they're going to believe it. And when they find out you were lying about your alibi, they'll be even more certain you were involved. That's why we've got to be even more active on the case, find the real killer before it's too late." Too late for me was what I really meant. Lauren could pick me up and snap me like a rotten twig.

She picked up the phone receiver, unplugged it from the phone base, and tossed it across the room. "The only way they'd ever find out would be if you told them."

It hadn't taken her long to get to the crux of my problem. I'd gone from her ally to her biggest threat. Considering what had happened to the last person who'd been a danger to her, that wasn't a good place to be.

"That just isn't true, Lauren. Sooner or later, some genius in the D.P.D. is going to realize that Nagle's description doesn't match up with me. They always suspect the spouse, especially when there is evidence of some friction in the marriage, so they'll look into your alibi. I won't have to tell them anything. I mean, why would I want to? It isn't as if I owe them anything."

She wheeled on her heel, stepped into my kitchen and returned with an ice cream drumstick.

If my brain had been working, I would have used the moment her back was turned to get up and run for it. By the time I thought of it, though, the opportunity had passed.

Lauren sat down behind me and licked a nut off the top of the drumstick.

For the first time since we'd been together, she didn't offer to share. I had to hope that meant she was grouchy, not that she didn't want to waste food on someone she was planning to kill.

I eyed a path from my computer desk to the trailer door trying to calculate how I could get past her. Once I got to an open area, I thought I could outrun Lauren. In the enclosed space of the trailer, her longer reach gave her the advantage.

"If I were to die or turn up missing, the police would be over you like butter on bread," I said. "They know we've been spending time together. Having your husband die is an unfortunate event. Having him die and then having the woman all the cops think is your lesbian girlfriend show up murdered would be too big a coincidence."

She glared at me, then sank her teeth into the chocolate coating on the outside of the drumstick.

My teeth clenched in sympathetic brainfreeze, but she didn't seem to mind. Maybe she wasn't just a killer. Maybe she was a pure psycho.

"There's no way you wouldn't get caught, Lauren."

She took another bite, then moved closer.

"You know what?"

I didn't think I wanted to know. "What?"

"You're assuming that I'd stay around waiting for the cops to come and pick me up. With a couple hundred thousand in cash, I could simply vanish, create a new identity in another city. As long as you don't have to get a job, nobody looks too closely at your identification."

I'd forgotten about Fred's money--money that Lauren had desperately wanted to take.

She was right. So what if the Dallas cops thought Lauren Herbert had killed her husband, Fred, and me if she'd fled the scene? None of us would be considered any great loss to the community. It wasn't like the FBI would put her on the ten most wanted list or she'd make *America's Most Wanted*. Within a few months, Lauren would be forgotten and be able to integrate into whatever community she chose.

I wondered if she had picked up anything besides the drumstick when she'd walked into the kitchen. Like a knife.

I grabbed my stapler as the closest substitute for a weapon and gave Lauren a smile that probably looked about as convincing as it felt. "If you're going to run anyway, you don't need to kill me. You can just walk out of here, Lauren. I'll tell the cops what I know, but what do I know about where you're planning on going underground?"

She considered and I inhaled, sort of gasped really. I hadn't been breathing in a while.

"No, I don't think that's going to work."

I stopped breathing again.

"How about getting one of those drumsticks for me, then?"

Lauren looked at me, then glanced toward the refrigerator.

I figured getting her to look the other way was about as much of a break as I was going to get and took off toward the door.

In two steps, I was past her. My trailer wasn't that big so I was almost at the door already.

I reached for the knob and something hard hit my leg.

I fought for my balance but it wasn't happening. I smacked my head against the door and collapsed to the floor.

"Sorry, Kim," Lauren grabbed me by the armpits and hauled me back to my couch. "Is your head all right?"

Like that mattered. Okay, I was dead but at least my head didn't hurt too badly? Give me a break.

In the movies, this is where the heroine suddenly remembers that she has a black belt in some top-secret martial art, keeps a gun hidden in her couch, or converts a lipstick into a secret weapon. All I remembered was that my underwear and bra didn't match and my mother was going to be embarrassed when she came to identify me at the morgue.

I tried to make my mouth work, remind Lauren that we were buddies and that she didn't need to kill me, didn't want to kill me. All that came out was a little whimper.

"Kim, you've got to cut this out."

That was what I needed. I got mad. "Whatever you say, Lauren. Tell me what you want me to do."

Although if she expected me to make things easy for her, she had another think coming. I'd bleed all over her if that was all I could manage.

"I want you to start using your brain again. You're the smart one, remember, the one who was going to keep us out of jail."

"Right." I'd played along with Clark, pretending sympathy for him when I'd thought he might be the killer. I could hardly do less for Lauren. After all, her husband had been boffing her sister. If ever a case for justifiable homicide could be made, this would be it. If she could just get a jury of twelve women, each of whom had younger sisters, Lauren would be acquitted so fast the Judge wouldn't have a chance to settle his judicial butt into his chair.

"How about this?" I suggested. "When you found out about Sean and your sister, you were angry and you confronted him. But he became violent. He'd just had a tough run-in with Clark and decided to take it out on you. You struck back in desperation. It was purely self-defense."

Yeah, right. And then she'd had to defend herself against Fred as well. If that was the best my so-called brain could come up with, Lauren might as well kill me. I wasn't going to be much use for anyone.

Her eyes narrowed perilously. "You're not helping. I've already told you I didn't kill Sean. For sure, I didn't kill the fat-boy. Remember, even when the evidence against you seemed strong, I believed in you. I never doubted your innocence. And the first time things look bad for me, you're ready to throw me to the wolves."

It wasn't quite the same. The cops didn't have beans for evidence against me, which is why I'd been able to make bail. Dallas isn't big on letting murder suspects walk the streets--not, at least, unless they have more money than Big Bob would lend me. Against Lauren, the evidence seemed inarguable.

But I *wanted* to believe her. Wanted to believe that the woman who'd become my friend had picked me because she liked me, not because she intended to use me to cloud the evidence and maybe with the idea of finding Fred's blackmail money.

"You swear you had nothing to do with Sean's death? Absolutely nothing?"

"The first I knew about Sean and my sister was when I saw them in that video."

"Which doesn't answer my question."

She smashed the remains of the drumstick into my waste paper basket. "Of course I swear it. I didn't kill him."

"And you didn't kill Fred, either?"

She shook her head. "No way."

I had no reason to believe her and she had no reason to tell the truth. I knew she was a liar and an actress. And if she was the killer, I'd be in more danger if we left my trailer than if we stayed. But a part of me wanted to believe her so badly that I just went along with it. I didn't have very many friends. I decided I'd be loyal to this friend if it killed me. Which seemed quite likely.

"In that case, I think we'd better get out of here. Since we know the cops are bugging us, they now know everything about Sean and your sister. They're probably on their way."

"Oh, shit. I completely forgot about that."

I gathered up a couple of changes of clothing and led Lauren out to our rental van. There wasn't a row of cops outside. That probably meant they didn't have a team of people listening in real-time. It would be more efficient to use voice-activated recorders that would automatically eliminate the dead-time and then just listen to the tapes. If that thrifty behavior meant me getting killed and them finding out about it too late to help, I suspected no one in police headquarters would lose much sleep about it.

I loaded my bike in the back of the van, carried out the computer and the box of pictures and disks we'd taken from Fred's motel, then dumped in a pillowcase I'd filled with clothes. That was all. I was ready.

Lauren stood there, hands on hips, not getting into the van.

"Come on, we've got to go."

"You do believe me, don't you?"

Instead of answering, unlocked the passenger door for her, walked around and got into the driver's seat.

She waited for a moment, then scurried to catch up. I was getting out of there. If she wanted to play silly games, she could explain it to the cop.

She fastened her seatbelt and I headed us toward my bank, where I used my ATM card to withdraw the maximum. After that I turned in the opposite direction--toward Arlington.

Two minutes after we got on the freeway, Lauren's phone rang.

"You'd better dump that," I said.

"Hey, it's your landlady, Tina... what's up Tina."

A pause.

"Really? That many?"

I grabbed the phone from her and heaved it into the center median. "The police can track that."

"Tina says there were fifty cop cars. They're going trailer to trailer looking for us. Guess we got out just in time."

"I guess we did."

* * * *

Dallas is a strange city. Its mentality is south to north. Even with the economic downturn, upscale suburbs and high-tech campuses are built ever-further north, along the U.S. 75 freeway and sprawling along the George Bush. But there's an entire separate universe just to the west of Dallas. Arlington and Fort Worth are closer to downtown Dallas than Allen or McKinney, but they're not really part of the Dallas urban system or mindset.

I hoped that the cops would share my north-south mentality and wouldn't think to look to the west.

"I love that water park." Lauren gestured out the window to where long lines of high-school age bikini-girls showed off for admiring boys. "Maybe when this is over, the two of us can go there and hang out."

I resisted the urge to growl at her. I'd weighed two hundred and fifty pounds when I'd been sixteen. Men would have paid me to cover up rather than look at me and any time I took a step toward a pool I'd inevitably hear supposedly amusing calls of *thar' she blows*.

"Nobody has seen me in a bathing suit since I was ten," I said. "And that's not going to change, either. Even if we do find the real killer."

"Well, excuse me. And there's nothing wrong with your body that a few meals wouldn't fix."

There is a complex of motels around the multiple amusement parks, roadside attractions, and the Ballpark. None looked to be as colorful or historic as Fred's Rock Cliff No-Tell Motel, but nondescript suited my purposes perfectly.

I pulled into a two-story green monstrosity that advertised free HBO and free breakfast buffets.

I paid cash, got a weekly rate, and nobody asked for any ID when I signed the register with a fake name.

I hadn't answered Lauren's question about whether I still thought she was guilty because I didn't know the answer. I was going to act as if she was innocent, treat her as if she was innocent, while the thinking part of me continued to scream in terror.

In a way, I was surprised that I was still alive. But the longer she went along with me, the more I started questioning myself. Would she be going along with me if she was the killer? Or was she simply taking advantage of me, letting me get money, setting up a hideout, figuring out a way to ditch the car--after which she might go ahead and finish me off? For all I knew, I was just digging my hole deeper, making things rougher for the cops when Lauren got bored of her cat-and-mouse game and decided to end it.

Then again, if she really wanted to kill me, how would waiting help? The longer she waited, the more likely it was that the cops would find her, and get Fred's money before she did. If she was guilty, why was I alive?

"You want to dump our rental?" she asked. "Go deep underground."

I nodded. "I've got an idea for that."

"Cool."

My only slightly brilliant idea was to return the van at Love Field rather than the hotel lot where we'd originally rented it. If the cops came across it at Love, they'd assume that we'd flown away, running from the law. I didn't want to leave it at DFW because Dallas-Fort Worth is closer to Arlington.

First, though, I stopped at a Salvation Army Thrift Store and bought a cheap bike for Lauren. I wasn't going to let the cops trace me by talking to one of the SuperShuttle drivers. It was time for Lauren to join the ranks of those who got around by human-powered transportation.

* * * *

It took a couple of hours, a lot of complaining from Lauren, and one quick tire repair job before we made it back to our motel.

Lauren stomped across the street to a convenience store for food while I flipped on the T.V.

The local news anchors were going on about new developments in the Sean Herbert case. Lauren was now listed as suspect number one, with me as a lesbian sidekick. The police spokesman indicated that their meticulous research had raised doubts about Lauren's alibi.

From somewhere, they'd located a telecom-vintage photo of me and splashed my three hundred pound blob look across the tube. In contrast, Lauren looked glamorous even when they showed her mug shots.

What the reporters didn't mention was anything about finding a big stash of money in Fred's motel. I didn't think that meant much. Piles of cash seemed something the police would want to keep quiet. Especially if they weren't certain whether we'd counted it.

One enterprising reporter had gotten a quick interview with Vito Lindner, labeled as my boss although he was multiple levels above that. Lindner claimed that I'd already been in trouble at the post office, that a few postal workers were holdovers from a previous administration, protected by overzealous union rules, and that I brought shame to the organization through my bad attitude and drug-using habit.

Preston might still be hoping I'd be able to clear my name, but Lindner had obviously washed his hands of me.

Lauren returned with a huge bag of tortilla chips, dip, Cokes, and a couple of soggy-looking tuna sandwiches.

Also some hair die and self-tanning product.

"Time for us to change our appearances," she said. "Did you know we're on television?"

"You bought hair dye from somebody who was watching pictures of us on the tube?"

"I kept him distracted."

She considered her loot. "I'll go the Goth look. You can be a redhead. Because you're tiny, the red hair thing will look cute on you."

I don't know about cute, but by the time Lauren had finished with me, my mid-back-length brown hair had been converted into a sort of Cockatiel do, with short, bright red spikes sticking up and a bit of a crest sticking up even higher straight over my head.

She smeared the self-tanning product over skin I had religiously protected with sunblock since I'd left the dim corridors of telecom, turning my skin a shade of orange that might, possibly, look natural to someone with a severe case of color-blindness.

"You look really good, Kim," she assured me for the tenth time as I studied myself in the mirror and tried not to cry. "Completely hot."

She didn't cut her own hair, of course. No way was she going to let me anywhere near a two hundred dollar cut with a pair of scissors. But jet-black dye gave her a completely different look than her usual blonde. She looked exotic, like a gypsy, maybe.

"We'll have to get new clothes to match the new looks," she announced happily.

"No credit cards," I reminded her.

She pouted a bit, but she knew I was right. "Maybe we should stop by the No-Tel Motel and pick up a handful or two of cash," she suggested. "That would keep us going."

"We'd just walk into a police trap."

"Yeah." She sighed. "I guess we missed our chance. I can't believe I talked about finding the cash when we knew we were being bugged."

"Well, you did."

"Because you accused me of being a killer. That was crazy."

"Sorry." I didn't really mean my apology, but if we were going to stick together, I had to make an effort to put my suspicions behind me.

She snagged the remote and started flipping through channels, finally ending up on a home decorating show that showed a group of *friends* completely destroying a couple's nice suburban home.

I'd been so intent on getting away from the cops, finding a place to hide, that I hadn't really thought through the logistics. My money wouldn't last long and we couldn't accomplish anything sitting in a cheap motel with no phones, no Internet, and no connection to the outside world.

I took a bite from the sandwich Lauren had brought me and shoved the rest of it over to her. "We'll figure something out."

"Or are you just waiting for a chance to turn me in? You still think I did it, don't you."

"No, Lauren. I believe you. If you were a killer, I think you would have killed me when I made you ride your bike across town."

"Damned right. Whoever invented bicycles had it in for women."

We both laughed, but our situation was anything but funny. We we'd gotten out of my trailer just ahead of a huge police raid, but we were in no position to do anything. And all we'd managed to do with all of our investigations to date was make the police even more convinced they had the right suspects.

Chapter 14

"We've got to get other people involved in the investigation," I decided.

We'd spent twenty-four hours in the motel, watching pictures of us on the TV and listening to cops and local news anchors pontificating on what the world was coming to when women, rather than men, became serial killers. I was bored, but I had the beginnings of a plan.

Lauren looked up from her third bagel. "Brilliant. So, how are you going to persuade anyone to work for us?"

The motel's free breakfast buffet was worth about what we'd paid for it. It consisted of some sad-looking bagels, cream cheese that squirted from little packets, corn flakes that were soggy even before I added milk, and cheese Danish that came individually wrapped in plastic and preservatives. But at least we were the only people eating it. We could talk.

Lauren gave me a rundown on the negative health consequences of each part of the meal, but she also managed to ingest a thousand calories or so, anyway.

I ate a spoonful of corn flakes and two bites of bagel. Neither created any bliss.

Lauren palmed one of her little white pills, swallowing it with coffee when she thought I wasn't watching. "They'd have to be an idiot to help us. Everyone already thinks we did it. Even you thought we'd done it this time yesterday."

Lauren raised a good point. I just hoped we could be persuasive.

"Preston Rolin has been willing to give us some info. At least we could get him to give us an update."

She shook her head. "Maybe Rolin *was* helpful, but his boss has sold you down the river. Lindner is in this so deep, he'll be embarrassed if you turn up innocent--maybe you can even sue him. No way will he let Rolin help. Besides, Rolin will turn us over to the cops if we try to contact him. For one thing, he'll have to. For another, being the guy who captured us would make him a hero. He seems to me like a guy who wants to be a hero."

That was my impression as well. Given the choice between having to work real hard and maybe doing something useful by finding the real killer, or not having to work at all and becoming a hero by handing over the two women, Preston would take the easy road.

"I'm pretty sure we burned our bridges with the D.E.A. guys," Lauren added. "You as good as accused Clark of killing Sean. No favors from that direction."

"If *you* didn't kill him, Clark is our only suspect," I reminded her. "He admitted to being there. He admitted that Sean was alive when he got there. He admitted roughing him up. We know he was there only an hour or so before you found Sean dead. Of course I accused him. What was I supposed to do?"

It wasn't as if Lauren hadn't done the same thing the first time we'd met with them, with a lot less evidence.

"I don't know what you were supposed to do, but I do know we're going to have a hard time getting Pete and Clark to cooperate from now on."

"We've got to finish with Fred's blackmail stuff." If we didn't find anything we could use, like Pete or Clark or some cop coming in and threatening Fred, I'd have to make another plan.

We still had about a million hours of Fred's videos to go through and didn't need any external help for that. I set up my computer and started plugging through the CD-ROMs and DVDs.

Fred had his disks labeled, of course--he'd been every bit the practical blackmailer. Unfortunately, his organization system seemed based on the value of the blackmail opportunity rather than the time and date of the event. Since his sense of importance didn't match mine, I had to watch all the recordings.

Lauren looked over my shoulder occasionally, but when she saw it was mostly compressed images of Fred in his office signing in one disreputable couple after another or looking at dirty magazines, she managed to find a book to read.

It was deadly boring. Watching the progression in Fred's photography skills added the only hint of interest. He added wipes, experimented with camera angles, and occasionally introduced sound to the video. Nothing helped, though. The amusement of watching people come in, sign in, head to their rooms, and finally get it on, all in fast motion, wore off quickly.

Something was nagging me about the videos though and I had the sense that I was close to a discovery.

After all, there was nothing wrong with signing into a motel. For the most part, the hookers waited out in the cars or taxis while the men came in and got the room. So, why did Fred take those pictures? He might be vain, but I couldn't believe he simply wanted hours of footage of the back of his bald head.

When I finally got it, I felt like smacking myself in my nearly-bald and bright-red head. It was too obvious.

"He videoed the sign-in so he can get full facial shots of the blackmail victims," I finally deduced.

"So?" Lauren was now painting her nails a pale shade of lavender.

"So he was killed in his office."

She inspected a nail, touched up the polish, and then blew on it gently. "Remind me why I should care."

"You should care because it means he videoed his own murder."

That got through to her too. "And the idiot police managed to screw up his computer. All of this could have been avoided if they'd just been a bit more careful."

"I thinking it was no coincidence the key piece of evidence got trashed. Considering they didn't look too hard for the blackmail backup, I don't think it was to protect any police captains or patrolmen. The only files that were lost were the ones Fred hadn't had the chance to put to backup."

"You think the killer was a cop?"

"Either a cop, someone who could get a cop to do something for him, or maybe someone who already knew Fred was taping and sabotaged the hard drive before the police got there."

"Except we know the cops checked out some of the video when they got there. The sabotage took place after the cops grabbed the computer. Who could make policemen destroy evidence?"

Lauren squeezed my arm so hard I almost cried. "The D.E.A."

She was right. With their boatfuls of federal money, Pete and Clark would have a web of informants and gofers within the D.P.D. They could have easily asked one of their snitches to run a magnet over Fred's hard drive.

"We can already place Clark at Sean's place near the time of death. If we can place either him or Pete at Fred's, we'd know for sure."

"How are we going to do that? If we had the tapes, we could prove they were there. But if we had the tapes, we'd already know who killed Fred." Trust Lauren to point out the problems with my idea.

"I'm working on that."

* * * *

I was still working on that the next day--without making any progress. It was so bad, Lauren managed to persuade me to get out of our room and go shopping.

She was still on a kick about heading for the water park so I was keeping her company while she tried on swimsuits at *Just Add Water*, a bathing suit store, when the mail arrived.

I didn't recognize the delivery person--Arlington has their own main post office and their own routes, although Dallas does a lot of the bulk processing for them. Still, I hunkered down in the bikinis. Postal carriers notice things.

The carrier chatted briefly with the store clerk, dropped off a couple of packages and a stack of invoices, and left.

I watched her go.

"Hey, girlfriend. I'm going to get jealous if you don't look at me more than you're looking at her."

If I'd been a guy, I wouldn't have thought about looking away from Lauren. She'd just come out of the changing booth wearing a thong so tiny it almost disappeared.

But I wasn't a guy so I looked away quickly and watched the carrier chat up the clerk in the next store down the mall.

"I think I have our answer. And I've got a plan."

* * * *

Buddy wanted nothing to do with my plan.

"If you're innocent," he said, "you need to be helping the cops, not getting in their way."

"I'm not getting in their way, Buddy, I'm trying to keep out of jail."

I was using voice over IP through my computer and the free Wi-Fi service at an Arlington coffee bar. When I'd been in telecom, it had been almost impossible to track Internet calls, once they'd been routed through the thousands of anonymizers available, but I didn't know how technology had changed and I didn't want to stay on the phone long.

Buddy sighed. "They think you're guilty because you ran. What were they supposed to think?"

They were supposed to think I was innocent until proven guilty. "If we find evidence that points at me, you can turn that over to the cops as well."

"The police will already have canvassed the neighborhood. What makes you think postal carriers can do anything more?"

"Get real, Buddy. Cops?"

He thought about that. "Yeah, maybe you have a point."

I *knew* I had a point. Nobody wants to talk to the cops because you're never sure whether they're trying to trick you. Texas's prisons are full of people who talked to the cops--some guilty, others innocent. Every one of them is written up as a solved crime--good statistics for the cops, bad luck for the people tricked into playing along.

But nobody is afraid of the local postal carrier. The worst thing they do is bring bills.

"Lindner will never approve." Buddy was definitely weakening.

I faked a noisy yawn. "Lindner sits in his office and diddles with his spreadsheets. If it doesn't make the five o'clock news, Lindner won't ever see it."

"You're asking a lot of people to give up their free time just on a long shot."

"I know, Buddy. And I'd feel guilty if the prospect of a lethal injection hadn't reset my priorities."

He paused for long enough that I wondered if he was working with the police, helping them trace my call. "Finally, though, he spoke. If you're guilty and this is just some sort of makework, you won't live long enough for a lethal injection. I'll kill you myself."

"That's fair."

Another pause. "All right, Kimberly. I'll talk to some of the guys and see if they're willing to help."

"Great. I'll get with Larry and see if I can get union support."

"Larry might think he's the union, but the union doesn't think that."

"He's the best I can do."

Larry wasn't happy to hear from me. He hadn't figured out about his missing shirt, though.

After I'd apologized about twenty times for hinting that he might possibly have something to do with the murder, Larry finally loosened up, told me to forget about it, and agreed to listen to my plan.

Going Postal

My plan was to have post office carriers chat with everyone in Fred's neighborhood and see if we could put Pete or Clark in the picture.

According to what the police had released to the papers, Fred had been killed around seven in the morning. Lauren and I had pulled out of his motel a bit after dawn when we'd burglarized it, and there had been plenty of traffic already. And with the blind turn, we'd nearly sideswiped three cars. Seven would be practically rush hour as Oak Cliff residents poured north, into downtown Dallas. I just had to hope that Clark, or whomever was driving after killing Fred, had been as conspicuous as Lauren and I had.

Surely someone had seen something. I was betting that an army of postal carriers could find out what no number of cops could.

"Strictly speaking, this isn't a union function," Larry reminded me. "If the Postal Service asked us to do this, we'd be within our rights to turn them down, or to demand overtime payments."

"But the Service isn't asking for anything. It's me, Kimberly. You know, the woman who's going to vote for you in the next election."

"Yeah, but--"

I wasn't past groveling. "You told me that the union wanted to protect me, Larry. You know the bosses want to put the screws to the working stiff. If they do this to me, do you really think they'll stop there."

Playing to his romantic notions of union solidarity was dirty pool, and I felt a little guilty for doing it. Not guilty enough to stop, though.

It turned out, I'd played the right chord.

"Damn. I'll do it. I'll talk to union management and make this my priority. We won't let them railroad you, Kimberly. We'll stand shoulder to shoulder. We shall not be moved."

It was good stuff and I let him know how much I appreciated it before hanging up.

"So now we wait for those other guys to do something?" Lauren had been pushing her head against mine so she could hear what Buddy and Larry and been saying.

I just laughed at her. "No way. Ten zillion postal carriers hanging around Davis are going to make a great cover. We're going to blend in--fish swimming in the sea."

"Huh?"

"Sorry. Larry has me deep in liberation-thought."

"Huh?" she repeated.

She still didn't understand, but I didn't feel up to explaining Chairman Mao's analogy. My parents had been radicals way back in the 70s and I'd been brought up with that kind of stuff.

"Okay, here's the plan. We're going to put on postal carrier uniforms and go asking questions ourselves."

She wrinkled her nose. "I saw a Cheers episode about that. You can get in trouble for impersonating a postal employee."

"You can get in bigger trouble if you're convicted of multiple murders." I met her stubborn stare and had a brainflash. "Besides, we'll get to go shopping again."

It took a couple of hours but between a costume store, a uniform store, and a well-equipped Good Will store, we gathered together leather pouches, shorts, uniform blouses, and all of the patches and paraphernalia of a modern postal carrier.

If I'd thought ahead, I would have brought a couple of uniforms with me and saved a lot of time and money. But then again, if I'd thought ahead, I would have extended my vacation in Acapulco and missed this entire disaster.

* * * *

We waited until the carriers had been working for two days without finding anything before heading back to the No-Tel area ourselves--time enough for the cops to get used to the idea of a small horde of postal employees wandering around asking questions but not quite enough time for the enthusiasm to wear off and my postal brothers and sisters to vanish back into their real lives. Not that I didn't think they could do the job, just that I was a lot more motivated than they were. Besides, I was going absolutely nuts with Lauren force-feeding me all the time.

On the third day, I woke Lauren up early, slathered sunblock over my fading orange skin, and put on my uniform.

"Would you do me?" She held out a big blob of sunscreen, looking pathetic in her jog bra and panties. Poor baby. Being gorgeous, she'd probably always had a long line of studly males lining up to smear lotion over her body. That wasn't a problem I'd ever had and so I'd become self-sufficient. That and back when I'd been a three hundred pounds, I'd had plenty of acreage to practice slathering on.

Remembering didn't make me more cheerful.

"Here." I swiped some of the sunscreen out of her hand and rubbed it on the back of her neck and upper back where the helmet we carriers wear provides too little protection. "You can do your own legs. That's a little personal for me."

"I appreciate it, Kim."

"Yeah. Well, do me a favor and don't mention it to anyone. They'll just be more convinced I'm your boyfriend."

We skipped the free breakfast, not wanting to ride with lead bullets in our guts, and rode our bikes back toward Dallas.

An hour later, Lauren was groaning about her legs and crotch, but we were back in home territory.

"Let's lock up our bikes at the Food Mini-Mart," I suggested. "We'll blend in with the other postal workers along the street. I'll take the northbound side and you can take southbound."

Normally I would have let her have the heavy traffic side because drivers were more likely to stop for her than for me. Today, though, Lauren looked grumpy. Commuters might stop, but I doubted she'd get any answers if she bit their heads off. The whole purpose of the postal carrier dodge was to be nonthreatening.

"We need to eat first," she insisted. "Now."

The Food Mini-Mart isn't anyone's idea of gourmet cuisine. But they did have some tired-looking biscuits stuffed with semi-melted American cheese and mysterious-looking sausage.

Lauren bought three and told me she wasn't going anywhere until I'd eaten at least one.

Their coffee was pretty good and I managed to wash down half the biscuit, then I distracted Lauren by pointing out some of the really tacky rear-view-mirror ornaments the Mart sold. While she wasn't looking at me, I trashed the second half of the biscuit.

I'd eaten at the Mart before, but I'd never seen anything approaching personal service. With Lauren there, all glowing with sweat, her slightly-too-small uniform blouse sticking to her curvy breasts, we got all sorts of attention including hand-poured coffee refills and a couple of bonus donuts in case our stomachs could make room for anything else.

"Talk to them, Lauren," I urged.

"I'm not sure they speak English."

"Don't be an idiot. They're from India. Of course they speak English. They just have an accent."

It turned out they were from Iran, not India at all. But they spoke English with no problem. As long as I didn't block their view of Lauren, they seemed willing to talk all day.

"You guys work here every morning?"

After a brief discussion in what I guessed was Farsi, they agreed that the three of them were the normal workers--in the morning and the rest of the time, too.

"Bet you get a lot of strange people through here."

That just got some shrugs. They weren't going to label any of their paying customers strange.

"Did you have any customers on Monday morning a week ago?"

The third question got a couple of raised bushy eyebrows. "You know," the oldest worker demanded, "you're about the eighth postal worker asking us about that. What's going on here, some kind of scavenger hunt?"

"One of our fellow postal workers was accused of murder. We're trying to find the truth."

"And you don't trust the cops to do their job?"

"Let's don't get sarcastic. They only have so many man hours."

While the guys were sympathetic, they remembered no blood-spattered military-looking men stopping in for a cup of coffee or wash-up the preceding Monday.

"I can unbutton a button or two." Lauren made her offer to me in a whisper. "They seem real interested in my tits."

"It's because you dyed your hair black," I lied. "Unfortunately, I think they're telling the truth. Getting them to lie wouldn't help."

"Okay." She settled back down and let the youngest of the employees refill her coffee cup.

"You ever see a guy with sort of sandy brown hair, about six feet tall but almost as wide?" I got as detailed in my description of Clark as I could and when I'd exhausted that, I did the same with Pete.

They weren't sure. They had a lot of customers through. Possibly they looked at the women a little more closely. And Anglos tended to look alike to them anyway--hey, they said it, not me.

"These guys would have guns," Lauren put in.

That got their attention. Another brief huddle led to the agreement that there had been a guy with a gun in that Monday morning, but earlier than seven. More like six. He'd picked up a coffee and bought gas.

"What kind of car was he driving? Do you remember?"

They didn't have to huddle about that. Anglos might all look the same to them, but they liked cars. The youngest one, who looked like he should be in high school rather than working for a living, had checked things out. "Government-type car. Unmarked but boring. Sort of gray, or maybe beige. Five years old, probably. Maybe six. Can't remember now if it was a Ford or GM."

"Bingo," Lauren said. "We've got Clark placed. He drives exactly that kind of car."

Just about every non-uniformed cop and federal agent drove that kind of car, so we didn't have anything close to a slam-dunk case. Still, if their evidence wasn't enough to convict Clark, it encouraged me.

"What we need is a witness who saw a gray or beige governmental-looking car turning out of the No-Tell motel sometime around seven," I reminded Lauren. "So, let's hit the road."

* * * *

People may not think of postal carriers as threatening. But that doesn't mean they like to stop and talk.

The nearest signal to the No-Tell was Hampton and Davis, and traffic was heavy as commuters made their way into the city for their day jobs.

I glanced at my watch. Almost seven. Time to get to work.

"Do you guys have any cardboard?" I asked the Mini-Mart guys, who were still in helpful mode.

They brought me a couple of donut boxes and I borrowed a *Sharpie* and wrote signs for Lauren and me.

Did you come this way last Monday? That was all.

Lauren wanted to add something about the ugly American-made car, but I didn't have room and I didn't want Lauren finding some male with more hormones than sense willing to swear he'd seen the car in hopes of ending up between her legs even if he'd been in Houston last Monday.

"If you're going to be out there for a while, I'll bring you some coffee." The youngest one was fawning.

"Cool. And maybe a couple of donuts, too," Lauren suggested.

I think he was about to promise that and more but one of his brothers or cousins or coworkers cleared his throat.

"Ah, you'll have to pay for that, though. We don't get the donuts for free."

I left Lauren to negotiate how she was going to feed her food addiction and went to stand outside.

We could have saved ourselves the time making the signs. There were already half a dozen lying outside the Mini-Mart with different variations on the theme. The postal guys had gone to bat for me and I was grateful. Still, according to Buddy, they hadn't found anything. And they'd been at it for two days.

I didn't really have any reason to believe I could do better myself--but this was the only idea I had.

They were on their way to work. I would have thought they would pray for a semi-official excuse to be late. Not to be.

Lauren joined me after a few minutes, complained that she was moving out of range of her personal coffee and donut service.

When the light turned red, I walked down the middle of the lanes and knocked on windows.

A couple of drivers thought I was collecting money for charity and shoved crumpled bills at me. One guessed I was a streetwalker and offered me twenty dollars to blow him on the way to the office. But most listened, shook their heads, and told me that they hadn't seen anything.

After half an hour, my feet were killing me, my head was pounding from inhaling too much carbon monoxide, and sweat was wearing stripes through the orange food coloring Lauren was convinced made me look tan.

"Learn anything?" I shouted to Lauren who was on the opposite side of the intersection.

"One guy told me he'd give me five hundred bucks for a blowjob."

"Good to have a second income." I didn't tell her I'd only been offered twenty.

"I told him I'd have to stamp his doodle *highly perishable* first. He didn't think it was funny."

Another wave of traffic cut off the conversation.

By nine, I was ready to give up. Fred had been killed at around seven. Clark, or Pete couldn't have waited around too long after that. First, who would hang around with a bloody corpse for two hours? Second, if they'd stayed, they would have cleaned out Fred's computer and the police would never have had a chance to destroy evidence.

I was about to suggest calling it a day when a woman actually stopped in the middle of traffic and rolled down my window.

"You're looking for that crazy guy, right?"

"I'm sorry."

She shook her head impatiently. "I'm blocking traffic here. Why don't you come over to that Mini-Mart in the next block and let me tell you what I saw."

I waved at Lauren to let her know I was moving and managed to get across

Sylvan without getting run over and only getting beeped at a couple of times.

The driver took a wild 'u' turn, almost snagged three cars, and shot into the Mini-Mart at seventy miles an hour.

I nodded to myself. Anyone *she* thought drove like a madman would have had to be severely motivated.

My new best friend's name was Kathy FitzJones.

"I'm running a few minutes late today," she admitted. "I got this new haircut and I just can't make it do what my stylist manages." She reached out a tentative hand and touched my cockatiel do. "You've got to tell me who does your hair."

"She does." I pointed to Lauren who had managed to talk the Mini-Mart clerk out of a couple more donuts despite his earlier get-tough attitude.

"Oh. That is so cool. I didn't know the post office had their own stylists. I thought you had to take your chances with the rest of us."

A million cars were going south, carrying in them two million eyes that might have seen something, and I was talking to a woman who wanted her hair to look like a mass of feathers.

"Not many people know all of the Post Office's secrets," I admitted. "We're actually aliens. I mean, you see us everywhere, but do you actually know anyone who works for the post office? Have you ever been in their homes?"

Her eyes got wide for a moment, then she laughed. "That's a pretty good one. You had me going for a minute, there, you know. Because, you're right. Who actually knows anyone who works for the post office? Besides saying hi to them when they deliver the mail, I mean. And leaving something for them around Christmas time, of course."

She'd added the last with a furtive glance toward Lauren. I figured that meant she didn't really tip her carrier but felt guilty about it.

I didn't mind. A little guilt could come in handy about now.

"Did you really have something to tell me about last Monday, or did you just want to discuss my hairdo?"

"Oh, I forgot. That's why I pulled over. Your sign doesn't say, but I guessed you wanted to talk about the accident."

"Accident?"

"I always see those ads in the paper. You know the ones. They say something like, *if you saw the accident at someplace and wherever, call this number.* Except, I'm the only person I know who reads the paper and I didn't even see an ad for this one. I guess they were smart to use the post office to get their information for them. I didn't know you guys hired out like that."

"Not many people know all--"

She narrowed her eyes. "You aren't really aliens, are you?"

I shook my head. "I could introduce you to my co-worker, Larry. He's about as non-human as you can get and still hold down a job."

"I'd be nervous about dating an alien." She scrunched her face in thought. "Uh, is he single?"

Kathy wasn't bad looking. Maybe thirty-five with a few extra pounds that mostly turned into extra curves. Her hair was a wreck, but her skin was good and she had a pretty smile. If a nice-looking woman like her couldn't do better than Larry, I was going to have to hang up my heterosexual badge and date Lauren. "Trust me, you wouldn't be interested."

"If he's male, straight, single, and lives in Dallas, he's a valuable commodity. Oh, and above eighteen. No jailbait for this girl."

Male, straight, single, urban, and over eighteen just about exhausted Larry's positive qualities. But hey, I owed Larry for what he'd done in setting up the postal investigation and Kathy seemed anxious.

"Give me your phone number and I'll check with him. But do yourself a favor and meet with him in a public place. He's a bit scary."

"Cool." She scribbled her number on the back of a gum wrapper. "Was there anything else you wanted to know about that accident? I'm running a little late for work."

She hadn't told me *anything* about the accident yet. When I reminded her of that, she just giggled.

"Right. Sometimes my brain is a million miles away."

This was definitely not the witness I wanted to rely on to get me off the hook.

"What, exactly, did you see, Kathy?"

She fished out her pack of gum again, offered me a piece, then took it herself when I refused, stuffing it in with a large wad already there.

"I was just driving along, sort of like when I noticed you. I was going maybe ten miles an hour over the speed limit, but people were still zooming around me like, hey, they're real important and they have to get to work or the world might just run down before they wind it back up."

"Got the scenario. But then?"

"Well, one car, an Audi TT, I think, had just passed me on the right, crawling out into the shoulder to do it, when a beige car pulled out of the No-Tell."

"And they hit each other?" All of a sudden, I had a life again. I'd check with Clark and Pete, see which of their cars had been in a recent accident, and compare the paint to whatever they used to paint Audis with these days.

She looked at me funny. "Of course they didn't hit. What are you trying to do, confuse me?"

I almost hurled. My hopes had been raised and then she'd shattered them. "But you said there'd been an accident."

"The Audi. It veered out of the way of the beige car and smacked into a tree. The big government car went on its merry way without even stopping to make sure the air bag deployment hadn't hurt anyone."

"Was the driver of the Audi all right?"

Kathy looked at me like I'd gone crazy. "How the hell would I know? I was already running late."

"Did you happen to notice the license number on the Audi?" It was a forlorn hope.

"Call the cops. Don't you government people work together at all?"

The postal service is a quasi-public corporation, ideally run without any subsidies from the government. Explaining that to Kathy didn't seem worth the trouble.

"What about the beige car's driver? Did you get a look at him? Or her?"

She shrugged. "Not really. I was making sure I didn't run into anyone."

Lauren grinned at me when Kathy finally left. "We are so close, I can smell it. Let's eat."

* * * *

After an early lunch at the Food-Mart, Lauren and I rode our bikes back toward our motel.

"I think," I said when we hit a quite patch of road, "we're onto something. We need to track down the Audi driver. Maybe he, or she, got a good look at the driver of the car that nearly hit him."

Lauren moaned something about trying to breathe.

"You're in Texas," I reminded her. "It's practically flat."

"Yeah, except this mountain we're going up."

What looked flat to drivers turned into something more significant to bicyclists. Still, with all the donuts she'd eaten, she should have been full of energy. "If the airbag deployed, the police were probably called," I reflected.

"If you say so. Say, do us postal people have those composite sketch artists, like the cops use on T.V.? We could get him to whip up a picture, then go and nail it on Clark. No need for anything fancy."

"I don't think we can get that much cooperation," I said. "But I do have an idea that might work."

The Texas sun beat down my energy, but I needed to put some distance between me and our hiding place before I took the next step. Lauren refused to pedal the extra miles, so I sent her ahead and rode my bike into the affluent enclave of Las Colinas, found a grocery store with a payphone, and dialed the Dallas Police.

Because I was out of Dallas, I didn't dial 9-1-1. I didn't think they taped normal calls but I let my fatigue disguise my voice, just in case.

It took me a while being routed around the police department but I finally found a clerk willing to listen to my story.

I explained that I'd witnessed the accident, basically telling Kathy's story as my own, and asked to talk to whatever officers were handling the case.

It turned out that *case* was an overstatement. The one-car accident had been written off as driver negligence. Every bad driver gives the excuse that someone else cut him off. No one wants to admit that they just suck behind the wheel.

But a cop had been dispatched, had taken down the details and, for a miracle, was at his desk.

I almost sickened myself with my girlish whining and cajoling, but I channeled Lauren and I wheedled the name of the Audi driver out of the cop. Sharing that info probably wasn't department policy, but I wasn't about to turn him in for it.

We had a go.

Then I called Preston.

As I'd guessed, the Dallas branch of the Postal Service didn't have sketch artists and with Vito's position that I was a menace who needed to be arrested and drummed out of the postal service, Preston wasn't sticking his neck out.

"Do you still think it's those Drug Enforcement guys?" he asked after he'd shot down all of my suggestions.

"That's where the evidence points."

"Well," he hesitated. "I shouldn't tell you this, hell, I should have hung up the second you called. But don't do anything crazy. Definitely don't try taking them down yourself. Since we talked last, I've been doing a bit of discrete digging. Those two guys have a dangerous reputation."

"Dangerous like how?" I wasn't sure I wanted to know.

"Dangerous like people who mess with them end up dead."

"Oh. That sort of dangerous." I'd been right. I *didn't* want to know. "So, you're volunteering to help out, provide a bit of muscle if we need it?"

The pause seemed to go on forever.

"Still there, Preston?"

"I knew I should have hung up on you the instant I heard your voice."

"Is that a yes? It really would be good for the post office, even if it isn't good for Lindner."

"Tell you what. You let me know what you want to do and I'll see if I can round up a couple of guys to help out. No guarantees, but I'll do the best I can."

"Sure, Preston." He wasn't as bulky as Clark, but Preston was a big guy with hard muscles and he carried a gun. If he was afraid to confront the D.E.A. guys, then they really were scary. All I had was Lauren, and a lipstick was her most deadly weapon.

"Why don't you give me a contact point in case I learn something?" Preston suggested. "Can I call you back at this number?"

I almost froze. I'd been standing there like a lump for better than ten minutes. Preston hadn't gotten off the phone but there had been that long pause. The cops could be coming for me now.

"I'll call you, Preston. Bye."

He was trying to say something when I hung up on him, but the phone was already on its way back to the hook and I didn't have time to listen.

My legs groaned at me when I swung my butt over the saddle, but I told them to shut up and move. Alarm bells were sounding in my head almost as loudly as the sound of the pay-telephone's ringing.

I circled around the grocery store, ducked down an alley, and watched as an Irving Police black-and-white moseyed into the store parking lot.

I tried to blame it on my fatigue, but blaming didn't help. I'd almost blown it. I had known I couldn't trust Preston and I'd still let him keep me on the phone long enough to get myself in trouble.

Three miles away, I found another phone booth, called Larry's answering machine, and gave him Kathy's phone number. Who knew? If I didn't solve my case, maybe I could become the prison matchmaker.

After that, I headed back to the motel and turned the water on full cold, and sagged against the shower wall while the water beat on me. The Texas sun and full noon bike rides were taking a toll on me.

Lauren barged in about a second after I'd tied a towel around myself and forced me to drink most of a bottle of Gatorade--something I barely managed to do without losing the towel.

"Well? You were gone forever."

"I got contact info on the Audi's driver. And Preston won't try to go over Vito's head to bring in a sketch artist. Oh, and I set Larry up with Kathy."

Lauren giggled. "I wish I could see her face when he introduces himself. If she liked your do, what do you think she'll make of Larry's?"

I shook my head. I didn't want to think about it, just like I didn't want to think about the way my own hair stood up straighter than my body was. "Preston offered to help if we have to go after Pete and Clark ourselves."

"That's got to be good news. Those two are scary."

"But I'm not sure I can trust him. He has to be working with the local police because they traced me through the call."

Lauren patted me on my arm. "You're smart, Kim. You'll figure something out."

Lauren, I realized, was pretty smart herself. She manipulated people into doing what she wanted--and made them feel good about it. Maybe I should send her to manipulate Preston into helping us without turning us over the cops. In the meantime, we needed to talk to one William Evertt, the driver of the wrecked Audi.

"Nobody can possibly know our witness," Lauren assured me. "How could they guess you found Kathy, then suckered some doofus in the police department into giving you his name?"

I wasn't so sure. As far as we knew, the cops hadn't connected an ordinary traffic accident with a murder that had been discovered only a few hundred feet away from it. They probably wouldn't, either, since it couldn't help pin the blame on me. But Preston was smart--and wanted to be a hero. He might put things together. Still, it was a chance we had to take.

A few minutes with a phone book, and we had an address for Evertt. Unless he'd moved since the phone book was printed, he lived in a neighborhood a couple of miles south of my mail route, not too far from the light rail.

I consulted with my thighs and crotch and they reported that they were on strike. There weren't going to be any more bike rides that day.

Relying on north Texas's public transportation system for a possible quick get-away was risky. I'd already taken so many risks, I hardly noticed this one when I cajoled Lauren into grabbing the Trinity Rail Express, linking with light rail, and heading with me out to Evertt's neighborhood.

Chapter 15

The sun was still up when we got there around six that evening, and I was sweating like a pig--again. Lauren looked as cool as always. She'd bought a Popsicle from a street vendor and savored it as we walked, sucking on the end of it until it faded into a pastel version of the bright green it had started out as.

She made eating a Popsicle look sexy, which didn't seem fair to me. When I ate them, they just looked messy.

"Nice house." She pulled out her compact and checked herself out. Where money was involved, she wanted to look her best.

Although Evertt lived in a neighborhood of mostly 1950s brick ranch-style homes, a few enterprising sorts had knocked down the aging properties and built mansions similar to those springing up in Highland Park. Evertt's was four stories high, and extended to the edge of the property line.

"Maybe he doesn't like mowing the lawn," I suggested.

"Yeah. And maybe he's the type the cops will listen to. A guy in a house like this has more credibility than a woman in a trailer."

The woman answering the door was as gorgeous as her house. Her skin was the color of coffee with just the hint of cream and her figure put even Lauren's to shame. Not even the telecom V.P.s I'd worked with would have been able to pull of the combination of professional and high-fashion style of the short skirted gray suit she wore.

She looked down her noses at us. "Yes?"

I didn't take it personally. We still wore our postal disguises. The better to remain invisible as we passed through the dangerous streets of Dallas.

"We're looking for William Evertt," I said. "Just following up on the accident report."

"Really? The postal service is working vehicular accidents these days? Who knew?"

"Ma'am, if we could just talk to Mr. Evertt. This shouldn't take too long."

Her dark eyes flashed at me. "I don't know what sort of scam you're pulling, but William is a good driver. If he says that someone else caused the accident, you can take that to the bank."

"We may have a lead on the vehicle which nearly struck Mr. Evertt's Audi TT," Lauren volunteered. "It would help us a great deal if we could spend a few minutes with him."

"Not without me present."

"Who is it, honey?" A male voice as smooth as melted chocolate sounded from inside the house.

"A couple of postal workers. They say they learned something about your accident."

"Hell, show them in. It isn't like I'm going anywhere in a hurry."

William Evertt had his right arm in a sling, a beige butterfly bandage across incongruous against the dark skin of his forehead. Not even his skin color hid deep bruises under each eye. The airbag might have saved his life, but it hadn't left him undamaged.

Which was unfortunate because merchandise that looks that good doesn't come along too often. He was something more than a foot taller than me and had a great build, but with long lean swimmer's muscles rather than Clark's steroid-enhanced bulk.

His smile was so bright it could have guided ships to safety. His cream-colored suit, a tiny gold cross in the lapel, provided a sharp contrast to the dark ebony of his skin.

"Come-on in and take a load off." Evertt waved at a couple of upholstered chairs.

I caught his wife's glare before I sat down and let her arrange an afghan on my chair to keep me from sweating on her nice fabric.

"You two want something to drink? I'd love a beer myself, but the doctors tell me it might interfere with the Codeine they've got me on."

"A glass of water would be nice," I ventured.

"Skinny little thing like you should drink something with some substance to it. Get the woman a Guinness, honey." He turned to Lauren. "You look more like the Martini type. Do I have you right?"

Lauren grinned. "Great."

Mrs. Evertt rang a little bell and whispered something to a tired-looking servant. No way was she leaving her husband alone with a couple of dangerous-looking postal workers.

Evertt insisted that we call him William, introduced his wife as Clotelle, and talked about the weather until the drinks had appeared and the servant vanished.

"Now, how can I help you?" he asked.

"We have a witness who says that you were driving by the Rock Cliff No-Tell Motel when a vehicle abruptly exited the No-Tell parking lot, causing you to veer out of control."

He glanced at his wife, caught her slight nod, then gave me a grin that showed rows of perfect teeth. "Glad to hear someone believes my story. The way that cop looked at me, made me blow into his little balloon like I was a drunk, I felt like I was the criminal."

The cop hadn't told me he'd suspected alcohol. I desperately wanted to ask William what the blood-alcohol test had shown, but I couldn't figure out a way to pose the question without offending him--or offending Clotelle, which seemed even more dangerous.

"Cops go by patterns," Lauren agreed. "They're busy so they try to make things fit."

"We're Black." Clotelle rolled her eyes. "This, we know."

Despite her mansion and thousand-dollar suit, Clotelle seemed to resent us.

"A serious crime was committed at the No-Tell Motel that morning." I needed to get the conversation back on track. "It seems possible that the driver of the vehicle which nearly struck yours could have witnessed something."

"Or done something," Clotelle observed.

Well, yeah.

William made a little pyramid out of his fingers and gazed at me like he was reading my soul. "I see. Before going on, perhaps you would explain to me why the postal service is involved. Usually talk of serious crime involves the police, not delivery people. Meaning no offense, of course."

I opened my mouth to blurt out a confession, but Lauren beat me to it.

"One of our fellow workers has been set up, William. Dozens of Dallas-area postal workers are volunteering to help clear her name. If you've been driving down Sylvan lately, you may have seen some of us asking questions. That was how we learned of your accident."

"A bit of solidarity, is it?" William gave us one of his million dollar smiles. "Glad to hear it. Too many of us are caught up in our own affairs and don't make time to help others."

That would describe me, all right. I liked to think I would have volunteered if another carrier had been accused of a crime but I wasn't sure. If a miracle happened and I got cleared of the murder rap, I was going to work at being a better person.

"Anything you can tell us about the car that almost struck you, and especially about the driver, would be extremely helpful to our investigation," I added.

William looked at me, at his wife, then at Lauren. "This is about that murder, isn't it? The postal worker who, ah, went postal."

"The police grabbed onto the easiest solution, not the truth," I said.

I was hoping that William's own experiences would let him believe that.

"If my husband describes this driver, would it put us in danger?" Clotelle asked.

That was a fair question. One that deserved a better answer than I was prepared to give. Fortunately, William answered it for me.

"Hell, honey. Even if I didn't see anything, I'll still be in danger. Seems to me I'd be safer describing what really happened to these women. The driver might think it was too late to shut me up."

"Their recollection of your description would be hearsay, inadmissible."

Oops. Lawyer talk. No wonder Clotelle had insisted on being there. She just wasn't being a protective wife, she was being the protective attorney.

William shrugged, wincing when the gesture conflicted with his injuries. "Maybe you're right and maybe you're wrong, honey. But if I lie, what right do I have to stand in front of the congregation and teach the word?"

Despite the cross on his lapel, I wouldn't have guessed that William was a minister. I hadn't seen much of his house, but the living room where he'd planted us didn't have any obvious religious iconography. Still, minister training could help explain the wonderful voice.

"I'd really appreciate that," I said.

"Right." He glanced toward the gray slate fireplace, shuttered and cold for the summer, but I didn't think he was seeing it. Instead, I thought he was looking again at the car that had nearly killed him.

"My Lincoln was in the shop that day and Clotelle was down in Houston on a case, so I borrowed her Audi. One of my parishioners is hospitalized at Medical City and I was running late due to construction. It's possible I was going a bit over the posted speed limit."

"They don't need to know that, honey."

I nodded encouragingly.

"A car zoomed out of the Rock Cliff Motel parking lot right in front of me." William shook his head, getting into the story. "I don't think he ever noticed me. He just drove away while I jammed on the brakes, fought the steering wheel, and ended up driving straight into a Live Oak tree that put a dent the size of Mississippi in Clotelle's Audi."

"Can you describe the car that nearly hit you?" I had taken out my notepad and was jotting things down but I hadn't really heard anything yet that offered anything new.

He shrugged, a bit abashed. "Back when most of the boys my age were studying up on cars, I was reading the good book. I can tell you it was a big American car. Not a Lincoln Town Car: I'd recognize that. More like an Impala, or maybe a Crown Vic."

"Color?" Lauren asked.

"It kicked up a major cloud of dust when it exited the motel parking lot, but it seemed to me that it was a sort of tan."

"Not gray?" Kathy had thought it was gray. I was starting to understand why cops grab theories rather than investigate facts. Everyone saw something different, even when they saw the same thing.

"I'm pretty sure there was some brown in it. Maybe a faded yellow. Not sandalwood--nothing metallic. Course it was dirty. Hard to tell what it would have looked like with a decent detailing."

I wrote that down feeling grimmer by the minute.

"Did you happen to note the license number?" Lauren didn't sound much more hopeful than I felt.

"You know, I think I could describe every branch of the tree I hit, but I didn't much study the car I was trying to avoid."

"How about the driver?" I asked.

"Didn't get a good look at him."

"But it was a man?" Lauren grabbed that one even before I could. I knew why, too. She was still steamed that I'd accused her of being the killer and figured she needed the vindication.

"It was a man all right. Big white guy."

"Big like fat?"

William shook his head. "I couldn't see his body. Just head, neck, and shoulders. But his head didn't look fat and his neck was all muscle."

"Hair color?"

"He was wearing one of them gimme hats. Couldn't make out the hair color."

"Would you recognize him if you saw him again? If we were able to show you a picture."

William considered that, then shook his head. "Probably not."

"Distinguishing marks?" Lauren suggested.

"He was a big white guy. That's about all I can say."

"What color was the cap?" William was getting a little worn out with our questions he couldn't answer, but Lauren kept pushing.

"That I can answer. It was black."

I could almost feel our time running out. Clotelle was making some vague motions that were going to translate into kicking us out soon and William was looking like he wished he'd never let us into the house. I figured we had time for one more question and needed something brilliant. Nothing came to mind.

"You say you don't really know cars," I said, "but did you notice anything unusual about the car that almost hit you. Were there any dents, any unusual markings, anything that would let us pick it out if we happened to see it?"

"I told you it was dirty, right?"

I nodded.

"It seemed like it was most dirty right around the door handle. Like someone with muddy fingers had been opening it."

"I think that's about enough." Clotelle got up and opened the door. "My husband is still recovering from his injuries and I simply can't let you take advantage of his tolerance any further."

I glanced at Lauren to see if she had any ideas for a parting question. She looked as blank as I did.

"We appreciate your time," I said.

"Leave a phone number and I'll call you if I think of anything else," William offered.

"We're sort of in transition right now," Lauren said.

Clotelle left her door open, watched us carefully as we walked down her walkway to the sidewalk, then turned and headed toward the train station.

"I think she knows who we are," Lauren said.

I thought Lauren was probably right. "Think she'll turn us in?"

"Does milk come from a cow?"

* * * *

We didn't make it back to our cheap motel until almost midnight.

Lauren insisted we get off the Light Rail at 8th and Corinth, hang out at a bar where the male-only clientele gave us strange looks and carefully avoided talking to us for a couple of hours, and then take a series of buses rather than the train back home.

We didn't see any cops, but that didn't mean they hadn't been out looking for us. One thing for sure, our postal carrier disguises were thoroughly blown.

Lauren tossed her costume-uniform in the corner, pulled on a baby-doll-style nightgown, and sat on the bed. "So, what are we going to do next?"

I sat down at the other end of the bed. "We don't exactly have a slam-dunk, but all of the evidence says it's Clark. We already knew about the drug connection. Now we've got multiple witnesses who saw what appears to be the same car at both Sean's place and at the No-Tell Motel."

"That's not much."

Well, it wasn't. "Still, we've also got the black ballcap, the muscular no-neck look." Every time I saw Clark, he was wearing a black cap, even when he was inside and didn't need it for the sun.

"Yeah. Okay. So it's Clark. Just as we've suspected for a couple of days."

"But now we're *more* sure."

"But the cops are just as sure it's us."

I pondered that. "You've got a point. But we seem to be running into the same answers every time--it seems like Clark but we get nothing definite. Do you really believe my friends in the post office are going to learn more?"

She shrank a bit. "It seems hopeless."

Back in my telecom days, I'd bucked up plenty of development teams that had started getting the hopeless attitude. I chose to forget that they'd generally been right and my bucking them up had just made them work harder and not bother with sending out resumes until they actually got laid off. "It isn't hopeless. It's just time to try something else."

"Like what?"

"We need to go after Clark directly for more evidence. And when we get that, we need to set a trap for him."

Lauren clapped her hands. "I like the sound of that. How are we going to manage a trap?"

I was clueless. "Go to bed for now. Maybe we'll dream something up during the night."

* * * *

Lauren got up early, brought back donuts and really bad coffee from the motel buffet, and was waiting when I finally let the smell of coffee lead me back to the world of the living.

She pushed a cup of coffee into my hand. "I'm ready to work on the trap."

She looked it, too. She was dressed in a silk blouse that was held together by two buttons just north of her belly button and hip-hugging harem pants so low she must have spent some extra time with the razor that morning.

"Ufgh."

"Drink some coffee and eat a donut. Come on, we've got to get a move on it. The cops are going to find us before long."

That was one problem, all right. The newspapers and T.V. were keeping up a steady barrage of disinformation about us, telling everyone to be on the lookout for us and to report us to the local police as armed and dangerous. I thought Lauren might have a deadly nail clipper somewhere but the closest I got to being armed was my dog spray.

My bright orange cockatiel-do and Lauren's Goth-black hair made us look somewhat different from our normal selves, but some people looked past that stuff. I was pretty sure Clotelle had.

TRU TV was running a special on us, but they went back to their normal crime shows--police actually working on solving crimes. I watched them paint Luminol over a wall smacked my forehead. "That's it."

"What?" Lauren ripped a donut into quarters and stuffed one into my mouth.

I gestured at the show. "The mud on the car door that William mentioned."

Lauren followed my gaze. "You think it was blood?"

"What else?"

She jammed another hunk of donut into my mouth. "Keep eating."

Since I couldn't talk, Lauren took over. "We'll get some Luminol at the Spy Store in Addison. Clark always parks outside the donut shop. Even if he washed his car, traces of blood should still be there."

I chewed and nodded. This would be better than a trap.

I hadn't had a donut for years--not that I hadn't been tempted when Tina had brought that bag of them into my trailer.

The rich mix of fat grams and carbs melted in my mouth and I savored the slightly crunchy texture of deep-fried dough and glazed sugar--until I thought about how many miles on the bike each crunch would cost me.

"I can't go on eating like--"

She stuffed another donut chunk into my mouth before I could finish the thought.

"If you don't eat, you won't have the strength we need to trap Clark and hold him captive."

I snickered, then blew my nose because I'd sent donut crumbs up it.

Two girls with a combined weight of maybe two hundred pounds physically holding Clark captive was not going to be a happening thing. Not to mention, D.E.A.agents probably get all sorts of training in how to beat up people and I hadn't been in a fight since I'd been in fifth grade when Milly De'Angelo had called me a fat pig and I'd still been in denial.

Come to think of it, I'd lost that fight.

"Let me get showered and then we'll see about getting Luminol," I promised.

Lauren smiled and popped another donut chunk into my mouth. "All right. Oh, by the way, I used both towels."

That was nothing new. The cheap motel only gave us two tiny towels--and since we'd signed up for the weekly rate, they didn't even bother changing them.

I gathered up clean underwear, a pair of jeans and a t-shirt, and headed into the bathroom.

Lauren tried to follow me in with another chunk of donut, but the feeding thing was getting past my comfort zone, especially in the bathroom. I shut the door on her and pulled off the t-shirt I wore as a nightgown.

I hated looking at my body. I had stretch marks from all the weight I'd lost, my boobs were practically non-existent, but I still had a little pouch in my belly that wouldn't go away no matter how little I ate.

I sucked it in without much effect, then gave up.

My face wasn't in much better shape than the rest of my body. Half my hair still stood straight up, the other half matted down from sleep, and my eyes had black shadows from exhaustion. Maybe I needed to turn myself over to the police in order to get some rest.

"Don't obsess about how you look," Lauren shouted through the door. "With the right clothes and some makeup, you'll look great."

As if. I doubted Lauren, who looked perfect all the time and had every man in the planet panting after her, could have any concept of what ordinary women went through.

I sighed, climbed into the shower, and let the water rain down on me.

I must have zoned out there because after a while, Lauren pounded on the bathroom door. "Come on. We don't have all day."

"Oh, sorry."

I turned off the water, dried myself with already wet towels, and put on my clothes. Unlike Lauren, I didn't get any kick out of parading around in my underwear.

Lauren waited for me with a pair of scissors in her hand. "Okay. Time to change disguises."

* * * *

Twenty minutes later, I was a different person--but not a person I'd ever wanted to be.

Lauren trimmed my hair, dressed me in a baggy t-shirt and baggier jeans, and declared that I was her teenaged son who just happened to be fascinated by spies and police stuff. She didn't disguise herself much at all, other than wearing a pair of movie-star sunglasses. I, she reminded me, was the one the police were really looking for.

The media was treating us like a latter-day Thelma and Louise, so I suspected she was wrong. She was right, though, that people would pay less attention to a lady with a kid than they would to two women. As I was short and had no figure, I figured to be the kid. Still, it wasn't the kind of decision that improved my body image.

Chapter 16

I'd never been inside a spy store before.

Seeing myself on two dozen monitors at once was a bit intimidating, especially since I looked a lot like the annoying teenager who lived in the trailer next to mine and was always setting fires and trying to capture Tina's chickens. Even more intimidating was the assortment of dangerous stuff just anyone could buy.

They had eight flavors of mace, stun guns that were guaranteed to leave any hapless mugger writhing in agony, cameras the size of a pea, digital tape recorders that fit on a key chain, and at least six books with detailed lessons on hypnotizing women so they'd become willing sex machines.

It looked like the kind of store Fred would have appreciated--sex, blackmail, and violence all in a convenient shop.

In the back corner, I found a cardboard box filled with Luminol.

The shop manager gave Lauren a little spiel about how we needed to be sure to use everything legally, taking himself off the hook if anything went wrong, and proceeded to ring up Lauren's purchases of a flask of Luminol, a digital recorder, an aluminized space blanket, a UV light source, a twenty-five dollar digital camera, a stun gun, and three cans of what was labeled as military-grade mace.

I put down my foot when she tried to buy one of the hypnotism books.

"Not to hypnotize you, sonny," she assured me.

Even so--I didn't see us asking Clark to focus on the shining ball.

Afterwards, we launched an epic bus journey involving seven transfers before we got anywhere near to the Chinese donut place where the D.E.A. agents hung out.

When we finally got to the Wynnewood Village area, Lauren insisted we eat before checking Clark's car.

We sat at an Arby's across from the donut place. Lauren ate. I looked around for anyone who looked like an informant, and tried to avoid Lauren's attempts to feed me.

I'd already read the Luminol instructions five times, so I paid more attention to the cars.

Which one belonged to Clark?

There were eight cars parked there and every single one of them looked like government issue.

"You know those guys better than I do," I finally admitted. "Which car is Clark's?"

Lauren gulped a swallow of chocolate shake. "The one with the blood on it."

"Thank you."

Two were black and one a midnight blue so dark it looked black except where the sun glistened off of it. I ruled those out--they didn't match the descriptions.

That left one beige one, two light gray ones, one really filthy one that looked like it might be white underneath, or maybe gray or even brown, and one tan-colored one.

"Either the tan one or the dirty one," I guessed.

She put down her sandwich. "Maybe."

Like I really needed that kind of support. "Finish up your food and let's go."

When she didn't lecture me about eating more than the two French fries I'd forced down, I realized Lauren had to be as nervous as I was.

"Keep your stun gun handy," I suggested.

"Oh, that'll work. I'll stun them and we'll make a quick getaway on the northbound bus."

Put that way, this was an even stupider idea than I'd envisioned. Without a car or even our bikes, our getaway would be slower than O.J. Simpson's.

"I've got a better idea. Let's not get caught."

Lauren smacked her forehead. "Now why didn't I think of that?"

The really filthy car was farther from the Chinese restaurant so we started with it.

William had described the car that nearly sideswiped him as being covered with dirt, so this one looked like a possibility until we got close. Unfortunately, there weren't any obvious bloody fingerprints near the car door where William had reported seeing them. It certainly didn't look like anyone had wiped it in the past week--or the past year for that matter.

I still had Lauren hold the space blanket over me, held my breath and sprayed the Luminol, then shined the UV light on the mess.

The whole thing glowed, but there were none of the distinctive splatters or fingerprints that we'd seen on T.V.

Still, I snapped a couple of pictures with the digital camera, almost blinding myself on the first one before I found the knob to turn off the flash.

"Right. That sucked," I said. "Let's check out the tan car next."

The smells of boiling fat and soy sauce nauseated me as we got closer to the D.E.A. hangout. I ducked low to minimize the chance someone might look out one of the restaurant windows and spot me but Lauren just laughed. "Any way you can think of to look even more suspicious to the hundreds of drivers going past?"

As if huddling under a space blanket with an ultraviolet light source wasn't going to look suspicious enough.

The tan car was clean. In fact, it glistened.

"William said the car he saw was dirty," Lauren reminded me.

"Clark isn't a genius, but he might have noticed the evidence and gave it a wash."

She nodded. "The guy at the spy store said Luminol will detect faint traces. Give me the can and let me spray it on while you get ready with the blanket. We need to make this fast."

I checked to make sure the flash was still off, draped the blanket around my shoulders, and was as ready as I was going to get.

"Shit."

"What?"

"The creep must have waxed his car. Look at the way the Luminol is beading up."

The highly raised beads of the liquid chemical looked more like a commercial for car care than a crime scene but I figured it was as good as it was going to get.

I turned on the UV lamp, huddled under the blanket, and took the shot.

Again, the entire car door glowed wherever the Luminol had hit it. "I didn't see anything that looks like bloody fingerprints," I admitted. "Do you think the wash and wax would have smeared it around completely?"

"You're the genius."

The scritch of tire against gravel jerked me back to the present. "What the hell is going on here?"

I dropped the space blanket and looked at the bearded man leaning out the open window of his dually pickup truck.

"Nothing."

"You vandalizing that car, son?"

We were so totally screwed.

"No way. Uh, we think my dad is in there with his *boyfriend* and mom suggested we take some pictures for the divorce lawyer."

"That right, ma'am?"

Lauren rubbed her eyes and gave a good sigh. "I gave Biff the best years of my life and he doesn't even have the good grace to go off with a trophy wife. Instead, he wants a trophy boyfriend."

The truck driver scratched his head. "Can't say that seems like a smart decision to me, ma'am. But neither does involving your son in something like this."

"Oh, you're so right." Lauren flipped her long now-black hair. "Recently I've really begun to doubt myself."

"Man would have to be crazy not to find you attractive, Ma'am."

"I just don't know how I'm going to raise Chip here by myself."

Self-defense battled the driver's hormonal drive--and won. "Well, I guess I'll just be moving along here, assuming there's no trouble."

"No trouble beyond another jerky male. Thanks for asking."

His big diesel pickup kicked gravel on the shiny car as it spun back onto the highway, almost causing a wreck as it went. Now that would really have made the day perfect.

"I think it's time we headed for the bus stop," I said.

Lauren shook her head. "I'm not going back to that creepy motel. I didn't mention it, but I think the manager suspects something. He really gave me a once-over this morning when I picked up the donuts."

I suspected it was because she'd hogged half of the donuts he'd put out but I couldn't be sure.

"The Luminol didn't do the job," I said. "Time for our trap."

"You never did tell me how we were going to do that."

"Let's get away from here and I'll go over it with you."

* * * *

We headed for the nearest public library and signed up for an Internet computer.

"If we had some way to blackmail Carl," I whispered, "we'd be able to get him apart from Pete, get him talking, admitting things when he tried to bribe his way out of whatever we threatened him with."

"Good thinking. And if we had the winning lottery ticket, we'd be rich."

"Well, you're partly right. *We* don't have anything to blackmail Carl with, but we know Fred did. Because we're ninety-nine percent certain that's why Fred got killed. Not because he dealt in drugs, but because he was blackmailing Carl."

"So you think--"

"Carl knows he ruined Fred's computer, but can he know for sure he destroyed everything? He didn't find Fred's backup--he can't know Fred didn't make copies of whatever it was before he killed Fred. When we tell him we have something on him and prove we've got access to the backups, he'll believe us."

"I think he'll come kill us."

"That's the reason I put off our trap for last." The fact that he'd killed Fred despite the possible existence of backups bothered me--a lot. "I'm open to alternatives."

Lauren shook her head. "Let's do the trap, but make sure we don't get killed."

"Hey, I like it."

While we waited for the computer, we roughed out an idea. We'd contact Clark, let him know we had Fred's blackmail backups, and suggest he pay us off with enough money to run to Mexico. That was, I'd learned, what one of the other women in my trailer park had done and she'd lived.

"Right. What if he asks why we don't just turn it over to the police and clear our names?"

I'd given Lauren the idea of picking holes in our plan and she was good at it. Frustratingly good. If we had definitive information that would take us off the hook, why would we bother with blackmail?

"He'll know we don't have the video of him killing Fred. So, we're afraid we'd still end up in prison--but we'd make sure he ended up there, too."

Lauren nodded. "I guess that makes sense."

"Okay. So, what stops him from killing us?"

"I'll tell him we've got the info in a drop. If we don't retrieve it, it'll go straight to the cops."

Lauren grinned. "I think I saw that one in a Hitchcock film back when I was in college. Good plan."

"Yeah. There is one thing, though."

"You mean about after he's spilled the beans and tells us what he did and gives us the money, then when we try to arrest him and he kills us? That problem?"

"That's the one."

She considered that. "What about your postal cop friend, Preston? He wants to be a hero, right? He might help?"

"He might help, if he couldn't become a hero by turning us in to the police first."

"Good point."

I thought for a moment. "Okay, got it. We clue him in, tell him where to go, how we'll make contact with him, but he won't know whether he's getting to our location until he's there--and it's too late for him to bring in the Dallas police."

Lauren considered. "That might work. But what if he's wearing a tracer?"

"We'll have to time things, not give him a chance to connect with the police. We'll tell him we're watching and if we see the cops, the deal is off. Besides, we'll tell him we want to surrender to him--if he brings in the police, he won't be the hero."

Lauren slapped the fashion magazine she was pretending to read down on the table. "I like that--I like it a lot."

As traps went, this was slightly better than the one Winnie the Pooh and Piglet had set for the heffalump. We argued a little about the exact wording we'd use to trap Clark, but neither of us came up with any big improvements.

Finally the librarian called our name and we got our Internet computer.

Lauren started by searching for Luminol+Car Wax and came up with nothing. Still, Luminol detected hemoglobin from blood and Clark probably knew that. He might not be a genius, but he could figure out how to clean up the evidence.

That was when I figured out why both cars had glowed when we'd sprayed them. "Hemoglobin is iron. Which is what cars are made out of. And metallic paints have more metal. No wonder we got the glow."

"Next time I find a dead body, I'm just going to deliver his mail and keep walking," I assured Lauren.

"You'd better. Because I want a closet with my own clothes, I want to be a blonde again, and I'm not sure I'm ready to have a teenage son." She glared at me as if it were all my fault. "I'm worried about you, though. What are you going to do if I don't make you eat?"

I pinched my poochy stomach. "I'm going to lose this gut."

"As if. Anyway, next question. Where are we going to do this and when?"

"Tonight. We'll call Clark when he's on his way home from the donut

145

place. And we'll do it at Lakeside Park. They've got a semi-enclosed picnic area there where Preston can hang out without being seen while we tape Clark's confession."

"Damn, girl. This is going to rock."

I wasn't so confident, but I nodded. "Now we need to do two things. First, we need Clark's personal cell number. That's your job. Second, I need to set up some calls to Preston that nobody is going to be able to use to trace us."

"I thought if you kept the call short, they couldn't trace you, anyway."

"You've been watching too many old movies. Now it doesn't take any time at all. A two-dollars-an-hour outsourced worker in India can read back the calling location in twenty seconds."

"Oh." Lauren's face fell. "I guess I'll see if they'll let me use their phone and you can play with the computer."

"Good plan."

* * * *

Just because I'd been laid off from the telecom industry didn't mean I'd forgotten everything I ever knew.

It took me about thirty seconds to find a site that would convert text to speech for me and I typed in the messages I wanted delivered to Preston. One, to be delivered immediately, just told him to keep his cell nearby. The second, for six that night, told him to head to Southwest Center Mall. The third, I directed to all of the payphones anywhere in the mall--since I figured at least a few of them would be out of order. It gave him directions to the park where I said he'd get further instructions.

"And don't bring your Corvette," I added to the six o'clock message. "It's way too obvious."

If our timing went well, Preston would arrive a couple of minutes before Clark did. We'd agree to let him turn us ove to the cops--but only after we'd met with Clark. In case he arrived late, I warned him to approach the picnic area from Hill City Drive rather than Steger so Clark wasn't likely to see him. Besides, I didn't think they knew each other. As long as he didn't drive the Corvette, he would just look like another park user.

I didn't need to tell Preston to bring his gun--he always carried that.

It took a few minutes to hack into a voice over IP site, connect in my messages, install a timer and connect in an answer detection object. The whole thing should be untraceable, at least for a few hours. And, if they ever did find someone smart enough to trace it back to the library, well, we'd be long gone.

I felt like I was ready to get back into telecom engineering by the time I'd finished and the feeling was surprisingly good. Who would have thought I'd ever have any fond feelings at all for the years when I'd earned six figures, spent more, and sweated my overweight buns off for a company that gave its senior management team bonuses for doing a good job laying off all their American engineers?

* * * *

Lauren wanted to eat again, but not even her nagging could make me force anything down into the tight knot that was my stomach. So I watched her chow down a couple of tacos and a burrito and thought about all the things that could go wrong.

Maybe Preston wouldn't be enough--Clark had killed twice that I knew of already. Maybe I should have just turned over what we'd learned to the police and let them run with it. Maybe I should have--

Lauren interrupted my thought trainwreck. "You're muttering to yourself. Someone is going to think you're a crazy person and call the white fishnet society."

"People don't see crazy people any more," I reminded her. "The men in white coats are out of business."

"I don't want to hang out with an invisible person, either. Come on." As if I hadn't been sitting there waiting for her to eat.

I had to dig deep into my bag for bus fare. I was running low on cash. If Clark no-showed, I was going to have to turn myself into the cops just so I'd have a place to sleep. Naturally, Lauren didn't seem to be having the same problems. And she'd spent twice as much as me. Of course, whenever she'd had the chance, she'd spent my money.

Despite the late-summer heat, the park was awash with running children, young men showing off their shirtless bodies, and mothers pushing strollers as they chatted with each other.

It took us a while to find an unoccupied picnic area, but when we finally found it, we both knew it was perfect. It was close to a nearly full parking lot, which meant that Preston's car wouldn't be obviously related to the picnic area. But it was far enough away that everything we said could be relatively private.

We tested out the tiny digital recorder. Incredibly, even when we stuck it to the bottom of the picnic table with chewing gum, it picked up everything we said perfectly. The trick was going to be to get Clark to confess in the first ten minutes because that was all the memory it held.

"We should have bought the higher capacity model," I said.

Lauren wrinkled her nose at me. "With any luck, he'll kill us right away so we can get everything on tape."

"Okay, I'll stop complaining."

A couple of early-teen girls hopefully poked their heads into the picnic area and asked if I wanted to play catch with them. I had to remember that I was supposed to be a kid myself. It was a good reminder to keep my cover for another few hours.

"Go ahead, Chip," Lauren offered. "I'll wait here. You've got to get over being shy of girls."

Talk about blowing my cover. The first time I threw a ball, everyone in the park would know I wasn't a boy. "Sorry," I told the girls. "I hurt my foot."

"Oh? That's too bad." The girls came into the picnic shelter and plopped down at the table with me.

"Do you go to school near here?" the taller of the two girls demanded. "How come we haven't seen you around?"

147

Obviously Lauren had known what she was doing when she'd dressed me in baggy jeans, a baggy t-shirt, a baseball cap covering my practically shaven head, and no makeup at all. From the way the two twelve- or thirteen-year-olds were looking at me, I was the perfect pre-pubescent boy.

For just a moment, I let myself consider the possibility that I really did have an eating disorder, that Lauren's constant force-feeding of me had something to do with me rather than with her own addiction to the amphetamines. I mean, a grown woman isn't supposed to be mistaken for a boy.

"Have a seat, girls," Lauren offered. "I've got some Coke in my bag. Do either of you want some?"

"Do you have diet?"

"You're too young to drink diet." Lauren poked me with her bag as she pulled out a couple of Cokes. "Smile at them," she hissed at me. "We've got time to kill and they'll help us blend in."

I tried. I smiled, let the girls sit down and, when they got off their conversation about the soap opera they were watching, we got into a really nice chat about Harry Potter books and on how come Harry wasn't interested in Hermione when she obviously had a lot more on the ball than any of the chicks Harry got hot over.

"I'd take Harry," Lupe, the smaller of the two girls insisted.

Tawdry shook her head. "Hermione is looking for someone who will be loyal to her. Harry is always off adventuring. He's checking out the other girls, wondering if he has a chance. Hermione shouldn't waste her time with him. But Ron is going to be there for Hermione no matter what."

It was a surprisingly insightful thought and it led us into a discussion of relationships, the role of sex appeal, and who was going with whom to the school dance.

"Is something wrong with you?" Lupe suddenly demanded.

"Huh? Oh, my foot. I twisted my--"

"You don't talk about the things normal boys talk about."

"Like cars, you mean? I've got a cool bike."

"Not like that," Tawdry explained. "Most guys would want to start hitting us or something rather than talk about real stuff. Either that or they'd try to get into our pants right away."

"How old are you guys?"

"I'm thirteen and Lupe is twelve," Tawdry said. "We thought you were our age, but you're older, aren't you?"

"A little. And believe me, you're too young to be thinking about who gets into whose pants."

Lupe laughed. "I guess you don't go to school around here. Where do you come from? Mars?"

"Nebraska," I answered, more or less honestly, if you forgot about the ten years since I left what had been home.

"That's like in Canada isn't it?" Lupe seemed genuinely mystified that anyone could come from so far away.

"Getting up toward there," I answered. "Can we get back to Harry Potter?"

After they finished Lauren's Cokes and tried to persuade me to play catch again, they got up and started making leaving motions. They promised they'd be around if I came to the park again.

"We can teach you to throw if that's the problem," Tawdry whispered to me when they got up to leave. "Guys around here will think you're creepy if you throw like a girl."

"That would be nice," I said, trying not to choke up. I wouldn't wish being falsely suspected of murder on anyone, but the past two weeks had been an eye-opening experience for me. I'd made my first best-friend since elementary school, found that my fellow postal workers were ready to give up their holidays and spare time to help me out when most of them didn't know me from Eve, made friends with a couple of young girls who, I suspected, probably had more sexual experience than I did, and had broken out of my rut for the first time since I'd retreated there after telecom.

"Hey kid," Lauren said. "Little one, Lupe."

The friendly face dropped and an ugly scowl appeared. "Yeah?"

"Want a hundred dollars?"

The scowl deepened. "I don't do it for money and I don't do it with old ladies." She turned to me. "You didn't tell me your mother was a pervert, Chip."

"Nothing like that," Lauren said. "Let me borrow your cell phone for a couple of hours and the hundred bucks is yours." She dug five twenties from her purse. Which looked like about all she had left.

I wondered what we were going to do about sleeping. Neither of us had motel money any more. Heck, if we could scrounge together bus money, we'd be doing great.

"You going to call foreign countries or anything? Except Mexico? That's included in my plan."

"Just local."

"Let me see the money."

Lauren extended the bills but kept a firm hold.

Lupe winked at me. "It was worth a try." She slid the phone across the picnic table. "Here. Take the phone. We'll come back in a couple of hours. You'd better be here."

"Don't come barging in. If there's a guy here, it might be dangerous. We're supposed to be meeting with, uh, Chip's dad."

Tawdry shook her head. "You'd be better off just getting away from him. They never pay anything, anyway."

"Just stay away if you see anyone but us," Lauren repeated. "If we're not here, we'll hide your phone in the pipe over there."

"My mom will kill me if I lose the phone." Lupe looked at me. "Do you promise that you won't run off with it, Chip?"

"I promise."

She giggled. "Chip is a really funny name. Does anyone in Nebraska have normal names?"

I assured her that most of Nebraska was filled with normal humans. Chips normally just went with the buffalos.

She giggled again. "We hang here at the park all the time. Look for us."

Lupe headed out of the shelter and Tawdry started to follow her, then turned back. She glanced at Lauren, then whispered in my ear. "If you want to get over that virgin problem, you need to know that Lupe likes you. She likes you a lot, if you know what I mean."

"Thanks," I told her. "But I really think you guys need to keep your priorities straight."

Tawdry shook her head like I was crazy. "You don't know what you're missing."

Okay. I had a new resolution. If I got out of this mess alive and not in prison, I was going to volunteer in the StrongGirl program, which was a local group that helped girls. These were nice kids and they were setting themselves up for some pretty messed-up lives.

"Well that was interesting," Lauren reprogrammed Lupe's cell as the two girls vanished into the nearby playground equipment.

"I liked them."

"You should write it up for one of those true-confession magazines. 'I went underground as a teenaged boy. Do you know what your daughters are delivering?'"

"That's sick."

"Speaking of sick, it's time to call Clark. I programmed in his number. There's no way they'll have a trace on this phone, and I can't think why they would be listening into Clark's."

She shoved Lupe's phone to me.

The tiny cell was decorated with bright yellow Pikachus. The worn keys spoke of frequent text messages--probably sent when Lupe should have been listening to her teachers at school.

I took the phone and stared at the LCD screen where Clark's number glowed like a demonic incantation.

All of a sudden, I didn't feel so hot.

"Crap." Lauren barely snatched the phone away from me before I was sick all over the table.

"Sorry," I told her. "Sometimes when I get stressed--"

"I thought you were just anorexic. Are you bulimic, too?"

"I don't have an eating disorder. I sometimes get an upset stomach."

"Talk about denial."

"Said the amphetamine addict."

"I'm not an addict."

"See what I mean."

Unfortunately, squabbling didn't make me feel any better. It also didn't get us an closer to solving the case.

Lauren shoved the phone to me again. "Call Clark. Try to sound like a tough, no-nonsense woman rather than a frazzled kid. This is our last chance."

Chapter 17

"If you'd like to leave a message, press one."

I glared at the phone. "What do I do now?"

"Maybe he's on the other line," Lauren suggested. "Nobody expects their snitches to leave voice mail so you can phone back in a couple of minutes."

I filled one of the Coke cans with water and rinsed off the picnic table, then tried again.

Sure enough, this time he answered.

"Clark Study."

I'd been so sure I would get voice mail again, I almost pressed the disconnect button.

I swallowed hard. I was going to be tough on the phone. Vomiting during conversation wasn't going to do it.

"Uh--"

"I don't recognize this number. Who the hell is calling me?"

"Mr. Study. I thought you might like to know that Fred Turley was careful with his backups."

Clark's breath hissed over the phone. He waited just a fractional second too long before answering. "I'm not sure I know what you're talking about."

"Are you sure? I'm talking about murder and cover-up."

Another pause. "Go on."

"We need ten thousand dollars or we're going to the police with Fred's blackmail material. And believe me, you don't want that to happen. But I guess you do know that, don't you?"

He pondered that, but I heard his breathing so I knew he wasn't switching to another line to have the cops or his D.E.A. buddies try to trace Lupe's phone.

"Ten thousand dollars is a lot of money. I don't have that kind of cash lying around."

I laughed. Lauren and I had brainstormed his likely response and so far he was right on track.

"Don't give me that crap, Smart. The drug world isn't a credit card sort of business. You pay your informants off in cash all the time. So, write me up as an informant. Believe me, the information we're going to provide will be worth more than you normally get. It'll be worth your job--and your freedom."

"I see." He breathed a couple more times. I could barely hear his car engine but it sounded like it was idling, like he'd pulled over to the side of the road to talk to me.

At Lauren's raised eyebrow, I stuck a finger in my mouth and made the shape of a hooked fish. He was on the line. Now I had to reel him in.

"Obviously, we've notified our attorneys that we're meeting with you. If anything happens to us, you'll be the obvious suspect. So I advise that you not get any ideas about cleaning things up."

"I won't do that."

I wondered if he'd said the same thing to Fred and Sean.

I gave him directions to the park, told him he had twenty minutes to get here, and told him to keep breathing. I wanted to listen to him all the way in so I'd know he wasn't calling for backup. I didn't think he'd call the cops, but D.E.A. agents get to know plenty of guys who'll kill someone for the fun of it, or for a twenty-dollar rock.

"No sign of Preston," Lauren whispered.

I nodded and glanced at the time in the phone. I hadn't realized until then how much I'd been counting on having Preston for backup. I hoped Clark would rather pay us than kill us, but I was betting my life on it and wished that I thought my odds were better than fifty-fifty.

"I'm sure Preston'll get here." I whispered the lie. But what if I'd made a mistake in my coding that afternoon? What if Preston was out of town on vacation? What if he'd just been humoring me when he'd offered himself as backup when we finally took Clark down? One problem with using technology to make telephone calls is that you don't get to hear what the other guy has to say. Maybe Preston had told me to blow off.

It was after working hours and a number of full-sized American-made cars were pulling into the nearby parking lot, but I didn't see Clark's. I just hoped that Preston's would blend in if and when he got here. I'd told him not to drive the Corvette, but maybe it was all he had.

But Preston didn't show.

Clark did.

We'd been right about his car. It was the tan one that had recently been detailed. It looked like he'd tried to buff the Luminol off the door where I'd sprayed it and only been partially successful.

As always, he wore his black cap as he strode up to the picnic shelter. His broad shoulders and straight back nearly filling the structure.

"Give me the phone," Lauren demanded.

I passed it over. It had done its job.

She fumbled with it, then punched a bunch of numbers. This didn't seem to me to be the time to check her e-mail, but she was definitely doing something like that because she wasn't talking to it--or listening.

"Okay, so what's this about?" Clark came into the shelter blustering, putting on an innocent act that wouldn't have fooled a first grader.

"Have a seat, Clark." I gestured for him to sit at the picnic table--closer to the concealed recorder.

He glared at me, but he sat when I stared back at him.

When I didn't say anything, he went into attack mode. "If you two had any sense at all, you'd be in South America by now. The police are steamed that they let you get away. Any deal about taking over Sean's business is definitely off the table."

Interesting. Without Pete around, Clark seemed a lot more articulate, on the ball. I'd thought I'd detected an act in the donut shop, but I hadn't expected Clark to step so far out of his role.

"The thing is, Clark. We're running low on cash. We need help."

"Remind me why this is my problem."

"Sure, Clark. Two names. Sean and Fred. It's a funny thing that a blackmailer like Fred Turley gets killed right after Sean's death, isn't it."

"What's funny," Clark sneered, "is that nobody killed him before. Fred has made a lot of enemies over the years."

I nodded. "I'll bet he did. What with pictures of mayors and congressmen and rich businessmen doing the nasty with cheap hookers, he'd have a lot of people wishing he'd just drop dead."

"Fred's computer was ruined. There wasn't any evidence found on the scene."

"Is that what you heard, Clark? Because it happens to be wrong. It is true that the *cops* didn't find anything when they searched his office. But they didn't look very hard, did they? They knew a lot of people would be embarrassed when Fred's little photos and videos turned up so they deliberately looked the other way. Or did they get a little federal encouragement to keep their noses out of D.E.A. business?"

Clark took off his cap, spun it around in his fingers, and slowly returned it to his head. "I suspect you're right about the way the cops searched. But even if they'd found embarrassing evidence, do you really think they'd have gone public with it?"

Lauren was still busy playing with Lupe's phone so I was on my own.

"I don't really care, Clark. As far as I'm concerned, who sleeps with whom should be between a man and his religious advisor." Unless she was twelve, like Lupe. "Same with drugs."

"So, what's your--"

"But murder is a different story."

Clark leaned forward, his suit jacket gaping just enough to show the leather straps of his shoulder holster.

"I suppose it was you who screwed up my paint job."

"We had a witness who saw a bloodstain on your car. Funny that you had it detailed right after the murder, isn't it."

"I didn't have it detailed. I washed and waxed it, like I do every weekend. And your Luminol didn't pick anything up, did it? Because there was nothing there for it to find."

Because I'd sprayed the wrong door. Suddenly I saw it clearly. The car had turned left in front of William--showing William the passenger-side door--and

I'd tested the driver's door. What an idiot I'd been.

"For ten thousand dollars, we'll leave the evidence with you, head for South America, and you'll never have to worry about us again."

Clark nodded slowly. "Why don't you tell me what you've got?"

I laughed. "Think about it like poker, Clark. You want to see our hand, you pay. You don't want it, we'll turn it over to the Dallas Police Department and cheer when they drive out and arrest you for murder."

The 'm' word hung there like a huge turd no one had wanted to mention. Mention or not, it still stunk up the neighborhood.

Around us, the sounds of the park all faded: screaming children, shouting parents, the shrill sound a million cicada, and the racket of thousands of grackles settling on a few trees so thick they looked like black leaves.

"If you had positive evidence I killed Fred, we wouldn't be having this conversation," Clark said. "I want to know what my ten thousand is buying. Right now, I'm thinking it's buying nothing but hot air. If I was in the market for that, I could get it without leaving the donut shop."

He was right, unfortunately. But admitting that wouldn't get us anywhere.

"We don't have the murder on tape, obviously. That we would have turned over to the cops. When you sabotaged the computer, you destroyed the real-time stuff. But Fred made an audio of his blackmail offer."

"Oh, really?" He stood and stepped away from the table, moving away from the microphone. This wasn't going well.

"I already told you what's going to happen if you don't play, Clark. We've got more than Fred's info. We've got your admission that you were at the scene of the crime late the evening of Sean's murder. We've got a description that matches your car and you leaving Fred's motel the morning of his murder. You have nothing in terms of an alibi.

"We've got motive, we've got opportunity, and a big guy like you would have no problems with method. When you add the blackmail on top of it, I think the evidence will persuade any jury in Dallas."

"Persuading a jury in Dallas isn't hard," Clark told me. "There are three things wrong with your list, though."

"Funny, it seemed pretty convincing to me."

Clark rubbed the bristles of his G.I issue haircut, then shoved his hat back down. "I'm starting to believe that maybe you didn't kill those two. Otherwise you wouldn't be trying to persuade me I did it. But listen to this. First, I paid my little visit to Sean at around seven, on my way home from work. According to the medical examiner, Sean died around eleven."

"Everyone knows estimating the time of--"

Clark shook his head. "He couldn't be *that* far off."

"Doesn't matter. I've got a witness who saw you there after ten."

Clark ignored my outburst. "Second, Fred never tried to blackmail me. The man wasn't that stupid. So, if you have anything at all, it's a fake."

"I guess you'll find out." It was weak, but it was all I could come up with.

Unfortunately, Clark gave it all the attention it deserved--none.

"Third, I didn't kill either guy. Not that I'm crying over a couple of dead druggies."

"I think the police--"

He shook his head. "No, Kimberly. I've listened to you plenty and now you're going to listen to me. You've been running around stirring things up. You've got me convinced that you're innocent. Good work. But someone is guilty. And that someone isn't going to worry about your little blackmail scheme. He's just going to figure the two of you are two more little speedbumps on the way to his goals."

"I think--"

"If I were the two of you, I'd change my names and stay underground. Because when whoever really killed those druggies finds you, you're dead."

Either Clark was tougher than I'd hoped or we'd picked the wrong guy. With the right car, the right build, the witness statements, I'd been sure he was guilty but his confidence shook me. I was set to bluster and threaten a bit more, but I was running out of hope. He just wasn't admitting anything for the tape.

"Listen, Clark. I already said we'd go underground, but--"

Lauren had been quite through our entire conversation, not even nodding to reinforce the threats and promises I'd been making, but she jumped in here, putting her hand across my mouth.

"What." It came out muffled. We definitely weren't impressing Clark.

She passed me the phone.

The text message was written right over the phone-photo of Clark twirling his cap. *Not the guy*, it read.

Lauren's fiddling with the phone hadn't been nervous behavior after all. Lauren had snapped Clark's picture and e-mailed it to William.

Well, shit.

* * * *

Clark's car peeled out of the parking lot and Lauren put her head in her hands. "We are so dead."

"Okay, so it wasn't Clark coming out of the motel," I said. That doesn't mean he didn't do it. I mean, a lot of guys could have been coming out of the motel."

"At seven in the morning?"

She was right. While that would be a normal time to leave a regular motel, the Rock Cliff No-Tell Motel was anything but normal.

"Okay, let's use our heads. Review the evidence. If it's not Clark, who is it?"

Lauren shrugged. "Who the hell knows?"

I pulled out the little notebook I'd been carting around on my neck and went down my list. "It's not Buddy. He drives a Volvo."

"Hey, great. We're clicking them off fast. That only leaves maybe another three hundred million Americans to check off before we have it." She paused and gave me a bright, fake smile. "You do think he's an American, don't you. I mean, we haven't even started ruling out all of those Asian people."

I didn't need the sarcasm so I ignored her. "And it can't be Larry. He drives a beat up Volkswagon van with flowers on it. I don't know what Rev. Nagle drives."

"A Cadillac."

"Okay. I don't think William would have mistaken a Cadillac for a cop car."

"What if Clark was telling the truth about everything," Lauren suggested. "What if he really did visit Sean at seven or so. That means he wasn't the military-looking guy Nagle saw."

This was supposed to help? "That just means it could be anyone. Some cop. Some army guy who thought he'd made a bad drug deal and wanted revenge. You're right. We've got less than nothing."

Lauren shook her head. "Oh, no. I was just being negative for a moment. But we still have a lot. We've got a muscular, military-looking guy who drives what looks like an unmarked police car and wears a black ballcap. We've got a guy who knew Sean and Fred. We know there's a drug connection, a reason he ransacked Sean's records."

"It could still be a million people."

"Come on, Kim. Help me here."

The more I thought about it, the more I thought of the angle the cops had been working--the Postal Service connection. Both murders were on my route, but we'd ruled Larry out and Buddy was a million miles from the description. Who did that leave?"

"Someone," I said, "associated with the Post Office with a muscular military build, driving a police-looking car."

"You mean--"

She and I hit it at the same time. "Preston."

"He warned me to be careful of anyone who was too helpful," I said. "I never thought that he might be talking about himself."

"We invited him to back us up," Lauren said. "Let's get out of here."

I looked around but didn't see any sign of Preston or his 'Vette. Maybe he had missed the call. Still, leaving was a good plan. I grabbed Lauren and dragged her away.

We'd gone a couple of hundred feet when I remembered Lupe's phone. "Shit."

"We're getting away." She sounded breathless.

"We promised we'd leave her phone. Her mother will kill her, remember?"

I took it from her and headed back. "I'll leave it in the picnic table tubing, like we promised."

"And Preston will kill us." She trailed after me.

"For all we know, we're walking toward him rather than away from him. Besides this won't take any ti--"

Lauren grabbed my arm. "Oh, shit."

* * * *

Preston nodded to me and gave Lauren a grin. "I got here a bit late, so I hid behind the shelter."

"Right, Preston. Uh, thanks for coming." How loud had Lauren and I been talking? Was it possible he didn't know that we'd figured him out?

"No problem."

"Turns out we were wrong about Clark," I said. "Which means we've come up with a big fat nothing. I'm really sorry we put you to this inconvenience."

I was trying not to meet his eyes and glanced out into the parking lot. One of the big American-built cars there had just a bit of a dark handprint on the passenger side. Preston had taken my advice and driven his other car--the car he'd used when he'd killed Fred.

He shook his head slowly. "I told you before and you didn't listen to me then, but I'll tell you again. I think you should give up the investigation."

"Right, Preston. Good idea. In fact, I absolutely agree with you. We've been wasting our time, accusing a bunch of innocent people. We'll just turn it over to the cops, same as we should have done from the start. What do you say, Lauren? Let's call and give ourselves up."

Preston swatted Lupe's phone from my hand.

"Then there's the matter of you thinking I did it." He shook his head sadly. "Ridiculous."

I looked at him carefully. He wasn't as square as Clark, but he was built. He hit the weights hard, for sure. But he also had the bald spot and skin blemishes that could be natural, but could also come from illegal steroid use. His navy blue Post Office cop cap wasn't a ballcap, but it could easily be mistaken for one. The blue was also dark enough that it could also be mistaken for black, especially by a frightened driver about to pile into a tree.

"Why would we think you did it? You've been helping us."

He pointed a finger at me. "I think you're lying, Kimberly. I think you've got another of your crazy theories going and you don't want to give it up."

Lauren edged toward the picnic table, trying to put it between herself and the killer but Preston called her on it. "Don't move."

She collapsed. "What are you going to do, Preston? Kill us too?"

Oh, great, Lauren. Let's put him in a spot where he has to kill us, why don't we?

Distaste and anger warred with a faked amusement to control Preston's face. With a visible and unconvincing effort, he picked amusement.

"You have an incredible sense of the melodramatic, Lauren. Sean always said that about you."

Putting together Preston's apparent steroid abuse and Sean's reputation as the guy to go for when shopping for non-hallucinogenic drugs and the evidence was becoming overwhelming. Sean had supplied Preston, but he hadn't known Preston was a cop, could be blackmailed. When Preston showed up in his nice uniform after Andrew had bit Larry, Sean had recognized him.

Could I be jumping to conclusions again? More to the point, could I use my previous false certainty to save our lives?

"Preston, I've been convinced that Buddy did it, that Larry did it, that Lauren did it, that Clark did it, that Fred killed Sean and some gangster killed him. If I didn't suspect you for at least a few minutes, you'd feel like you were left out."

His smile seemed a bit sad. "I wish I could believe you, Kimberly. But you're going to go running around stirring up dirt, trying to find evidence to pin on me, aren't you."

I shook my head firmly. "I'm out of the detective business, Preston."

"Well, you're right about that."

The words were okay. The way he said it, his voice as smooth as glass, but his eyes glistening with anticipation, made me more than nervous.

I edged away. *Maybe I can run.*

"Stay still."

"You had to kill Sean after he saw you in uniform, right?" Lauren guessed. "It must have surprised both of you when you followed up on Larry's dog-bite and found your drug supplier at home. Did you normally deal with him in Northpark? He did a lot of his business there. What I don't understand is why you had to kill Fred too."

Thanks, Lauren. So much for my plan to persuade Preston we didn't think he was guilty.

"Oh, Lauren. Do you really think I'm going to confess for your little tape recorder? Kimmy here already let me know about your plan, remember."

He reached under the table, felt around, and came up with the digital unit.

"Cute little toy, isn't it?" Then he dropped it on the ground and crushed it with the raised heel of one of his cowboy boots.

"I'm just curious about how you think you can get away with this." Lauren appeared completely cool, like she was chatting about the weather. "If I were you, I'd forget about us, jump in my car and head for the hills."

"Why would I run? I'm a cop. I'm on the short list to transfer into the FBI. If I have to go through a little inconvenience to get there, I don't mind."

"The only problem is, you got Sean and Fred to turn their backs on you so you could slit their throats, right? But Kim and I aren't going to do that. And I don't think you've got the balls to kill someone face to face. Not just because they shriveled up because of your steroid abuse, either."

Lauren's plan was apparently to make Preston mad enough to kill us in a hurry rather than to drag out the inevitable. My own thinking was that dragging out sounded better. But she was ignoring my glares and my head shaking.

Preston reached into his slacks pocket, then withdrew his hand slowly, almost sensually.

He held something long, black, and rigid.

A blade snicked out when Preston pushed a button on the side. His grin opened almost as wide as the switchblade knife.

Chapter 18

"Ohh, a switchblade. I'm so frightened." Lauren said the words as if reading from a bad script.

"Shut up, Lauren," I commanded.

"Oh, hell, Kim. You know he's too much of a chicken to kill us face to face. He's trying to persuade us to run so he can stick us in the backs."

Preston's face glowed red. "You want to know the funny thing? You think your brave sacrifice is going to result in me getting caught. Well, you're wrong. Nobody is going to catch me and your sacrifice is pure stupidity."

Where was everyone else? It wasn't dark yet. There had been hundreds of people at the park earlier, which was one of the reasons we'd picked it. But right when we could have used a couple of really big guys with baseball bats to ride to the rescue, nobody was around. Outside of the bugs and birds, the park was silent.

"Hit me with your best--"

Before Lauren could finish her latest taunt, Preston lunged at her.

He came straight in, keeping his knife close to his body rather than making the kind of big swing I would probably do.

My adrenaline cranked up and the world seemed to slow down. I saw the glint of the blade, the edge of the black handle where it extended beyond Preston's swollen fingers, the thin sheen of sweat on his face as he fell victim to 'roid rage.

Lauren was reacting, bringing up a hand to deflect the thrust, but I couldn't see how that could possibly do any good.

I seemed to be caught in a dream sequence, my muscles responding only sluggishly to my commands.

Lauren's high-pitched scream shattered the silence, creating circles of sound just as a rock, thrown into a still pond, creates concentric circles of waves.

Her hand gushed blood where Preston had struck, and she grabbed it with the other hand, dropping whatever she'd held.

But Preston didn't finish the job. His own scream was a cursing echo of Lauren's. His knife clattered on the picnic table.

My brain, overwhelmed by excess adrenaline, finally interpreted the sound I'd heard. The buzz of a stun gun. Lauren had zapped Preston just as he'd cut her hand.

My muscles finally responded and I surged the rest of the way to my feet.

"There's mace in my handbag," Lauren groaned. "Spray him down good."

Preston was groggy, but he had pulled himself together enough to reach for

160

his knife. I kicked it as hard as I could before he could get it.

Only after it bounced under a bush did I realize that I'd just knocked away a weapon I could have grabbed and used. Although, maybe not. Everything I knew about knife fighting, I'd learned from watching Cajun Chef reruns during the first months after my telecom layoff. If I'd tried to use his knife against him, Preston would just take it back and carve me up.

The blurb on Lauren's stun-gun had promised that it would render anyone helpless for long enough to call for help or escape the attacker. The blurb lied.

Preston shook short-circuits out of his head and moved a bit slowly, but he was very much conscious, and very much pissed at what had happened.

I fumbled for Lauren's purse, pulled out the spray tube, aimed, and sprayed. Nothing.

For a moment, I was afraid I'd pulled out the wrong tube and was trying to stop him with hairspray, but I risked a glance. The bright yellow skull on the red aerosol can said I'd pulled the right weapon. What wasn't right was that nothing had come out.

"This just isn't your day, is it, Kimmy." Preston knocked the tube out of my hand.

"Stick it," I told him. I was sick of sucking up, sick of pretending I didn't know it was him, and sick of letting this pond-scum representative of the human race chase me out of my trailer, cost me my job, get me in trouble with the police, and send me hunting after all sorts of innocent people to make their lives as miserable as mine was.

"Maybe I'll do that." He shoved himself to his feet and gestured to his groin. "I bet you don't get a lot of action, since you look like a boy but hey, I'm into pity-sex. Especially since I can tell you're the kind of girl who likes it rough."

I kicked in the general direction of his balls.

In the movies or the romance books I like reading, it works every time. In real life, things weren't so great.

He caught my leg before I connected, and yanked.

For a moment, I was flying.

That moment ended abruptly as my butt hit the ground. My head followed shortly afterwards. I saw stars. At least I didn't lose consciousness.

Preston was fumbling with his belt--which provided a bit of distraction. I tried kicking him again, this time in the knee, but he just moved out of the way and then slammed his own kick into my hip.

Something went crunch.

A red wall of pain shot through my body like a hurricane-flood-surge through a coastal town. Without meaning to, I curled up into a ball, helplessly hugging by arms and legs to my torso.

A thump next to me forced me to open my eyes but it was only more bad news. He'd yanked Lauren away from the bench, knocked the zapper from her hand, and dropped her next to me.

"You're the smart one." Her voice was contorted with pain, but she managed a slight smile. "Better come up with a plan, quick."

Lauren's purse was next to my head and I grabbed it hoping she had another of her clever devices inside.

I came up with another aerosol can and sprayed Preston's eyes as he yanked down his uniform pants and pushed himself between my legs.

He knocked the can away from me, slamming my hand into the concrete slab in the picnic shelter hard enough to really hurt, but he stopped for a second, his knees between my legs, as he tried to rub gooey hairspray out of his eyes.

I shot a fist toward his groin but he felt me move and planted a hand in my chest, his steroid-enhanced weight behind it. "You really are skinny, Kimmy. Don't you ever eat? A man likes a bit of meat on the bone, if you know what I mean."

I tried to breath but I couldn't fill my lungs with his weight bearing down on them.

"How would you know?" Lauren demanded. "A steroid freak like you can't get it up anyway."

Despite the blood gushing from her injured hand, she was getting to her feet.

"Shut up and run," I wheezed, using the last of my breath. If one of us could get away, Preston would have no reason to kill the other. No reason other than rage, that is. And from the bloodshot look in his eyes, he was mad as all get-out.

He grabbed Lauren's bleeding hand and yanked while I sucked in a life-sustaining gasp of air.

Lauren collapsed next to me once more. "Sorry," she murmured. "My big mouth got us in trouble."

"You two are such incompetents, I can't believe you actually guessed it was me," Preston said. He grabbed my jeans and yanked them down.

All of a sudden, I hated the baggy jean style. He didn't even have to unzip the things, just unhooked the button and yank. Bam--there I was ready to be raped.

Since he'd pulled my legs up in the air, I tried a kick. Not with a great deal of conviction, though. Preston had to weigh over two hundred pounds, all muscle. Even with everything Lauren had made me eat lately, I was still under a hundred pounds and calling much of that muscle would be an exaggeration.

He raised a hand to block my leg, then dropped it, looking momentarily confused.

I didn't understand what was happening, but I took advantage of his confusion. My kick landed right on his ear and he collapsed.

Which sounds better than it was because when he collapsed, he landed right on top of me.

"What the hell--"

I put a thumb on his throat and pushed.

He gobbled the last of whatever he was trying to say, rose up, and then collapsed again.

This time, I heard the thump.

A battered, much-used baseball bounced on the concrete. As it rolled, I saw a bloody spot on it--the type of spot a ball might get if someone threw it into a man's head.

I shoved Preston the rest of the way off me.

He looked groggy, and looked groggier yet when I caught him with another kick along-side an ear that was already dripping with blood--a baseball injury if I guessed right.

He rolled away from me--and came up with the knife I'd thought I'd taken out of the fight.

"Now you die, bitch."

The baseball had rolled back within reach and I picked it up and heaved it at him.

He didn't even bother ducking, letting the thing bounce off a shoulder with no damage at all.

I hated throwing like a girl.

"Now it's my turn." Preston tossed his knife from hand to hand, then moved in for the kill.

* * * *

Another baseball hit him, bouncing off his ribs.

Preston gave a sort of moaning wheeze and collapsed, dropping the knife as he fell.

I bent over and picked up his knife. I might not know how to use it, but leaving it around definitely hadn't worked.

"I never seen a boy wear underwear like that," Tawdry announced as I straightened up.

I pulled up my pants. "If anyone can find Lupe's phone, call 9-1-1. We need the police before Preston tries anything else."

I checked on Lauren, but she was already up and had found a paper napkin that she pressed to her injured hand.

"I'm all right," she assured me. I didn't believe her. She looked pale and her blood was all over the picnic shelter.

"You're going to call the cops on a cop. That's pretty funny," Tawdry said.

That must also be why the park had emptied out so completely when Preston had walked behind the shelter. Picnickers had seen the police uniform and made the practical decision to vacate before bullets started flying, questions were asked, or police brutality was exacted.

"Word on the street was you were getting busted," Lupe said. "I told Tawdry we'd better go back get my phone back before it got confiscated or something." She paused, then added, "You need a place to stay, I've got friends who can hide you."

"No, I mean it," I said. "We really want the police."

"Ha, ha, ha." Tawdry just spoke the words, but cloaked them with that thick layer of sarcasm that only teenagers seem capable of delivering. "You white folks don't have a clue, do you?"

"Maybe when they find out he was trying to rape a boy," Lupe said hopefully.

"Got bad news for you, Lupe," Tawdry said. "Your new boyfriend is a girl. Didn't you get a look at that underwear? No concealed weapons there at all."

Lupe turned on me. "Is that right. You're a girl?"

I nodded grimly. "Sorry."

She looked pissed for a moment, then smiled. "Guess we won't be doing it after all, huh?"

"Not going to happen," I agreed. "But could you please call the cops?"

"Only if you let me teach you how to throw a baseball. When you threw my ball, it was embarrassing."

By the time I got through trying to convince the girls that it was safe to call the cops, Lauren had handled it for us.

We used the leather straps from Lauren's purse to tie Preston up so he wouldn't go anywhere and waited for the cavalry.

A few picnickers wandered up, told us we were crazy to just sit around with a trussed up cop, and shook their heads and skedaddled when we told them we'd phoned for more cops.

Lupe and Tawdry evaporated when a helicopter swung overhead, beaming down its searchlight, and Lauren and I were left alone with Preston, who fully recovered his voice and told us exactly what he was going to do to us once he got free of the straps.

I'd laughed at him the first time he threatened me, but when he really bulged out his muscles, the leather started to stretch.

"I'll kick him a few times," Lauren offered.

She walked close to him, jumped over him when he rolled toward her, and reared back to kick.

"Drop your weapons. We have you surrounded."

"Looks like the end for you," I told Preston. "Guess your days of rape and murder are over."

"Officer down," Preston shouted. "I need assistance."

Before I could say anything, a beefy cop tackled me, throwing me on the ground and clicking handcuffs behind my back.

Chapter 19

It took a couple of hours to convince anyone that I should be put in the woman's side of the jail rather than with the men, but once the police realized they'd finally caught the two women they'd been looking for, they locked us away--separately, presumably because they thought we might not have gotten our story straight in the week we'd been on the run together.

I hoped they got Lauren the medical attention she needed, but they didn't even bother having a doctor look at my banged up head, hip, or ribs. They also hadn't bothered to look for Lupe and Tawdry, who had disappeared before they could give statements.

Since I could barely walk, I spent a lot of time in bed--and my new roommate, Shaneal, refused to let me have the lower bunk so getting there was trouble.

Shaneal wasn't very good company. She was the most obvious police squeal I'd ever met.

"Must have felt good to put the hurt on that cop," Shaneal offered as I lay in my bunk trying not to moan from pain. "A lot of times, I'd like to hurt some cops myself."

"He was trying to kill us," I told her for the hundredth time. "Can you find out if Lauren got medical attention?"

"Do I look like I've got some power here, girlfriend? I'm just a prisoner, like you."

She might be a prisoner, but she'd clearly been told she would be turned loose if she could get me to say something incriminating and was mining for it as hard as she could.

"Have the police even followed up on our evidence?" I demanded. "Has Preston Rollin been arrested?"

"You're going to have to come up with a better story than thinking you can implicate a cop, gonna be an FBI agent," Shaneal said. "Course if it was all Lauren's idea, that might get you off with just a couple of years. If you were willing to tell the truth to the judge."

I asked for a lawyer every time a guard or cop came anywhere near, but they somehow managed not to hear my requests. So I was a bit surprised when, after I'd been there for about forty-eight hours, a guard unlocked my cell door and told me my lawyer was there for me.

I dragged myself down the corridor into a Plexiglas-fronted room with little telephones so the guards could listen in while you talked to your lawyer. In this case, I didn't think they'd like what they'd hear.

It wasn't my lawyer. It was Vito Lindner, head of the Dallas Post Office region and the guy who had basically given up on me as soon as things got hot.

"I thought I was getting a lawyer."

"I went to law school, even passed the bar exam. Makes me a lawyer as far as I know. Uh, what the heck happened to your hair?"

"I got it cut."

He just looked at me so I continued. "What are you doing here?"

He studied me for long enough I wondered if the phone was working. "I've got a problem," he finally admitted.

"You had a problem. His name is Preston Rollin. He's a P.O. cop and a killer."

Vito nodded slowly. "That's one take. The other is that I have a whacked-out carrier who is trying to frame an innocent cop."

"That one sounds easier to sell, if you don't mind ignoring the evidence or believing a lie."

Vito's smile was particularly nasty. "Do I look like the kind of manager who cares about a lie?"

"I've worked at a lot of places and I've never found a manager who minds lying," I admitted. "Still, knowing that you have an officer on the payroll who's already killed at least two people, tried to kill a couple more, and just might murder even more to make sure no one gets in the way of his transfer doesn't sound particularly career enhancing to me."

Vito nodded slowly.

"Look, Vito. If you want me to roll over on this, you can forget it. If the D.A. decides to charge me, I'm going to fight it. I'm going to tell everyone who will listen that the union tried to do right by me, but that management would rather lie and let a killer run loose than admit they made a mistake."

"I don't think anyone--"

"And I'll name names, Vito. One name in particular. Vito Lindner, the man who kept a killer on his payroll."

A single bead of sweat popped out on his forehead. "I'm here to listen. Run me through the reasons you think Preston did it."

Half an hour later, a guard banged on the door and told Vito my time was up. Vito told her to shut the hell up, which got him tossed out and me limping back to my cell.

"Guess it's getting near your last chance," Shaneal announced grimly when I climbed up to the upper bunk. "I hear your girlfriend turned on you. She's blaming everything on you, saying killing both men was your idea."

"I didn't believe that lie last time they arrested us and I hardly knew her then. Now, I know you're so full of shit your breath stinks. So shut the hell up or I'll smack you in the side of the head with a baseball."

For a miracle, it worked. She shut up and I actually got some sleep.

* * * *

I woke up with an appetite and an idea.

Over the previous couple of weeks, I'd had a lot of ideas, most of them bad. I hadn't had much of an appetite since I'd lost my job in telecom, though. I wondered if I was dying from where Preston had kicked me.

When I clambered down from my bunk, whatever was wrong in my hip just gave up.

I collapsed on the cell's concrete floor, both my appetite and my idea washed away by a red surge of pure pain.

I suspect I blistered paint off the wall with my language because even Shaneal responded, finally calling for a guard when I refused to shut up.

They threw me on a gurney, wheeled me to the infirmary, and stuck an I.V. in my arm.

I faded right after that.

* * * *

I had no idea how long I was out, but when I rejoined the mundane world, I was in a real hospital bed, had a fiberglass construction over my upper thigh and hip, and felt like I was floating on top of the world.

I'd never been able to understand people who use drugs before but then, I'd never done more than an occasional joint or stay-up pill. Whatever they'd given me this time was the real deal. I felt profoundly one with the universe.

Unfortunately, that universe still had Preston Rollin running around in it.

A pretty nurse dropped in a few minutes later so maybe waking up had set off an alarm somewhere. She stuck a thermometer in my mouth, took my blood pressure, and lectured me on how anorexia can cause bone deterioration, which can lead to the kind of damage they had discovered.

"I'm not anorexic," I told her.

She shook her head at me, told me she'd get me something to eat, and left.

I swiped her phone from the holster on her hip and called Detective Poll, the man who'd first accused me of murder. I told him about William and suggested he do a photo lineup.

Then I called Lindner and asked him for a huge favor. I even promised I'd forget he'd violated the union agreement in how he treated me if he went along.

He said he'd think about it.

The next couple of days were a blur.

There were police guards at my door at first, but when they figured out that I was completely immobile with a fractured hip, they gradually thinned out and eventually vanished. A doctor stopped by occasionally, gave me lectures on eating more, and checked the cast they'd put over half my body. The nurse brought me food, took her phone back from me, and told me that she would be coming after me if I'd used up her minutes.

At around eight in the evening of my third day, Poll walked into my room. I hadn't seen him since that last time he'd come out and accused me of being a murderer, but he was welcome.

He carried a stack of photos, which he showed to me.

I flipped through them. They were average looking white guys. Maybe a bit more built than the usual sort, but nothing special. One was Preston.

"Well?"

"Your witness guessed Preston, but he wasn't sure. A good defense would cream him."

"Crap."

He shrugged. "Juries love eye-witnesses, but it turns out their testimony is mostly plain wrong."

He sat down at the little chair next to my bed. "You've been busy."

"Did you find the money and stuff in Fred's motel?"

He nodded. "Yeah. Your buddy Fred was a slimeball all right. Still, the only thing we had on Rollin was that he was the P.O. cop who followed up on your harassment claim. That means he knew Fred, but it doesn't mean he killed him."

"Okay."

We chit-chatted for another half-hour, him asking me about the case, where we'd hidden, how we'd discovered William Evertt, and why I'd been harassing poor Clark Study.

At eight thirty, Poll took out the pictures again and started studying them.

He sorted them into piles, muttered to himself, and generally went through the full production.

Neither he nor I saw the handle of my hospital room door lever down.

"So, you brought your witness in to see you," Preston gloated. "Two birds with one stone. This is so handy."

"Preston. What the hell are you doing here?"

"You think I don't keep track of what's going on? When Lindner called my boss and told him to assign me special night duty tonight, I got suspicious. So I snuck into his office and read the e-mail. You had a witness and wanted to make sure I was out of the way. Well, good bye, witness."

The police had confiscated the switchblade Preston'd used on Lauren, but he'd found another one and he clicked it out now.

"Hey man, let's not go crazy." Poll stood easily, balanced on the balls of his feet.

"I'm sorry you saw too much," Preston said. "I understand you're a good sort, not a druggie like Sean, Fred, or Kimmy here."

"Hey."

"Look at you, Kimberly. Everyone in the post office knows you're lying there asking for more morphine all the time. When your so-called witness refused to identify me, I guess you just flipped out. You killed him and then overdosed yourself. Tragic, but what can the Postal Service expect if you hire losers like you?"

"Nobody is going to believe that, Preston."

He cackled. "They believed me when I told them you'd attacked me, didn't they? Of course they'll believe it."

"Why don't you leave me out of this?" Detective Poll said. "Now that I think about it, I can't identify you at all."

"Too late, I'm afraid. I've got to tie up these loose ends before I head to Quantico."

I'd suggested Poll for the job because he was black, like William Evertt, but also because he was kind of round and didn't look threatening.

When Preston came at him with the knife, though, Poll moved fast enough. He tossed the stack of photos in Preston's face, caught Preston's knife-hand between his arm and his chest and snapped the elbow, then yanked a gun out from under his jacket.

"Preston Rollin, I am placing you under arrest for assault on a police officer and the attempted murder of a postal employee. Other charges will be added at a later time. You have the right to remain silent and can refuse to answer questions. You have a right to a lawyer. If you cannot afford a lawyer, one will be appointed on your behalf. Do you understand?"

Preston goggled at him. He turned and headed for the door--and ran into a combination of Dallas's finest and his former brother officers with the Post Office Police.

They had him down on the ground with his hands cuffed behind his back in no time. "And resisting arrest," Poll added.

* * * *

"Good thing Rollin's resignation had just come through," Lindner told me. He'd stuck around while a group of detectives, two each from the P.O. and D.P.D., had taken my statements.

"I thought that might motivate you to get off your butt. If he resigned, he wouldn't reflect so badly on the office."

Lindner shrugged. "Hey, the service has a bad rep. My job is to make it better."

"You sure suck at your job, then, don't you?"

I expected him to throw something against the wall and march out. Instead, he just laughed. "Hate to say it but it looks that way. Want a promotion to assistant chief for labor relations?"

"If I wanted a desk job, I would have stayed in telecom."

"You *tried* to stay in telecom but they laid you off."

"You don't have to rub it in."

Lindner laughed again. "I'm glad your plan worked. I know you think I'm a stuffed suit. Hell, I am a stuffed suit. But you're a credit to the service."

I didn't know how to answer that so I didn't.

"Right. Well, you've got some back pay coming and I'm putting this down as a service-related disability so it won't come out of your sick-time. Oh. And you've got a friend waiting to see you."

He vanished and Lauren burst in.

"They wouldn't tell me how you were doing." She threw her arms around me, banging into my injured hip.

"Hey, that hurts."

"I brought a couple of friends."

Lupe and Tawdry shouldn't have been out so late on a school night, but they stepped into my hospital room, each of them carrying an assortment of flowers which, pretty clearly, they'd picked themselves at the park.

"You just get better," Lupe instructed me. "You can't learn how to throw if you can't get out of bed."

"Yeah," Tawdry agreed. "And better start eating. A man likes a woman with a little booty."

I'd had booty before and it hadn't helped me with men, but I wasn't arguing.

A cop ushered the girls out after a few minutes and Lauren reached into her purse and pulled out a cheeseburger. "Tawdry was right. Eat this."

"But that's for you."

Thanks to a week in jail, I'm in rehab now. I don't need to eat so much. I think I'll make it."

The burger was barely warm, but it bit into it anyway. It the best thing I'd ever eaten.

Lauren watched me like a hawk, probably making sure I didn't disappear the burger the way I usually did, but I wasn't stopping. I ate the entire thing and licked my fingers. "You know, I'm going to miss you now that this thing is over."

"Miss me? How come?"

"I mean, we'll be friends, I hope. But you're way up there in Allen. It takes forever to ride my bike up there and--"

"Girlfriend, you aren't going to be walking for weeks. I put my house on the market and talked to your Tina Anderson. We're moving up. I bought us a three-bedroom singlewide. We're going to be living in style."

"But--"

"And I think that nice Vito Lindner likes you."

I covered my head with a blanket. "Don't make me laugh."

"I think maybe we should become private detectives. That way, you wouldn't be working for him and the two of you could date."

"Lauren, you're crazy."

"Maybe." She raised an eyebrow. "I figure we'll call ourselves Herbert and Walsh, P.I."

"Walsh and Herbert," I said.

"Deal."

THE END

www.ingramcontent.com/pod-product-compliance
Lightning Source LLC
Chambersburg PA
CBHW072150170626
46813CB00004BA/1741